ELF STONE OF THE NEYNA

Published October 2023
Indies United Publishing House, LLC

Cover art design by Muhammad Kaleem and Sabrina Bedford

SECOND EDITION

ISBN: 978-1-64456-637-4 [paperback]
ISBN: 978-1-64456-638-1 [Mobi]
ISBN: 978-1-64456-639-8 [ePub]
ISBN: 978-1-64456-640-4 [Audiobook]

Library of Congress Control Number: 2023943163

INDIES UNITED PUBLISHING HOUSE, LLC
P.O. BOX 3071
QUINCY, IL 62305-3071

This beguiling novel will bring you to a turbulent world where Yanda, a woman with untapped powers, is snatched from her home planet, leaving behind a daughter she loves dearly. You'll root for her as she endures imprisonment and worse at the hands of an evil being who intends to exploit his captives to rule the universe. Yanda forms alliances, but after every victory, new perils arise, and you simply have to keep reading until the very end. – Laura McHale Holland, author of *The Kiminee Dream*

Elf Stone

of the

Neyna

Lost Xentu
Book One

Marie Judson

INDIES UNITED PUBLISHING HOUSE, LLC

Prologue

Yanda had no idea, getting up for work that day—that fateful day—that she had little time left on her home planet of Alland.

But was it her *home planet*? She'd never fit in. Taken in and raised by a couple in the small town of Balyou, she'd never known her real parents or where they'd come from. Her amber eyes, butterscotch skin, and tawny, unruly hair were unlike anyone she'd seen.

Her mother was never cruel but was suspicious of her ability to see through things, and constantly told her to keep her ability secret. Her adoptive father, a quiet man, kept to the background. They never told her how they had come to adopt her. If they knew about her bio-parents, they didn't say.

Yanda stepped to the window of her high-rise

apartment. She'd never expected to find herself living in such a place, so far from nature, after growing up in the countryside with Omshi and Nedri. She'd chosen the apartment because it was an easy distance from Shrapels Hospital, where she was a surgeon. She could take sky-tunnels and be at work in minutes.

Beyond the city, low greenery stretched to infinity, cut into patterns by deep water channels. Electric rail lines further bisected the terrain past the suburbs. Alland, a high-tech planet, had no oceans and no forests.

It was Yanda's ritual to look out each morning toward the rising sun, in the direction where her six-year-old daughter Seiti lived, raised by Omshi and Nedri as well. She called them gramma and grampa.

Aching for the weekend, when she would ride the rail home and hold her little girl in her arms, Yanda pulled her satchel onto her shoulder and left her apartment, catching the sky-tube one floor down. Other tubes snaked between the high buildings, and, far below, Yanda saw through clear plaz, streets teaming with early morning workers like disturbed insect nests.

She unlocked her office door, barely registering the name plate, "Dr. Yanda Selkeden" – a source of immense pride a few years back, now starting to fill her with doubt. She hardly saw the day to day changes her daughter was going through. It was healthier, she told herself, for Seiti to grow up in the country with other children, a family. The air was cleaner there. The usual sadness and doubt about spending so much time away from her young daughter gripped her but she shoved it down, not ready to throw away her ambitions of a high-status career.

Inside her office, Yanda waved the transparent panel

over her desk into life and checked her schedule. Nearly a half hour 'til surgery. Time for a hot cup of stimulating *cuffa*. She slipped into her medical coat, leaving her bright sweater in the closet.

The dining hall was abuzz with activity.

"Selky!" A woman of indiscernible age and springy orange hair called Yanda's nickname, waving from a table near the windows.

Yanda signaled back, purchased her stimulant and made her way across to join the other woman. "Gotta be quick." She dropped into a seat, blew on her drink, and took a tentative sip.

"You have a heart surgery, don't you? The one no one else'll touch?" Celly was a masterful plastic surgeon.

"It's a tricky one. I've studied the scans and just can't tell what's eluding us."

"Not a good one for robotic surgery?"

"Apparently not. Boss Konkle called it." Yanda had a niggling suspicion the head of the department might have set her up to finally catch her using powers during surgery. But this was probably just paranoia. There had been questions here and there as she moved up the surgery ranks swiftly. Why did she seem to see things others did not? That sort of question.

"Well then," Celly conceded as she broke off a corner of her breakfast pastry and popped it in her mouth. "Guess that takes care of it."

Yanda gulped the rest of her beverage and stood. "Time to scrub in."

•———•••———•

Poor Joe Hoskins, bellhop at a local hotel, was slipping away. Without thinking, Yanda slid her mind down through the layers and swiftly mended the man's heart, making healthy what was blocked, torn, ruptured. She glanced at the monitors. Vital signs had improved.

Her shoulders ached. She'd tried to stick to standard procedure, but she was losing him. Instinct had taken over. Sweat trickled down her hairline and into one ear, making her shiver as it tickled, unable to remedy it with gloved hands. She looked around at her surgical team. Mind-powers were not credited on this planet. Worse than that, use of them would be grounds for dismissal. So far, with discretion, Yanda had managed to use her ability without being caught. But she'd never gone this far. "It's done."

Her team stared at her, then began to close the man's chest. Vital signs were strong now.

Letting out a long breath, she set instruments on a tray and walked from the surgery. As she stood at the sanitizer, several of her colleagues approached.

"I didn't see how you solved it," Arjan exclaimed.

"It was in a tricky spot. I had to take a chance." When would they open up to *other* practices so she could explain honestly, without fear of reprisal from the magic-hunters? Though some of what she'd done, she couldn't explain herself.

This planet had gone through purges until all unique abilities had been driven underground. Yanda had never found any text that spoke of powers such as hers, to see through.

"Magnificent. You have some eyes," said her assisting surgeon.

Yanda suddenly stumbled and wrapped her hands around the edge of the sink to catch her balance, her head pounding.

"Are you alright?" someone put a hand under her

elbow.

Her world turned into confusion as a voice thrummed inside her head. She looked around and gave a shaky smile to the small group facing her. "I'm going to lie down in my office."

Her friend, Magali, a fellow surgeon who'd been watching from the viewing room, touched her shoulder in sympathy. "Yeah, that was intense. Great job."

Something was distancing her from those around her, like a swarm of buzzing insects in her head. She slipped away before she acted more strangely.

Inside her office, Yanda locked the door and flung herself on the couch. But a moment later she rose, pulled her satchel from a drawer, changed into her street clothes, locked the door, and hurried down the hall. She searched the empty corridor to make sure she was not followed, then stepped into the lift and punched in the sub-level that connected to the spaceport by an underground tube. A force drew her there and she couldn't seem to fight it or think for herself.

The swarm grew louder in her head. The only clear thought was, "Book passage on the Lark." The rest of her mind seemed asleep. Only the faintest voice deep in her mind panicked as her feet took her along the bright tiled corridors flickering with messages and images. She navigated a maze of *move-walks,* and infallibly arrived at a counter announcing the imminent departure of the Lark. When she showed her ID, she was waved through, no questions. No payment.

"No payment?"

"It's covered."

That should bother me. The thought did not rise up to real consciousness.

Robotic attendants settled her in a private cabin with a stasis-bed.

Chapter 1

Coming to, Yanda felt nauseous. Raising her hands to rub bleary eyes, she realized she was shackled, wrists and ankles. She writhed, clawing at the metal band that circled her neck as panic surged through her.

Then she noticed something else. Her abilities were gone. She could not see through anything. It made her feel smothered, closed in. She couldn't seem to think clearly. How had she gotten there? Her past seemed to start in that room. Who was she?

Two beings with the Lark insignia on their uniforms escorted her—none too gently—from the ship. She was vaguely aware of boarding an aircart and shooting through tubes, traveling between domes with occasional clear panels giving her glimpses of darkness outside and several moons. Night? A bleak place, it appeared. By the domes, tube travel, and lack of plant life, she suspected no atmosphere. For the first time in her life, she could not see through walls. Perhaps the metal clamped around her neck dampened her ability? It felt suffocating.

The transport stopped and lowered to the concrete between similar shuttles. An auto-door shfff'ed open and her escorts' gloved hands locked on her arms as they entered a hall illuminated by dim floor and ceiling lights.

Yanda's eyes widened as they passed caged humans and other human-like beings of varied appearances, one, two, three... She thought she counted nine. Their eyes followed her.

The uniformed escorts shoved her into the last barred cell. When the enclosure sealed, they left. Yanda stood in the center of the small enclosure and felt for her ID, comm unit, money. Nothing. Wobbly, she collapsed onto a hard narrow bed at the side, dropped her head against the wall and closed her eyes.

"What name haff you?

A tall, thin creature—Yanda thought female—peered through the bars from the cell across from hers. In the low lighting, Yanda made out what appeared to be feathered skin.

"I'm Yanda." So she did know her name. At least she remembered that much. She stayed seated, feeling ill. "You?"

"I person Aktat" The bird-woman—a Jejod, Yanda thought—spoke with clicking noises, pressing a long, bony hand to her chest.

Yanda had read of the Jejod but they'd seemed mythical. The female must be seven feet tall since she had to nearly double over to look through the bars. The creature did a series of acrobatic moves, rolling, swinging off the bars and landing on her bed mat where she proceeded to do push-ups, planks and other exercises, confirming Yanda's suspicion that the tall being must feel constricted by the small space.

Chapter 2

Kridenit pushed a button on a desk console to allow the Lark personnel into his office, part of his living quarters in a dome adjacent to the prisoners. The one with captain assignation on his uniform waved the other out into the hall as the door snicked open and closed again.

"This is it. This is what I needed. Brilliant find." The wizard Kridenit allowed a smile to form as he gestured the other to sit.

The Lark captain pulled his protective face mask off as he sat. He was of semi-stocky build with a mane of unruly brown curls and slightly surreal beauty—wide, expressive mouth, long delicate nose, nearly translucent skin. He kept his darkened glasses on, which irritated Kridenit. "You found her," he said and shrugged. "I picked her up."

"True. True." Kridenit sat up straight, rubbing his

hands, beyond pleased. "I caught the message. I knew it was coming from the Stone. Or the Stone's speaker." Unable to contain himself, he jumped up and strode to a round vault door embedded in one wall. Hesitating, he whirled toward the other man. "You felt it, didn't you? You know it's the Stone that called her?" The captain, called Tennan, did not answer. Kridenit went on, "Anyway, you captured her without trouble."

"As you said, you drew her to my ship. I transported her here."

"And I have added your reward to your account." Kridenit returned to his swivel-seat.

Tennan, to Kridenit's further annoyance, was not susceptible to his mind-control and did not open up about the Stone. Probably because he was not entirely human. Part Elf, he guessed; he'd not met many. Something about his mental imprint ...

"You know more than you let on." When there was no response, he blew air, angry. "We'll leave for Terlond in a few days. This newest. She's the key. The Stone will call her. And we'll follow."

Captain Tennan stood abruptly. "I have ship business."

Kridenit considered preventing his departure, just out of spite, but he needed the Elf-man's continued cooperation.

When the Lark captain had left, he pressed a comm button. "Bring me the newest."

• ——— • • • ——— •

Kridenit felt her powers the instant Yanda Selkeden stood in his doorway, despite the metal collar he'd had fastened around her neck to prevent any powers that might allow her to escape. Tall, she wore a bright, belted sweater over classy leggings and short boots. He was drawn to her like a magnet, wanting to own whatever she was.

He rose from his chair and crossed the room to stand eye-to-eye with her.

"Let me remove this."

She flinched when he lifted his hands toward her.

Pressing a hidden clasp, he removed the metal shackle that dampened powers. Immediately he felt her amber gaze piercing him.

For a moment, he feared she would detect what was in his mind, but then realized she was not reading his thoughts; her sight physically penetrated into whatever she looked at.

He delighted in this discovery. *Oh, what a skill to control,* he thought. His hunger grew, as it always did around anything with power.

But he tempered the rising greed, remembering discipline in order to seduce: seduction was his automatic recourse. He was not above making the woman utterly compliant. It didn't injure his ego one bit that most sex he'd had, the creature, human or humanoid, had been under compulsion. The best way to find out everything in someone's mind was through intimacy, and it was a perfect way to leave traces of his influence, for later control.

He was not particularly taken with intercourse—sharing body fluids, getting skin to skin. He could take it or leave it; it was merely organic, like bathing. But tasting the minds—in that he was a connoisseur. He'd left a few damaged brains in the wake of his earlier years, which didn't trouble him a whit, but he far preferred collecting.

"Are you hungry?" he asked, modulating his voice to insinuate caring.

Chapter 3

"I feel rather ill," Yanda said. This man gave her the creeps and his sudden unctuous manner unnerved her. He pretended to have nothing to do with the debilitating circlet, as if he were merely helping her with a distasteful problem, yet he knew how to remove it. "I haven't eaten since anti-grav and stasis."

"We'll remedy that. Please, sit." He took a seat on plush furniture, patting matching accommodation next to him.

She dropped onto the chair, nauseous and unstable, glancing around for the first time. Strange objects perched on shelves, especially odd stones, some glowing in colors; one pulsed violet, another shifted hue every few seconds.

Kridenit—she'd seen the name next to the door: Kridenit Sonn, Esquire—spoke to a small wrist device to someone he called Beri.

Soon a tall, gawky man with reddish brown hair entered, pushing a rolling cart. She immediately liked his intelligent, serious expression. There was something wholesome about him, contrasting with everything around them.

"Leave it." Kridenit flicked a hand to dismiss the servant.

The man called Beri glanced over at her and nodded once, merely seeming to acknowledge her, before retreating, though she caught sadness in his expression.

Sorry to see him go, she turned her attention reluctantly back to Kridenit. She knew he wasn't what had called her away from her planet. He had drawn her there but the call had been drawing her somewhere else. He was an enemy of whatever had called her into space. But who was the true enemy? Once on the ship, she no longer heard that mind-numbing call. And then she'd been in stasis.

She realized she still did not hear that throbbing call, like a drum pounding in her head. But with the shackle off her neck, her memories were rushing back. *My daughter. Seiti. I left her behind.* Her stomach rebelled. She lurched to her feet, hand to her mouth, about to retch.

Kridenit leapt up, eye on his expensive carpeting. He swiftly scooted her toward a door that slid open, revealing opulent accommodations for bodily functions. "In here."

She rushed into the tile-floored chamber and the door shushed closed behind her. She jumped to the can, but heaved up nothing. There was nothing in her. She retched and cried, falling against the wall in a heap.

After a while, she staggered to her feet. She could not huddle there forever. She had to find a way back to her daughter. She searched for a source of water to wet her face and found a small indentation in the wall that shot liquid onto her hands by sensor. She splashed and splashed, tears returning. Eventually she patted her cheeks with a disposable cloth of some unfamiliar fiber dispensed from the wall.

I'm Kridenit's prisoner. Her breaths sped up, close to panic. Consciously, she slowed them. *I must think.*

She heard the venomous toad's voice outside the door, offering sustenance, and dragged herself to the auto-panel, which allowed her back through with a shu-shush. Disciplining her face to neutral, she returned to her seat. He lifted a plate to her hands: cheeses and bread, delicate honeyed pears, a relish that smelled of exotic spices.

Nausea still threatened but she was starving after stasis flight. When steady enough, she nibbled bread, drank the wine he handed her, and finally ate ravenously.

The food was not entirely settled in her stomach, though she felt slightly more stable. She knew Kridenit's gaze was on her but avoided it, staying intent on her plate.

Then she became aware of his mind in hers. *I have no tools to keep him out.* All her life she'd held a special power she hid from others; secretly it gave her a certain pride. Never had she been in the position to rail against mind powers she lacked.

Without volition, her eyes jerked to his. Her thoughts became muffled. Not the same as the incursion of buzzing in her head she experienced on her home planet. Consciousness slipped away, as her mind spiraled down a disorienting tunnel of phantasms.

• ———— • • • ———— •

Yanda lay in her cell, staring up at three moons through a narrow slat of window high in the rounded dome wall. She didn't remember returning there. It must be late—lights were out. She wrapped her arms around herself and heaved a sob. She'd been violated, mind and body.

Sending her microscopic sight downward, she checked for signs of penetration. They were there. And a tiny zygote had formed. She could send it away now, before it implanted on her uterine wall.

A kind male voice came to her. "We're on a moon called Farn. Those are three other moons circling the planet Mir."

She turned her head to find who spoke. The auburn-haired man who'd brought food sat cross-legged on the floor outside her cell, looking in.

She wanted to be alone, to go into a dark place and cry. But the warmth in his tone drew her. Yanda brushed a wet patch from her cheek and turned on her side to face him. "How long have you been here?"

"Just a minute or two."

Despite her despair, Yanda cracked a smile. "I mean here on Farn."

"I've been here about a month."

She studied him. Silence lengthened.

"I brought you pajamas." He pointed to folded clothing inside the bars.

She tried to thank him but tears welled and she buried her face in her arm.

"I'm a captive like you."

She raised horrified eyes. "But you serve him?"

"It gets me out of my cell. You have to be careful what you think around Krid. He has mind powers." His voice dropped. "I'm afraid... he might have hurt you? Did he?"

"Molest me? Yes." She rubbed her face into her pillow, feeling a bout of crying about to rise, making speaking impossible.

"He does that." Beri's voice was gentle, but low and

angry. "That's how he learns about you—all your secrets. Even ones you don't know, consciously."

She sat up. "What?" Bile rose.

His hand gripped a bar, squeezed knuckle-white. "Most everyone who interests Krid finds that out."

"You?" she asked.

He looked away. The cells were quiet and she figured the others were listening.

"Yeah. He takes your will away."

She scooted to the wall and brought her knees up, hugging them. "What was his interest in you?"

"I read minds, to some extent," Beri said. "I like to be invited, though." He said this with emphasis, she thought, to convey that he was nothing like Krid. "And I can find things that have power. I'm also pretty good at getting my hands on them."

She rubbed her eyes across her sleeve, snuffling. "You're a thief?"

Beri laughed, a short bark. "I'm a journalist, by trade. I just... tried to help people get something back that they need."

"But then why does he let you roam free? Why aren't you imprisoned like us?"

She saw Aktat's bird-like head, listening from her cell.

"There's plenty of surveillance. And he has a tracking device on me," Beri explained.

"How'd you end up on Farn?" she asked.

"That," he said, climbing to his feet, "is a story for another night." He added, "I'd better not stay any longer." He called, as he walked down the row, lit only by dim floor lights, "'Night, Tik, Jat, Aktat," making the clicking sounds for some of their names. "'Night, Chin, Dele, Bonden, Chela, Shouma."

Each, in turn, called back "good night."

When he'd left, Aktat remained by the bars.

Shaky, Yanda crossed to examine the sleeping garment. It was clean, at least, if not soft. Pressing her face to the cold tubes spaced five inches apart, she peered down the row. Every fem had come to the corners of their cells closest to Yanda.

Slowly, she began to notice messages in her head. At first, they reminded her of Krid's recent invasion of her mind and she tried to shut them out. But there was a friendly kindness to the various tones and vibrations. She felt a little soothed. Still, as she tried to discern meanings, she found a jumble that strained her mind. Succumbing to her exhaustion and the aftermath of Kridenit's cruelty, not to mention the realization that she'd deserted her daughter, she slid to a crouch. Leaning against the bars, she gave a low moan and pressed her face into her hands.

There came a clear call for silence and a single voice touched her mind. Shouma, she called herself. Yanda did not need to be told that this was an elder; she had a strength and steadiness beyond the rest. Yanda sighed with relief and sat back against the wall, facing the mature speaker at the far end of the hall.

"Where do you come from, child?" the elder asked.

Yanda had not ever experienced voices in her head. She had no idea how to separate thought from communication in this form. She said aloud, "I don't know how to do this."

"There's something troubling you," Shouma persisted with mind-speak. "I will not try to detect anything you don't willingly share with me, but I feel you're deeply upset. Traumatized even. I imagine I know what has occurred."

There was a general feeling of agreement from the rest.

"It's difficult, from a distance, to teach you," Shouma said. "If I might suggest, quiet your mind and if you feel me, allow me in as much as you wish to share."

Yanda shook her head. "I don't... I don't know how." She picked up the sleeping garment and crossed to the back of the cell. In the low lighting, she changed and crawled between sheets, pulling up thin covers, her back to the cell bars. She needed to be silent.

Lying in bed, her thoughts grew and circled, amplified. Tears soaked the pillow.

Someone started singing. It reminded her of her foster mother, singing her to sleep. At first, she couldn't tell if it was in her head or aloud. Someone joined in with sweet harmony. The beautiful, soft tune lifted her out of brooding and, at last, she was lulled into slumber.

Chapter 4

Morning brought increased light along the curved corridor, though the sky remained filled with stars.

Beri arrived, rolling a cart. He slid a tray into each cell through a small opening.

When he'd left, a smallish humanoid with pale blue skin and aqua nubs on her head, two cells down, asked Yanda quietly, "What *ith* your name?" She spoke with a slight lisp.

Yanda looked up from examining what was under the lids on her tray. Strange smells wafted up from unfamiliar food: a sort of flat bread spread with sweet jelly, and an egg-like mixture dotted with desiccated green bits. "I'm Yanda Selkeden." She tested the food with her fork.

"I'm Vatu."

"Nice to meet you." Yanda took a tentative bite of a textured pile and pondered its flavor. Slightly tart and spicy.

"How did you come to be here?" Vatu asked.

Yanda felt shame for being overcome enough to desert her daughter. "It's hard to explain. I was drawn to get on a ship, then abducted here." She could not shake the feeling that she should have been able to keep control.

There was silence.

A large woman sat near the bars of their shared wall. "Did he rape you?"

"Yes. I mean, not violently. But he got into my mind and I had no control."

"Same thing. As far as we know, Krid is the law here. He owns everything on this moon."

"Why is he imprisoning us?"

"I think we each have a different story. But he 'collects.' Things and people with powers. I'm Chinkendit. Most call me Chin."

"Glad to meet you." Yanda tried a nibble of the bread. The spread was fruity.

"You said you were drawn?" Chin had a gruff voice. She stood and paced.

"Yeah. I'm still trying to figure it out," Yanda said, chewing. "Something called me. It was—impossible to resist."

"Krid?"

"No." Yanda surprised herself with her vehemence. "Not at first anyway. He got in my head and told me to book passage on the Lark but before that, something filled my head, drawing me to the spaceport." She leaned her head against a bar, throat suddenly constricted. "I left everything behind..." Her voice caught and she rasped, "My little girl. My work. My life."

She felt a storm of sympathetic thoughts from the

others.

"When I came out of stasis on the ship, I was shackled, and a metal band around my neck suppressed my mind, my powers... even my memories, some of them." She looked around. "Does he rape everyone?"

Some shook their heads.

"He wants something specific from you," said a stocky woman in a cell on the other side. "Something he's been looking for. That's what I heard."

"Heard from where?" asked one of the others.

"Someone in the kitchen. I can hear her thoughts. I don't try but she's a loud thinker."

A few chuckled.

"I have his seed in me," Yanda said.

They sobered.

"We can get rid of it," Shouma said. "Chela can help you. She's a healer."

"Wouldn't you need special herbs for that?" Yanda asked. "How would you get them?" Secretly she knew she, too, could get rid of it, the way she could repair a torn blood vessel with her sight, and more... what she'd done in her last surgery. But something stopped her.

When the voices went silent, she looked around and noticed the others glancing at each other intently. A meeting of minds she was not part of, she guessed.

"We will have to work on this. But there is time. You've detected it very early," the elder said.

"That's my sight, my ability," Yanda said.

Chela, the healer, said, "You can see into your body?" She came close to her bars, pressing her face to them, and peered toward Yanda, eager.

"I can see into anyone's body. Or through a wall."

The awe in the prisoner dome was palpable.

"That must be what interests Krid," Chin said. She was playing with the covered dishes, spinning the covers.

But Yanda knew there was a deeper mystery to her being brought there.

Through the day, she heard the stories of the various women in her cell block.

• ———— ••• ———— •

Once in the morning, and again in the afternoon, they were brought to an exercise area, a few at a time, where they could lift weights and do pull-ups. Of course, it was indoor. There was no atmosphere outside the domes. Already Yanda missed the outdoors.

That night, lying in bed, Yanda sent her sight to the infinitesimal zygote floating in her womb. She would not destroy life. But she could move it out of her. She tried. It would not budge. She could not affect it at all.

She felt shocked. Did the zygote have power of its own? Was that mage power?

Later Beri came and sat by her cell, as he'd done the night before. He leaned against the wall on his side.

This time she came to sit by him, on her side.

"Where do you come from?" she asked.

"I'm originally from Romden. But I get around. I'm an interstellar journalist."

"Wow, that sounds fascinating."

The others conversed. A few played a word game. There was little else to do since their devices and other belongings had been taken. None seemed to pay attention to her and Beri.

"How'd you end up in Krid's snare?" she asked.

He studied her, as if weighing how much to say. "Kridenit collects power objects from around the universe.

23

You might already know that."

"I saw some strange stones in his... chambers." She cringed at the memory. "Does he use these objects to coerce people?"

"I don't know exactly what he uses them all for. But he became interested in obtaining the Sophis Tetra of Goncha — a thing of great value and importance to that planet, for which they hold great reverence. It helps them focus their mental energies. For this, it needs to be wedged in with its counterparts, high on a mountain that's basically unscalable."

"Did he take it?" Yanda's voice was filled with disgust.

"Sent more than fifty men and other intelligent beings to their deaths before he acquired it. More died in his exit from Goncha."

"Asshole," Yanda said.

"On my journeys, I often stopped at Goncha. They have healing pools that leave you tingling brightly for days." He grinned briefly.

"I'd love that right now." Yanda yearned for a mere bath. "What kinds of things do the pools heal?"

"My life, I was hoping," he said with a self-deprecating laugh. "I always visited a family there."

"Or perhaps a special woman who happened to belong to the family?"

"Maybe. Anyhoo, they are good folk. They told me about the theft of the Sophis Tetra. A girl of twelve had worked with its powers for years, preparing to be its next guardian. Since it was torn from the matching stones, she's been in agony, and the people suffer with her."

"Don't tell me. You promised to get it back."

"Of course."

"Very heroic."

"It would have been, had I succeeded."

"That's how you were caught by Krid."

"You got it."

"Have you ever seen the Sophis Tetra?" Yanda asked.

"No. I have a mental image, though."

"How?"

"My friends there can give a thought picture."

"Do you know where he keeps it?"

"I have a pretty good idea," he said, getting up. "I'd better go. I can't be gone too long."

* ——— ••• ——— •

Weeks later, in the first stage of pregnancy, Yanda once again boarded the Lark.

The fems were strapped onto stasis bunks, a few to each cabin.

* ——— ••• ——— •

On Terlond, Zamani felt the Lark approaching. More accurately, he felt Yanda nearing his planet. He knew her resonance, though they'd lost track of her after she responded to their calling, his and the Stone's.

He knew everything about her because she was the one the Stone needed. So he was able to tell, as he registered her approach, that a life was growing in her womb. His eyes widened.

* ——— ••• ——— •

One night, as they hurtled toward their destination, strapped into fold-out beds, Yanda dreamed of a stunning man—not altogether man, for his ears were leaf-shaped, curving up the sides of his head, pointed at the tips. His eyelids were long waves, lashes accenting the curled corners. His smile took her breath away. She felt a profound fondness for him, as one only does in dreams, in her bones and cells and soul.

They made love on a bed soft as clouds, on a platform tucked into treetops. She could have stayed forever.

"Tell me your name," she whispered against his lips.

"I won't. Not now." His voice was rich, like melted chocolate, and just as sweet. "There is great sadness in you."

She met his gaze. His irises seemed to swirl.

"I left my daughter behind," she told him, throat tight. "When I was drawn from my home planet."

"I'm sorry." His brows creased in consternation. Then he changed direction. "You had Krid's seed in you. I was not able to destroy it, so I transformed it."

"Is this a dream?" she asked.

"Yes and no."

"What did you transform it into?" she asked, calm as only in a dream when told something amazing.

"My child," he said.

"Oh." This seemed natural. It made her happy. He was her love and she wanted their child.

He told her that she had friends on Terlond but that she must wait, build her powers. "There will likely be battle."

"Battle?"

The Elf told her how Krid's father had been part of the attacks on Terlond, trying to obtain the Stone of the Neyna that had supported their Elven clans for thousands of years.

"How did it support them?"

"With energy. It is a beautiful force, when whole. But they blasted parts of it, diminishing its power. That's what called you. The Stone."

"How do you know?" she asked.

"I know. You sleep now." He put a long, slender-fingered hand over her dreaming eyes.

"If you knew, then you helped the Stone? Did you know it was taking me from my daughter?"

"We called," he said. "You answered, Yandawi. On Terlond, grow your powers."

"What is this name, Yandawi?"

"It is your right name."

Then he was gone and she slept on.

Chapter 5

Yanda watched with the others from the viewing platform on the Lark as they descended toward a red ball that gained details as they approached. Beri pointed out the toxic wasteland to the east of the one main city. He'd been there before.

She filed off the Lark with the others, stepping onto Terlond's surface for the first time. Strange orange sunlight glowered. They boarded a hover craft, Beri nowhere to be seen.

Traveling from the space port, they glided just above the ground, passing through slummy outskirts, soon entering a part of the city that must have been elegant in its day.

They came to a stop in front of one of the few mansions that had survived The Wars which decimated most of this planet's single continent. Guards led them into a long hall attached to servants' quarters, warning of a cadre of mage spies—who could read any use of psi--who would monitor their every move and thought from towers at the four corners of the property.

Yanda felt sad not seeing Beri; they'd formed a friendship in those few weeks. At least the community of women was no longer separated in cells. They were brought to a long room where apparently all were to stay. Narrow beds lined the walls, covers lacking any hint of comfort, a single small table next to each.

Chin tossed the small bag of belongings she'd been allowed to keep onto a narrow bed and grumbled, "I guess, now that he has his goons monitoring us, *Krud* trusts us to be together." She rolled onto it, feet sticking off the end.

Yanda appreciated the name Krud that the gruff soldier-woman, Chinkendit, and the Jejods had chosen for Krid. She wondered what Chin's powers were, other than being strong. As far as height, she increased the bed's length by pulling her assigned table to extend it, and stretched out feet over the edge.

"Probably wants to study us, see what we'll do now, out of cells." Bonden chose a corner bed and immediately began arranging her space, then flopped and tinkered with wires and small objects she'd managed to find and hide away in pockets.

Yanda moved toward a bed against a wall through which she could see a garden with birds flitting. The only windows were high up.

Vatu settled in the next bed over. On the simple side table provided, she arranged a few shells and stones, which seemed to be her only belongings.

The first night, Shouma called to them one by one,

making her bed a sort of consultation room. When it was Yanda's turn, the elder explained to her that she would train each of them to hide their thoughts. "We'll have to shield what you're learning from surveillance. Here on my bed, I've built a cone of silence."

Yanda felt elation that she'd be taught in this way. She shared with Shouma what she'd been told by the Elf in her dream, that they'd need to build their powers over the coming months, that Krid would be planning for war, to take the Stone as soon as he could find it.

"You think this Elf is here, on Terlond?" Shouma asked.

Yanda's brow creased. "I assumed so."

• ———— • • • ———— •

Months passed. Shouma's powers were formidable and she was a superb trainer. The women worked on their abilities until they had a hive-mind that could communicate flawlessly, with thoughts undetected by any outsider. They did mundane magic, like "pass me the sauce" in mind-speak. Meanwhile, Yanda's belly grew.

One day, a plump female Terlondian servant named Dew curtsied to Yanda, but eyed the exotic women around her with unease. "Summons from Kridenit."

Yanda followed her, heart thumping. Despising her rapist, her hand went protectively to her belly. Would Krid detect that the tiny fetus growing in her was not his? The others' eyes followed as Yanda walked down the long sleeping chamber. As she passed Shouma, the old woman sent her a mind-message. "I will hide your abilities. And your son's."

Son? She detected the gender of my child? And his abilities? If Shouma could, would Krid as well? She pressed her hands across her belly protectively, not wanting Krid to

30

know anything about her child, as they proceeded down marble-walled hallways, up sweeping, thick carpeted stairs to the greedy sorceror's chambers in the lofty central section of the estate.

She stepped into his tower-room, leaving Dew at the doorway. It gave views in all directions. Rows of tall trees hid most of what were said to be toxic swamplands to the east. In the west, beyond the town, ocean stretched to the horizon. To the south, only desert. Not many appealing escape routes. She turned hopefully to the north. There was this world's only spaceport—so Beri had told them. She longed to gaze in that direction, searching for possible transport away, back to her planet, but pulled her eyes away quickly, wary of showing too much longing for escape.

Kridenit lounged on a plush settee, bowls of fruits and chocolates within reach on a gold-filigreed table.

She thought about the contrast with the bland, almost inedible food they received in the prison-chamber and sizzled.

"I've heard rumors…" He placed a grape in his mouth and chewed, seeming to relish not offering her any, "that you're carrying my child." His eyes dropped to her protruding stomach.

Yanda resisted the urge to cover her belly with her hands.

"I assume it's mine since you were not with child when you arrived. We did have…" He unfurled his long fingers to indicate a search for words, "*intimacy* that first night."

The red heat of rage crept up Yanda's neck, prickling. The thought that he'd searched her body and knew she hadn't arrived pregnant was nauseating enough. But to call what he'd done intimacy?

What had Shouma said? Hold your anger. Let it fuel

future action. It will do no good now.

But *intimacy*? Her teeth clenched. As if some beautiful mutual connection had occurred. As if she had not been drugged by whatever tools he'd used to put her in a stupor, forcing her into intercourse for him to plunder her unprotected mind. Her belly roiled with fury. She felt her fetus respond, agitated, and tried to calm herself. She whispered into Shouma's mind, "don't let him tell it's not his." She felt Shouma's assurance.

Yanda had practiced concealing memories behind a protective wall in her psyche for hours, the other fems testing to see if they could detect her thoughts as she did theirs. She checked to make sure it was strong.

But he seemed more intent on something else now, as he rose and stared out the eastern windows.

Her dream returned to her. The lover who'd come into her sleep on the Lark had said Krid wanted her to find something for him. A stone?

The insidious mage turned, took her arm, and drew her to look out with him. "What do you see?" he asked.

She hated his touch. "Wastelands and a far-off ocean," she said. She could blast his hand off with her new powers. When she'd done surgeries, she'd thought she could only look through the layers, but it turned out she could affect matter. She *could* give him an electric shock. But Shouma had suggested they hide their abilities unless in dire danger. The power of surprise would be important.

Yanda glanced at Krid's face, holding her breath. Would he try to numb her and read her mind?

"Let's be frank, Yolanda." The words slid out of him like syrupy bile.

She winced at the erroneous name he gave her. She would laugh about it later.

"You were called by the Stone of the Neyna. I know that. Now you're on the Stone's world. I am not preventing it from calling you. You must be hearing it loud and clear." He sent an intrusive probe into her mind. All but recent banal events were hidden behind the wall of her and Shouma's construction.

The side of his mouth lifted in a sneer. "Dead as a rail." He shook her. "Are you keeping thoughts from me? You couldn't be that stupid. Need I warn you how ill-advised it would be?"

He must not know such a wall can be built to hide from him. She shrugged, as if she had no idea what he was talking about.

"Why would the Stone have called you if you didn't have great powers?" He gave her arm a last shake, digging his fingers in, and let go. "When you first came to Farn, I felt you looking into me. Now I feel nothing. Is pregnancy deteriorating your mind?" His lip curled again and he stepped away with a disgusted glare. "Go."

Something else Shouma was teaching them was to read others, even a difficult mind full of traps like Krid's. She caught a thought. He planned to let them escape and then follow them.

Yanda strode from the extravagant chamber, relieved to be away from Krid, simmering with fury that roiled in her belly. Dew waited at a discreet distance down the hall. They rushed along a covered outer passage suspended between buildings. By the look on her face, Dew was as anxious as she to be away from the foul mage's temper.

Yanda glanced out across the compound. Using her special vision, she saw figures within guard towers at the edges of the property. Surveillance mages. She simmered again with anger. Every day they had to carefully monitor their thoughts, sorting and separating mundane from magical, soup from escape-plan.

As they entered the sleeping, living, everything, 27-hour-a-day quarters, silence fell. Chin and the Jejods, beds pushed together, suspended their dice game, mid-roll.

Chinkendit, over six feet tall, moved like a soldier and cursed like one, too. She wore men's garb. About her face, gender was uncertain. She held the dice cup mid-toss. The three Jejod sisters, six-and-a-half feet tall, with their striking, bird-like features dusted in fine feathers, also froze, eyes on her, waiting. Clothed in black robes sashed at the waists, they were trained warriors, with keen, uncanny sight and hearing, much like the raptors they resembled.

Dele—a musician who could move through walls—laid down her flute-like *zhoun-zhoun*, waiting. Bonden—crafter extraordinaire, object-mover—gripped a mechanism she'd devised from found objects. Chela—healer and midwife—stopped mid-stitch, watching. Vatu, who appeared to be reading with nothing in her hands, sat up straight, cross-legged on her corner bed.

Shouma said to Dew, "You may go, child." Most everyone accepted Shouma as the elder, even the mostly Terlondian servants who delivered their food and other necessities.

When the local woman had left, the rest moved closer together. Yanda sat near Vatu. Shouma formed a protective sphere in the air around them so that no thought or spoken word could be detected by those who monitored them.

"Krid knows I'm pregnant." Yanda's voice sounded strange to her; spoken language was becoming almost a lost art among them. She projected hidden thoughts to the hive-mind: "He expects us to escape and lead him to the Stone."

"Good to know," Shouma thought into all their minds.

"We certainly won't take *his* escape. We must find one better, that he can't detect. I do wonder about this Stone."

The Ten Fems drifted back to what they'd been doing, with many small conversations. Chin and the Jejods' game grew louder, then quieter, then loud again.

Vatu moved onto Yanda's bed and rested a hand on Yanda's belly. "How's the jelly bean?"

Yanda chuckled, putting her hand next to Vatu's on the small hummock. "Good, I hope. Chela says so." She grew serious and put an extra barrier around them as Shouma had taught them. "He was agitated, wanting me to tell him where this Stone is. Some power stone." She didn't mention that the Elf who'd come to her in her sleep on the Lark spoke of a Stone as well. "He did threaten, if I hide information."

"He's such a beast." Vatu plucked at pilling on the old blanket. "We have to get you and your baby away. I'm going to start exploring outside of this room."

"But will you be safe?" Yanda didn't like this. There was something about the calm, delicate Mingal that eased the pain of their exile.

Vatu told Yanda then that she was a shapeshifter.

Yanda's eyes widened. "You are? Do others know?"

"Shouma does."

"You can... turn into other creatures? Or just put a glamor on so others think they see something else?"

"I think I really become something else on some level. Even my mind-waves change so someone would detect thinking like the other being. Most on my planet learn this skill for survival."

"Are you in constant danger on Mingal?" Yanda asked, starting to think the place might be frightful.

"Well, we're in the sea a lot, and there are predators that

might chase us. Plus, we think it's fun." Vatu giggled. "I should see if Shouma could teach me her ability to disappear and go from one place to another in an instant."

"She can do all that?" Yanda felt surprised that she'd not learned that about their mentor.

"Yes. I think she's been going outside the Citadel."

"Citadel?" Yanda asked.

"That's what I call this place." Vatu glanced at Yanda with a grin.

"It's a good name. Do you think she visits someone?"

"I don't know. Maybe I should try to follow her, if I can detect where she's gone."

"How would you do that?"

Vatu shrugged. "Maybe I could just detect her mind."

Yanda wondered what that would be like.

Lights went out at a strict time in their long narrow room. Few had the ability to conjure illumination, so most settled down to sleep when lights went out and rose with daylight. All was quiet except for the sounds of nine women sleeping.

Yanda heard Vatu's congested breathing. Dondar's foul atmosphere was weakening her, making her breathing labored. Yanda got out from her covers and knelt by Vatu's bed. Pressing her hands to the Mingal's small back, she concentrated, searching for blockages in Vatu's airways, clearing with precision until her friend's breaths came with ease, and she slept.

Then Yanda climbed back into her own bed and, lying still, tried to send her mind out beyond the walls, the way she did with her vision, mostly unconsciously. She searched for other minds but had no idea what she was doing and fell asleep trying.

Chapter 6

The next morning, as the others went about small pastimes —cleaning a musical instrument, sewing, inventing gadgets, playing dice games—Yanda sat in bed, her back to the wall, and again sent her senses outward as she'd tried the night before. This time she tried to find a specific mental frequency—Beri.

She sat up straight with a jerk. She found him, just a few blocks away! When she tapped lightly into his thoughts, he startled, looking around. Then, knowing the feel of her mind, he let her in. "Mirror," he thought, with an undercurrent of deep emotion.

Yanda thought of the first time he'd called her Mirror. Back on Farn, they'd glanced at a mirror and she'd asked about the candy stash she saw through the wall, in the neighboring storage room. Stuck on this far-away planet, she hugged herself, remembering the way he'd given her the nickname.

Through his eyes, she saw him on a stool in a leatherwork shop. She asked, "How are you?"

"I'm okay." His response was hesitant.

"How is it to be able to work and go around town?" she asked, envy percolating.

"Well, I'm indentured. My 'pay'—such as it is—goes to Krid. I can't save anything to try to leave, so... it's not great. I'm sorry you're imprisoned, though. At least I'm glad you're not alone. Can I see what you see?"

"Yes." She realized then she'd automatically blocked him from seeing her surroundings, for the privacy of the others. Tapping the hive-mind, she announced, "I've found Beri."

A stir went around the room—clapping, smiles, some jovial remarks meant for him if he could hear. A bit of "carrot top" teasing from the soldier corner.

"I heard that," he said into their minds with a grin.

"Can I let him see you?" Yanda asked.

Universal agreement erupted. They liked Beri.

So Yanda let him into her mind to see through her eyes. He studied the room, each fem's area either messy or neat according to personality.

After a long moment, he said, "I wish I could visit. I miss you guys."

"Good to see you, Beri," Dele said.

"You, too," To Yanda alone, he added, "I know no one in this city."

"I'm sorry," Yanda said. "Despite our limited quarters, at least we have each other. Maybe we can figure out a way. But we're spied on night and day."

She studied what she could see of Beri from his point of

view: mostly his hands on the workbench, stained with leather dye.

"I'd better get back to my work. Gerhog is already in a temper."

Yanda saw the burly Gerhog through Beri's eyes, barreling toward him. She watched Beri's hand pick up a tool to bevel a pattern into leather. "But drop by any time." He gave her a small smile she could feel if not see.

"Maybe you can figure out how to get on a spaceship," she said before they parted.

When they separated, she looked around for Vatu. Not seeing her, she got up and searched the bathroom. Knowing it was monitored, she never felt relaxed in there and came out quickly. Where was she?

Then she remembered their conversation the night before. Had Vatu gone exploring?

There was nothing to do but wait, so she sat on the bed again. She'd been trying to fashion baby garments from cast-off clothes but wasn't much of a seamstress. Others were stitching adorable infant outfits and blankets. She took them out and touched each one, smoothing it and carefully folding it again. One had embroidered ducks. That was Chela's work. Shouma was working on an extravagant patchwork quilt. Shouma glanced up from it and winked at Yanda.

Should she tell her? She didn't want to get Vatu in trouble but also didn't want Vatu *in* trouble and alone.

Her turn came to walk in the walled garden where they were taken twice a day, in small groups, for "fresh air"—such as it was in that toxic city—and exercise. She joined Dele, Bonden and Chela down two short hallways to the small yard area, following Assal, a Terlondian servant with stern shoulders.

To make the overgrown and neglected outdoor space more interesting, the women had formed a spiral, sorting stones into varying colors to line the path. To cultivate herbs along the borders, they cajoled seeds from kitchen staff, bringing water out whenever they could.

Chela worked on a section of the minimal herb border as Bonden arranged objects on a bench and worked on a low-tech mechanism, the purpose of which none were sure. They knew she could empower objects without any detectable data read.

Dele occupied another bench and played a melancholy tune on her flute-like zhoun-zhoun. Yanda thought Dele was more frustrated than the rest, based on her remarks. In her world, she loved dancing at large gatherings, jamming with other musicians, meeting lovers.

Yanda walked the spiral, sending out a feeler, trying to emulate her successful attempt to contact Beri, this time searching for Vatu.

She wouldn't have gone into the town, would she? Looking through the wall, Yanda sent her mind along with her vision, further and further outward.

"Ouch." Tall and willowy, Dele had her foot stretched out across the path.

"Sorry."

The attractive Qontaqian went on playing.

Yanda'd connected less with Dele than with the other fems. Though from the same planet as Chela, she and Dele were utterly different in demeanor. Where Chela was warmhearted and rosy cheeked, Dele could seem haughty.

Finishing the spiral, Yanda wandered to the corner closest to the street and sat on a stone bench under a scrappy tree whose fronds trailed to the ground. There she concentrated harder, seeing through one wall and then the next, along streets with storefronts and into residential neighborhoods. Like red light green light, she felt her senses getting farther from the now familiar Mingal's body register, and brought her searching tendrils back to explore along the corridor toward the servants' quarters. Through one wall, she saw two women having a private moment and quickly withdrew.

In a corridor approaching the kitchen and storage rooms, something tinkled in her mind, like a tiny bell or sensor. "Vatu?" Yanda asked tentatively.

Moments later, a cat rubbed her leg.

There had never been a cat out here before. She supposed it could climb the tree, then onto the wall. Maybe it belonged to someone in the building. "Hey, kitty." She reached down and stroked its calico coat.

The cat disappeared from under her hand. Vatu sat next to her on the bench, laughing. She stroked Yanda's leg. "Nice kitty."

Yanda's eyes widened. "You were… the cat?"

Vatu pulled her legs up, crossing them, eyes glowing. "I found some yummies I don't think anyone will miss. I had to become one of the servants to bring them back, hidden in my skirt. Or her skirt, really. Then to search for you, I became the cat."

"And they won't register the change, your sudden presence out here?" Yanda asked.

"I think they'd have to be following pretty closely to notice."

Yanda wasn't so sure. "Maybe you should ask Shouma what she thinks." It worried her for Vatu to take such risk without Shouma knowing. Though very likely the elder did know. Still. Yanda wanted to be sure.

"Okay, I'll check with her." Vatu wrinkled her nose,

rebellious.

Yanda rubbed where a flutter tickled.

"Baby moving?" Vatu asked.

"Yeah. I like how it feels."

"Have you thought about names?" Vatu put her hand near Yanda's. "Oo. Sweet tiny one."

"I've run lots of names through my mind but haven't settled on any. You should tell me some Mingal ones."

"I could."

Assal, the servant who'd brought them out, called time. Their outside stint was over.

Vatu shifted to a cat again before Assal could spot her. "Come see the goodies I brought," she said into Yanda's mind.

The cat stayed to the shadows as the fems strolled behind the Terlondian, back to their quarters.

Back in their long room, Assal called to the rest for their turn in the yard.

Vatu flopped on her bed. Yanda sat more gingerly on hers, aware of the cargo in her belly. Vatu sorted through delicacies she'd found in a pantry—raisins shoved back into a corner and forgotten, apples getting wrinkly but still edible. Even a bit of chocolate for each of them. She and Yanda passed it all out to cries of joy.

Though prepared food was brought from the kitchens, it was not to anyone's taste. Several of the fems could make fire, or heated spheres, and Bonden rigged a small stove they used for preparing their own dishes whenever they could scrape together ingredients.

Innovation wasn't just happening with food. A groundsman named Calden had taken to helping them, bringing random discarded objects from around the place. He seemed to feel sorry for their plight and was clearly fascinated by Bonden, who could make anything he gave her into something useful. She'd started building a structure for them to exercise on that stretched across the room over their heads. She said she was going to keep on until someone stopped her. It was a series of ladders to climb and play on. The Jejods already loved perching on it, for the ceilings were high; though it wasn't complete, according to Bonden, it seemed plenty sturdy and added interest to their lives.

They were told that their room's air was filtered. Yanda could tell the difference from the outside but it was not enough to keep Vatu healthy.

• ——— • • • ——— •

Seven months into the pregnancy, Yanda sat outside one day practicing a disappearing spell Bonden had taught her, with spoons. Nearby, Shouma guarded the area so that it looked like they played cards.

A voice came into Yanda's head. "Gamoo." She stopped her object manipulation, looking around. "Gamoo," it said again. Feeling the source, she sent her sight down into her belly where her beautiful, perfect boy lay curled inside her womb, sucking his thumb. She stroked near his head. "Are you calling to me, baby?"

He smiled around his thumb, kicked a foot.

"Kisses, baby. I can't wait to hold you and show you what a kiss is." Yanda looked up to see Shouma watching her.

"Baby's talking to you?" she asked.

Yanda nodded, shaky with wonder.

"I remember that," Shouma said with a wistful sigh. "But I couldn't see them inside my belly like you can."

"You have children?" Yanda felt a pang that she hadn't

43

known, hadn't asked.

"Oh yes. Several. And grandchildren."

"He's keeping you from your family. That's so wrong." New hatred for Krid rose in Yanda. The baby kicked, agitated. Yanda ran her hand down her belly to soothe him. "Maybe if I could tell him where the stone is... but it hasn't called to me again, not since it pulled me from my home." Yanda frowned at Shouma and said earnestly, "You could get away, couldn't you, with all your skills?"

"I wouldn't desert you, any of you," Shouma said firmly.

Her face creased in concern, Yanda protested, "But—"

Shouma lifted a hand to stop her. "I won't hear of it."

Yanda pulled distraught eyes to her lap, clenching her hands.

Watching her, Shouma seemed to make a decision. She said, "Child, I've found an ally. Or rather, she found me. We're making a plan."

Yanda stared at her. "Who?"

"I won't give details yet," Shouma answered.

"When then?"

"You must have your child. Things will be put in place —"

"No! I could go now. I don't want to give birth here." Tears welled.

Shouma scooted closer, laid a hand on hers. "You must be patient."

Yanda heaved in a long, shuddering breath. "I don't feel patient."

Shouma chuckled, despite herself. "I know. I know." She hugged the younger woman around the shoulders, pressing her head to Yanda's wild curls.

Chapter 7

Yanda went into labor late one evening. At her insistence, Shouma surrounded them with a shield that prevented anyone outside of their circle from detecting the activity.

Chela oversaw the birth, being a midwife by profession. The baby's tiny legs kicked wildly at the first contractions. Yanda felt his puzzlement in her mind over the sudden pressure. "It's okay, baby," she assured the infant in her belly, rubbing her side.

The infant, not yet born, brought his tiny hand up to suck his thumb.

Stabs of pain brought back stark memories of her first childbirth and she panicked. She turned on her side, biting down on the blanket. "I don't want to do this after all."

"Come, let's ease the pain," Shouma called to Chela who prepared an herbal brew.

Unlike Seiti's long drawn-out birth, this one was fast—one full contraction, a short bout of pain, and two pushes.

Bonden had made a clamp for the umbilical cord, too beautiful for a single use, Yanda thought when the brawny woman handed it to her; Bonden had welded flowers onto the metal's outer surface with her mind.

Now, Chela clamped it on and Bonden severed the cord with a stroke of her hand—they were not allowed sharp objects.

As Chela's skillful hands gently eased the baby's head out, Yanda felt a brief time-out-of-time moment: an elder Elf woman and man were there in her mind, experiencing it all with her, their heads surrounded by leaves. *Are they really here? she wondered. Or did I go somewhere else?*

Moments later, holding her son in her arms and gazing at his tiny wizened face, a name came to Yanda. "I'll call you Zami," she whispered. Then she held him to her breast to suckle.

Did she hear the Elven pair in her mind saying the name with pleased smiles and welcoming? It was so hard to tell. Dreamlike.

Zami latched onto her breast easily and eagerly, resting his tiny hand on her skin and telling her in drifty, feeling-language how much he liked nursing and being against her. She snuggled him, barely aware of the fems tucking pillows around her so she could sit comfortably and rest her head back.

After a while, Zami drifted off, mouth still working though he'd let go. She pulled her nightgown up, dried the area, and sought Beri. After all, he was part of their group at the start of Zami's life. She felt like he needed to be tied to their "family," not left out.

It would be further, she suspected, than his

apprenticeship, to his living quarters. Where did he live? She had no idea. They hadn't talked about it during the brief encounter.

As with searching for Vatu, she sent out her vision and awareness down one street, then another, seeing much of Dondar. She combed the city carefully, searching for Beri's mental register.

At last, she located him at the northwest edge of the city, past a military barracks. His shabby little room was in a block of worker sits, unadorned.

She tapped to see if he was sleeping deeply.

"Just started to drift off," he said, a mental mumble but with discernable pleasure at her presence. "What's up, Mirror?"

Yanda brought the sight of her sleeping boy into her consciousness for him to see.

Beri whistled. "Well, I'll be damned. Isn't he a beauty?" He spoke quietly, as if he might wake him, even though he was sending mind-speak from miles away.

"Yeah." Yanda let out a tiny laugh, half sigh, tinged with mother's love.

Vatu crawled onto Yanda's bed; Yanda curled her legs to make room and Vatu joined their mind connection, sitting next to her against the wall.

"Hey, Nubs," Beri said.

Vatu wrinkled her nose, not loving the name. "Carrots," she said back, using Chin's tease of his hair though it really was more of a dark amber.

"How was the birth?" he asked.

"Whisked him out," Yanda said honestly. "Comparatively speaking."

"Really?"

"Yeah, not like my first one." Her daughter had been a

difficult and long birth. Longing struck her with force, to show Seiti her new brother, and share her news with her adoptive parents. Tears suddenly ran down her cheeks.

Chela came over, carrying a hot mug of herbal tea, and sat on the edge of the bed. "You'll have to shoo everyone away for the afterbirth," she said.

"Oo," Beri said. "Well, I'll leave you to that. Let me see the little guy often, okay?" He sounded a little teary himself.

"I will." Yanda blew him a kiss.

Shouma joined them, sitting on Vatu's bed. She sent a message to Beri and the fems: "We'll be together soon and will be able to hug," that last part especially for Beri.

Thanking her, he disconnected from their mindshare.

"Vatu, can you hold Zami while we do this?" Chela asked. Gently, she removed the tiny infant from Yanda's arms, wrapped him in one of the soft blankets they'd made by hand, and gave him to Vatu, who stared with wonder, touching his puckered lips, his cheeks, his eyelids etched in blue at the edges.

The tea gave Yanda a light euphoria. The normally excruciating task of pressing out the afterbirth went by with little pain. Shouma, with Yanda's help to see the inner area, sent numbing to the tissues.

Yanda squeezed Shouma's hand. "Thank you."

Chela slipped the afterbirth into a small cloth bag covered in embroidered symbols. Before Yanda could get a good look at it, Shouma sent it away.

"Where'd it go?" Yanda asked.

Shouma was silent for a few heartbeats. "Where you get to where you want it to be, we'll find it."

Yanda, head on her pillow, blew halfheartedly through her lips. "Whatever."

"All will be fine." Shouma stroked Yanda's hair back

from her forehead, then bent to kiss Zami. "You did well and brought a magical boy into the world. Universe," she amended, then returned down the long row of beds to her own.

"Why isn't she telling us what she knows?" Yanda thought to Vatu, wanting to be part of the planning, aching to know what Shouma was setting up, what she, Yanda, would be bringing her baby into.

"I guess it would be too hard to monitor all our minds," Vatu responded. "If we were tortured, I have no idea what I'd reveal. Krid could probably break right into my thoughts." She wiggled one of Yanda's feet poking up under the blanket. "Right?"

Grinning, Yanda thought to herself, she's like the sister I never had. She sobered. "Shouma thinks we're all stronger than the spy mages now, for keeping thoughts hidden."

"But Krid?" Vatu asked.

"I don't know." Yanda frowned, touching her baby's delicate cheek. He seemed to stare up at her but she thought his sight couldn't be developed yet.

"What are you thinking?" Vatu asked. "Wondering what comes next?"

"Yeah."

"Everyone is." Vatu often caught errant thoughts people assumed they were hiding.

The other fems started drifting over and soon they crowded around, perching on the two beds, to get close to the new member of their hostage group. Some gave recently completed gifts: a blanket, booties. Each got close enough to touch his cheek or give him a kiss. Yanda worked a soft knitted hat over his light down of brown curls. Yawning, she settled her tiny new bit of family next to her in bed, on the wall side, and gazed at his now sleeping face. His ears were like small perfect seashells.

No points yet, she mused, running a fingertip over the top of one. Was it true, the Elven man coming in her dream and transforming him into his child, on the Lark? Or was he Krid's? She would love him either way. And she had to protect him.

Vatu climbed into her own bed. "'Night."

"Sleep tight." Yanda snuggled into her too-flat pillow, shoving the edge up to curl under her neck.

The others gave Yanda and her baby final pats and headed for their own beds.

• ———••• —— •

Over the next few months, Yanda went through the expected sore times and sleepless nights for everyone, as Zami had crying bouts, like any newborn.

Bonden fashioned earplugs for everyone out of beeswax they acquired from the Terlondian servants in exchange for embroidery and other skills the Fugitives had that did not involve magic.

• ———••• —— •

By six months, Zami communicated clearly, mostly in mind-speak. He also laughed and played like any baby starting to crawl.

Much was the same in the women's quarters. Zami loved their trips to the walled garden. Yanda tried to think up games out there and in their room. All the hostages did.

But there were subtle changes happening. Everyone was fashioning travel bags, hiding them under their mattresses.

Yanda had stayed in touch with Beri, and Shouma trained him to keep his thoughts hidden, just as she'd taught the rest. Yanda showed him how Zami was growing.

A new happiness had crept into his demeanor. When Yanda asked about it, Beri hesitated, saying he didn't know. Maybe it was just that they had found him and were giving him hope.

Vatu went on more and more forays. She collected more items from the parts of the Citadel she could reach by disguising herself. Shouma, Bonden and Chela suggested first aid materials, bandages and medicines. Yanda wondered if she ever went off-grounds. She would leave and come back, never telling where she'd been.

Shouma did the same, Vatu told her. When either left, they'd taken to leaving living replicas of themselves that moved around the place, acting in everyday ways. Even their minds were replicated, with simple thoughts. It was unnerving to see these living, breathing facsimiles. Yanda recalled reading of the homunculus from fiction: tiny perfect beings created first by alchemists in the old stories, later showing up in speculative fiction over the past thousand years.

Though excited that they at last seemed to be preparing for escape, Yanda was terrified. How would it be on the run with a six-month old baby? How could she keep him safe? With him starting to crawl, she couldn't just keep him in a carrier all the time. Anyway, no one had said *how* they would get out of the Citadel.

She desperately wanted to envision a different life for him by the time he was walking. Fields to run in. Streams where he could swim.

One day, sitting on their beds, playing with Zami, Yanda said to Vatu, "If Shouma and whoever her ally is won't make up their minds, maybe you could leave those living copies of you and me, and Zami, and at least *we* could escape. I have to find a ship home, get back to my daughter, and your health is not going to hold up." She bounced Zami on one knee, giving him smiles she didn't feel, corners of her mouth tugging downward against her will.

"We're not as strong, just the two of us. Trying to keep Zami safe?" Vatu argued reasonably. "Also, the street air is even worse than in here. If we tried to travel to the spaceport..." She shrugged. "It might be awful."

"Beri's near the border of Dondar and Sheffed. I hear Sheffed is sort of a slum town where a lot of spaceport workers live. Maybe if we could get to Beri, he would know."

"Have you asked him?" Vatu asked.

Yanda shook her head. "I still feel a little worried about the security when my mind is stretched clear across the city, or even the few blocks to where he works."

Vatu nodded understanding, putting her slender fingers where Zami could grab them. He anchored himself to stand and reached for her nubs, one of his favorite things. She grinned and kissed his cheek. "I still think we're far better off with Shouma's abilities and Bonden's. Not to mention Chin and the Jejods to guard us. And Chela for healing." Her eyes searched Yanda's face, begging for patience.

So Yanda went to Shouma.

"When do we leave? My boy's growing up." Her mouth was set in a line of despair.

"Come. Sit." Shouma patted the bed next to her and opened her arms for Zami.

Yanda sat and let Zami first stretch on his toes, then lean into Shouma's arms. The elder woman folded him into a hug and he chortled, grabbing at her hair.

Yanda felt Shouma check the boundaries of their thoughts. "Now we have to find the old tunnels. If we can get to them, my contact will try to help us."

"Your contact has told you of tunnels that no one knows about anymore?"

"Yes. Vaguely."

"And these would help us get on a ship?" Yanda asked, wanting explicit clarification.

"Help us get away from here first. I think she has ways of monitoring the coming and going of airships."

"Where is she?" Yanda asked.

But Shouma shook her head. "I don't know."

It'd been months. At least six months since Shouma had first told them they'd have assistance in getting away. Yanda felt testy, suspicious, and above all, done with the mystery. Her daughter was growing up without her. The usual ache gripped her heart, then moved to her stomach where it turned to a churning turmoil. Zami crawled back to his mama and she put him to her breast. The first pull was always gratifying.

Shouma touched his infinitely soft cheek with tenderness. "It'll be better for him if he's off the breast when we leave here."

"That's not a reason to delay," Yanda snapped. Then she softened her voice, "Besides, when we can get it, I've introduced him to other plant milks. Soon I can start him on more foods. He doesn't have to have my breast milk."

"True," Shouma conceded, patting her shoulder.

· ——— ··· ——— ·

Yanda told Vatu about needing to find underground tunnels. "Shouma said they're deserted. They're in the lore about the past."

"This is according to Shouma's source?" Vatu asked quietly, picking at her blanket.

"Yes. They're thought to still exist. I guess Shouma's

informant is quite certain, but doesn't know how to access them, especially from here."

After that conversation, Vatu increased her searches, even trying the streets. Each time, she came back coughing and looking drained, her color ashen.

Chapter 8

Krid's mage spies never entered the women's quarters…

…until the day Vatu went missing.

Yanda paced for hours.

"Vatu hasn't returned," she told Shouma at last. "Worse, I can't find her mental register and… her copy is looking... weird."

Shouma searched, then pulled together the hive. After a time, with all sending tentacles of thought outward, giving all their power to scanning the city, Shouma stopped them to rest.

"She's weak somewhere," Dele said. Though aloof much of the time, her sensing of another spirit could be far-reaching. "It's tenuous."

"Can you tell where she is?" Shouma asked her.

"I feel like I should be able to follow a thread to her,"

Dele admitted. "It's just so weak."

"Show us. We can try to help." Shouma said to the others, "We'll need a light touch. Take Dele's lead, try to drip strength into the mix without drowning out any impulses."

All the hive-mind concentrated.

Almost immediately, an unpleasant presence emanated from the doorway.

They ended their shared trance to stare at a pinched, sour man, hovering, ghoul-like, head extended forward on a skinny neck.

Yanda recognized him. She'd seen him in the towers when she'd studied the mages who spied on them, like a sore tooth one can't keep one's tongue from touching.

"There's one of yours in the gardens." His voice was nasal and rasping, as though seldom used. "You can't go out there. The gardens have access to the streets. You..." he seemed to search for a reasonable explanation, now that he faced actual beings in the flesh, "wouldn't be safe."

Wouldn't be safe. Yanda wanted to laugh. But she was terrified for Vatu.

Shouma, elder and their leader, stood. "We'll fetch her."

"She is being taken to our...infirmary...for healing. She appears passed out."

Chela said with unusual force, standing, "*We* need to heal her. We know what she needs. They *must* bring her here."

The spy-mage seemed to turn inward for a moment. Then he focused back into the room. "The Honorable K-Sonn approves. He does not wish to lose a valuable asset. He will give you twenty-seven hours with her, then she will be punished for leaving the boundaries." He spoke like an automaton, as if someone controlled him.

"One day is not enough. We need a week, at least, to heal her," Chela said firmly.

His eyes glazed over again.

Coming back, he droned, "One week then." His eyes flicked to the homunculus which had now run down and was making strange movements, lifting her hand compulsively. He smirked before he left.

So, the mages knew about the facsimiles Shouma and Vatu had been making. Had they informed Krid? Vigilance would increase. How would they escape?

A groundsman carried Vatu in, limp in his arms.

Yanda said, "Put her here," pointing at Vatu's bed. Shouma had made the fading Vatu-replica disappear by this time. The man, a stranger to them, dumped her, glanced around at them and left with a curled-lip and growl. Some around the place didn't like those who were different.

Chela rushed to Vatu, Yanda and Shouma close behind.

Once Chela had checked her vital signs to decide what herbs to brew among the limited supply she'd cached, Yanda and Shouma sat close to her and set about clearing her passageways.

Eyes filled with tears, Yanda choked out, "She's so toxic." She blamed herself. "I've put too much pressure on her about getting away," she said quietly to Shouma.

"Don't blame yourself, child," Shouma said, keeping her steady healing energy pouring into Vatu.

Bonden approached them, holding a strange apparatus. "Can I try this?" She held a kind of hood attached to tubes and a small tank made of a stitched hide bag. "I've found a source to pull good air from. I don't know where it is. Somewhere on this planet. I can just pull a bit at a time."

"Try it," Shouma said, holding Yanda's gaze for agreement.

Yanda nodded.

Bonden sat on the side of the bed, gently lifted Vatu, still limp with unconsciousness, and slid the gray material over her head. A clear panel showed her face. The neck fitted to enclose her. Bonden flipped a switch. "I'll stay with her, pulling healthy air in, until she's better." She settled herself by Vatu's head and closed her eyes, holding the small tank.

Yanda sat on her bed, gazing warily from Vatu to the apparatus, to Bonden.

A plain woman, Bonden had the straightforward manner of an engineer, or an accountant. No nonsense. But she had a deep affection for Vatu, as they all did, and now her face held the pinched look of someone with another's life in her hands.

Yanda scooted to the head of her bed, where it touched Vatu's, and crossed her legs, sitting back against the wall near Bonden. Arm pressed to the other woman, she sent energy into her. Wanting to join this effort as a partner, she asked if she might learn.

Zami crawled up and plunked down against her, toys in his small fists, and proceeded to play quietly. Yanda absently stroked his back as, in her mind, she felt Bonden calling for high quality air. This was an elemental skill. To learn it, Yanda had to release some notions of human thought and existence. Her expertise had been comprised of the elements of human blood and tissue. Willing suspension of superfluous thought, she traveled with the other woman's seeking, drawing. *That* she could help with. Once found, they drew the good air into the small chamber that lay in Bonden's lap.

Yanda thought she felt a tiny bit of her son's energy present with theirs in the effort.

• ——— • • • ——— •

For days, Vatu lay limp, losing weight, the color drained from her face. Bonden stayed at her side, feeding her lungs from the small tank that mysteriously filled again and again with clean air. Yanda, who now knew how to draw the good air in, took turns with her.

Krid had Terlondian servants spying more frequently, as Yanda had expected, along with increasing the sentient spies' invasion of their minds.

The breathing apparatus was a blend of primitive and magical; the non-tech, primitive aspects meant it was not confiscated. Or it was allowed because it kept Krid's "asset" alive, Yanda thought with disgust.

After Vatu's collapse, Krid called for Yanda nearly every day.

"Where's the Stone?" he'd ask over and over. "I detected it calling you across the universe but I haven't once felt it here, on its own planet." He gripped her shoulders. "What do you know?"

"Nothing. I've never known anything about it," Yanda said truthfully.

"I can take our son," he growled.

Each time she returned to the women's quarters after these sessions, she felt more desperate to get away. Vatu had to recover soon.

On the fifth day, Vatu pushed weakly to sitting. Yanda, beside her with the air tank, quickly shoved pillows behind her and checked her congestion, elation surging through her.

In her surgery work, Yanda had used her sight in a limited capacity to detect blockage, to see what did not show on x-rays. She was honing her skills for clearing passageways and mending.

"It was the toxicity of the streets, wasn't it?" she asked Vatu.

Her friend nodded, pale limp nubs bobbing with the motion.

Softly, Yanda asked, "But why were you on the streets? Don't we want to find tunnels under? They could be beneath this building."

"I've checked everywhere and not found them under this compound." Vatu gripped Yanda's wrist. "But I may know now where they are."

"What do you mean? You've been lying here unconscious. Haven't you?" Yanda felt panic rising that her friend might have risked her barely returning health. Had she pretended to be unconscious?

"It was in my unconscious state that I traveled. Maybe it was a dream. I need to verify what I think I found."

"Vatu, no. You're not strong enough. And to transform? It's too much too soon."

"Shouma can make me invisible," Vatu said, stubborn. "I feel much better."

"You've not eaten for days."

"I barely need to eat. On my planet, we sometimes go dormant. I can take my heart rate down to almost nothing. And not eat or drink for... a long time. Like a salamander."

Yanda stared at her. "You never told me that."

"I guess it didn't come up." Vatu shrugged. She did seem stronger by the minute.

Tik, the youngest Jejod, came over. "Hey, you're awake," she said to Vatu.

Others called out or came to check on Vatu. Spirits lifted all around the room.

"Can I take Zami over with us?" Tik asked Yanda.

She eyed the four beds pushed together in a far corner, where Chin and the Jejods were cleaning weapons she couldn't see but knew they were there by the fems' thoughts. She made a face.

"We'll be careful. Anyway, *he's* cautious. And smart."

"I don't know," Yanda said.

"I'll play with him here, then." Tik dropped onto Yanda's bed, long legs stretched far out onto the floor.

Zami jumped to her with a lurching crawl. Yanda wasn't sure who enjoyed their games more.

"My punishment comes in less than two days." Vatu sat forward, taking Yanda's hand. "Who knows where they might put me."

"How did you know that?" Yanda asked.

"I heard it."

Yanda was wondering more and more just how aware Vatu had been through this time. Now she knew her hunch had been right. Yanda pulled Vatu into a hug and enclosed them in a shield, even a layer stronger than the protection Shouma kept around the room. "We have to find a way to escape."

Vatu nodded. She ate a little, went to the bathroom, returned and slept again.

Zami, nursing, drifted off to sleep. Yanda gently laid him down, a pillow blocking him, and scooted to the end of the bed, where she rummaged for a notebook.

Suddenly the real Vatu appeared beside Yanda and her copy disappeared.

Yanda gasped, realizing she'd again been taken in, thinking Vatu slept soundly on her bed.

Vatu scooted to the wall and hugged her knees, breathing hard. "Found something." In her excitement, the pale blue-green nubs stood up on her head, white corn-silk hair almost crackling.

"You snuck off." Yanda felt concern with Vatu's weakness and the fact that she'd gone off, tiring herself, no one knowing.

"I had to." Vatu let the other fems hear her thought-communication, shielding anyone outside the Ten. "I think I've found an abandoned tunnel. It's many feet of stone below us." She turned to Yanda. "I need you to look through, to be sure."

"I can't believe you already went out there," Yanda whispered, arms crossed, scowling.

"Shouma helped me keep my strength."

Yanda felt hurt that she'd not only fooled her but had gained Shouma's assistance to do so.

"I'll disguise you," Vatu said. "Come on."

"You've just been in a coma. You're pushing yourself too hard."

"I have to. What do you want to be?"

Yanda looked around at the others.

"It is dire," Shouma said. "We can't risk them taking Vatu."

Yanda's shoulders slumped in defeat. "Watch Zami?" she asked Chela, the healer. "What takes little energy. A cat?"

Vatu smiled and took the form of Dew's sister, who was off that day. She put breathing, energetic copies of herself and Yanda for the guard mages to detect.

Chela took Yanda's place at the end of the bed, fondly stroking the baby's tiny feet as he slept.

Yanda thought to them all, "Back soon."

Zami's lips puckered in sleep.

Yanda, now a sinewy black feline, rubbed her furry side against Vatu's stout chambermaid ankle as they exited their designated quarters, shielding their minds. Shouma helped with the shielding from her bed.

A long hall ran the length of the west side of the mansion, from south to north. Columned passages, imitative of Earth's ancient Greek architecture, reminding Yanda of stories she'd read on her home planet. They led off to the sides, connecting with the streets of Dondar. Yanda had never been along this hallway though she'd seen it through the walls. Now she took it in as a four-legged creature. From a very low vantage point, her eyes saw with cat accuracy and focus.

She reached out for a glimpse of Beri. Seeing him, blocks away, bent over his work, she did not contact him. What would it be like to speak to him as a domestic cat? Would he detect that mental register as well as her own? She wouldn't experiment now.

The hallway turned sharply inward toward servants' sleeping areas. Yanda had never seen the north end of the estate, even with her sight. They continued on into a little used corridor and then out the doors to an abandoned yard area, walled and full of brambles.

"I found this when in cat form," Vatu explained as she too became a cat and led the way along a wall packed with tangled vines. In a hollow covered with ivy, Vatu took her own form long enough to press against a hidden door. Remnants of old paint peeled from its rough surface. It pushed inward easily.

On the other side, they faced a long, shadowy stairway descending into black. Vatu pressed the door shut with her back and they breathed relief.

Yanda glanced around nervously.

"I sense no one's been here for a long time," Vatu said in a low voice as she rested a hand on a stair rail and started downward.

"I don't think the mages see us here, either." Even in cat form, Yanda applied the abilities Shouma'd taught them, including sensitizing them to the presence of mage-minds.

Still cat, she prowled down the stairs with perfect sight in the dark, appreciating the feel of her paws on stone steps and the grace of her muscles before Vatu shifted her back to her natural form.

She breathed in underground air then, delighting in the new and different pungency from their sterile prison in the Citadel.

"Why do you think this large basement space has fallen from use?" she asked, somewhat rhetorically, expecting no answer.

At the base of the stairs, she jumped off onto a dirt floor and whirled out into open space, dancing in the darkness. "Ah, freedom from being watched."

Vatu smiled and came to dance with her for a moment. Then she said, "Under us. Do you feel it? Hollow spaces."

Yanda didn't feel spaces that way. For her it had to be vision. Her sight sense. Sitting against a rough wall on hard-packed dirt flooring, she closed her eyes and reached her sight down beneath them.

It took a moment to pierce through many feet of stone but, sure enough, a labyrinthine set of caves ran far below, branching in multiple directions. As far as Yanda could see, it was deserted. She felt that it had lain untraveled for years; it had that dirt-strewn, cobwebby look of disuse and abandonment. Her heart raced. She opened her eyes. "You're right. Seems extensive. How could no one know of it?" Could this be their escape? Her heart was racing.

"But I've found no door. No access to tunnels. We'll need Bonden to get us through the stone if there's no door."

Vatu had come to sit next to Yanda against the wall.

"Yikes. That's a lot of stone to travel through. That will take huge energy. And will be very weird, for us. Zami? Can he do that?"

"He's very special, Yanda." Vatu's eyes seemed to see her clearly. They were luminous as they peered at her. "With Shouma and Bonden. Dele, too. She can move through so she can maybe help move us through."

"Yes." Yanda vibrated with hope, but also fear. *Get away to a ship. Not be separated from my son. Return to my daughter. At last.* Her stomach did flips.

They retraced their steps to the door into free servant areas. Vatu transformed them back to servant and cat. As they hurried along the north-south corridor, Yanda shot Beri a message.

"We think we may have found a way to leave, staying hidden. Will you come?"

"We'll have to see. Stay safe, Mirror." In his mind, he flicked her untamable auburn hair.

So he detected her mind, not the cat one. Yanda's throat gripped in a knot. Krid held a burning hatred for Beri for having contemplated stealing the cherished *Sophis Tetra*. She could only imagine what was in store when the vile techno-mage decided to turn his attention toward him. Especially once he found the Ten Fems and Zami missing.

Yanda and Vatu returned. All eyes were on them as they stepped into their quarters.

Sealing their shields as tight as possible, with Shouma's inspection to make sure, they shared what they'd sensed and seen.

All tried to act normal through the rest of the day, but surreptitiously, everyone checked over their few valued belongings and the food they'd stashed into whatever bags or bundles they could devise, hidden under beds or disguised as pillows.

Chapter 9

Late that night, with linens bunched up under the covers of each bed to look like sleeping women—easier to set the mind-imprints of sleepers and hold them—the ten fems, plus Zami, prepared to leave the room they'd spent most of their time in for more than a year.

"How will we bring our stuff?" Dele whispered, as Vatu was about to turn them into mice." She held her tattily stitched cloth bag to her, the shape of the treasured zhoun-zhoun clearly poking out, flute-like.

"It's all really there, just different energy for a short time," Vatu explained.

Yanda's heart raced as she felt herself changed into a small rodent. The mind of a mouse understood little of what was happening, but was acutely aware of smells.

Still, she could tell she carried her human soul and

mind.

They sniffed the air, noses twitching, searching for danger.

In the second corridor, the alarm went up.

Ten adult mice skittered to a halt, then darted in all directions. Zami, tiny baby mouse, clung to Yanda's mother-mouse body.

After a lifetime of practice, Vatu kept her Mingalian mind while in other forms. She called them back together and they made a mad dash for the outside door and streamed under, just as lights erupted and footsteps pounded down the hall.

Outside, Vatu led the way to the hidden door behind the eves. Taking her full form, she pushed open the old abandoned door, and the mice poured in and down the stairs to the basement.

On the dirt floor at the base of the stairs, Vatu shifted them. Then, having spent all her energy on transforming ten large forms into small ones and back again, she collapsed to the floor, leaning against the wall.

Yanda dropped next to her, Zami in her arms, gazing around. "Was mouse," he thought to her, having enjoyed the new game.

"The mage spies don't detect us here," Shouma panted out, joining them. She sent up globes of light that floated around the room. The rest sat as well, trying to bring their minds back to normal.

"They'll find us here," Bonden said, agitated. "Even if they don't sense our minds. You saw tunnels?" she asked Yanda.

"Far below us," Yanda responded. "There's a great deal of stone between."

Jat's bird-eyes peered around them, penetrating far into

the darkness. "No doors, though? I check." She, her sisters and Chin moved off into the shadows of the large, irregular stone-walled basement to search.

"We're sitting targets, trapped," Dele grumbled as she dug through her hand-stitched bag, most likely making sure all was still there and unharmed. Especially her zhoun-zhoun. "So how do we get to the tunnels?"

"We're hoping you'll help," Vatu said, unfazed.

Chin, hurrying around the perimeter, called out, "Just a storage. No exit that I can see. She threw her bulky six-feet down next to Yanda. Are you sure—?"

"She's sure," Shouma said. "Bonden, Dele, we'd better get started."

They heard pounding feet somewhere above them, increasing activity.

"How thick do you think, Yanda?" Bonden asked. "Thirty feet?"

"I'd say so." Yanda nodded.

Some fems gasped, eyes wide, at the thought of entering solid rock.

"Can you help?" Shouma asked Dele.

"I've never moved a person," she said.

"What if they get us halfway and then... peter out?" Chela asked. "Should we send an object through first?"

The noises inside and outside the Citadel were increasing. Sirens wailed.

Shouma shook her head, glancing outward. "I'll be supporting all of you." She projected her voice to the whole group. "I'll keep oxygen in your lungs. Let's get going."

"How about over here?" Chin strode to a corner out of sight of the stairs and outside door. Shouma put out the lights. Dele and Bonden signaled for them to cluster in a tight knot around them.

Yanda brought Zami's face up to hers, wanting to feel his breath.

Slowly, they sank into the floor. Pressure built as they moved incrementally through thick layers of stone and concrete. Zami stared into his mother's eyes as if he could see in the dark, trusting, but gripping the carrier straps tight over her shoulders with his tiny hands all the same.

Their heads were still poking out of the ground as the baying of dogs seemed to come from just outside. Beams of light hit some high window and they heard shouting. The fems held their breath, still sinking, as their heads slipped under, closed in stone.

Yanda pushed down panic as they slowly moved downward, pressure all around.

Encasement went on too long—minutes that felt like hours. Yanda's heart burned as she tried to keep her equilibrium amidst the fear of suffocating. A plaintive whimper came from Zami. She reassured him, pressing thoughts into his mind. "It's a game, darling. See how long we can do this. Then we'll come out and be free."

"Rock all around," he thought back to her.

How does he know so much, understand so much, at his age, she wondered, as she had many times.

We *must* have sunk at least thirty feet, she thought, coming to the end of her tolerance just as her feet emerged, wiggling in empty space.

Their bodies slipped into freedom, the tallest taking longest to unmask faces and breathe air again, until the whole group dropped, fast, then gliding lightly, thanks to Bonden's ability to float them.

As Yanda's feet touched solid ground, Zami clapped. "Again!"

"You imp." Yanda kissed his soft brown curls.

They stood in blackness, shoes crunching debris on tiles. Shouma sent small globe lights above them and down the tiled tunnel so they could take stock. The hallway stretched as far as they could see in both directions and kept going.

Dele leaned against the wall.

Chin growled, "Let's keep moving."

"I've got to rest." The slender flautist glared at the big soldier woman.

Bonden, too, sagged at the side of the hallway.

Shouma said, "They'll need to rest after bringing us through all that." Her steady gaze toward Chin was slightly chastising. "I don't think they can get to us."

"How do we know they don't remember these tunnels, and ways into them?" Chin demanded.

"I've been searching everyone's minds and found no trace of memory of them," Shouma answered.

Chin and the Jejods paced.

"Only your friend?" Chin said.

"And she doesn't know a way into this section under Dondar," Shouma responded. "Vatu found this."

Yanda whispered to Vatu, "Which way?"

She pointed.

"Is that... north?" Yanda asked hopefully.

"More east. But the other way goes directly under Dondar."

"Do you think there might be routes north from there though?" Yanda asked.

"I don't get that sense. I think they just go to the west shore. To go north, I think we'll need to head to the east first."

Shouma had her eyes closed. She opened them. "That seems right."

Yanda tried to penetrate the underground with her sight

but it took in only endless soil, not a network of tunnels.

"I'm ready to move on," Bonden said. She'd shared a sweet bar of some sort with Dele and chewed her part quickly.

Chin made her way to the front of the group in the direction Vatu pointed. The Jejod sisters took up the rear, dark martial clothing wrapped firmly around them, knife-forms strapped at their waists and thighs.

As they moved forward, Shouma created a floating seat and settled her elderly body on it, gliding among them.

"Want float," Zami thought to Yanda.

"We've barely started." Yanda nibbled his neck with a grin.

"Give him." Shouma reached out her arms.

Yanda set him on the older woman's lap, where he stood on tiptoes, eyes glowing back at his mother over Shouma's shoulder as he glided along. "Fun," he thought to her.

The corridor dipped sharply downward and to the left.

Chin stopped. "This must be north if we were going east."

"That's good," Yanda said. "Toward the spaceport. Shouma, do you have any sense of the mage spies now?"

"No, I think they've lost us."

"What about your friend?" Chela asked.

"I can't sense her from down here," Shouma admitted.

Yanda sent feelers out to try to find Beri, mindful of not giving away her location to anyone who might search for their mental registers. Nothing. She could only feel the nine others' and her son's mind around her.

Chin said, "There's going to be a hunt for us. They'll be anywhere we try to come out." She had some sort of weapon hidden below her baggy canvas pants and seemed to itch to use it. "Wish I had my laser equipment." She peered behind them, eyes trying to penetrate the dark.

Yanda stepped back to face the other women. "We need to reach the spaceport. Are we all agreed on that?"

"Maybe these tunnels lead all the way to the port," Tik suggested. "Did your friend tell you?" She stepped closer to Shouma, bending toward her.

"We don't have enough food," Dele said, her voice rising toward a whine.

"Some of us could go into Sheffed," Chin offered. "If the tunnels don't cross clear under the desert, we can look for off-market transport to the base from there."

"Beri heard a ship's leaving tomorrow," Yanda put in.

"Oh, did he? And you were going to tell us when?" Dele, hands on hips, glared at Yanda.

"Let's keep moving," Shouma said, ignoring Dele. "I expect my contact will be in contact as soon as she can. Maybe if we get closer."

They walked on until they came to a T, a solid wall running east-west.

"Should we send the Jejods east and west to check where we are in relation to the city?" Yanda asked. "I need to nurse Zami, anyway." Without waiting for a reply, she sat and lifted the baby from his carrier.

Others settled and found snacks in tacit agreement.

"If someone's heading West, I could come along and see if I sense Sheffed," Vatu offered, but she was sagging against the wall.

"You don't look up to it," Chin said. "How about riding on our shoulders? Mine or Jat's." Chin most often paired off with the oldest Jejod.

Vatu said, "I'm game," and Chin lifted her up.

Tik shrugged. "Why not me?" With the impatience of

youth, she liked to see things first.

"Could you go east, Tik?" Yanda asked. "You could see if any tunnels lead north."

Chela sat next to Yanda. "You need to keep hydrated. You can't just give, give, give to the baby and not take care of yourself." She held out a waterskin, which Yanda accepted with a grateful smile.

"Let's keep a guard with us," Shouma said. "Aktat?"

The middle Jejod nodded. "Tik, search to the east."

The thin bird-like youngest Jejod drew up to her nearly seven feet and made a preening motion toward one shoulder before her gangly legs took her out of sight in long proud lopes down the east tunnel.

"Why do we keep talking about Sheffed? What's there?" Dele grumbled.

Shouma responded, "Sheffed's a slum. And closest access to the spaceport."

"I know. Beri told us," Dele grumbled, still irritable, as she picked at a piece of overripe fruit. "I still don't get it. I mean, are we going to try to stay there? It sounds filthy. And Yanda wants to find a tunnel all the way to the port? How are we going to get across under a desert? I'm already starving. And thirsty. We have hardly any supplies."

Bonden handed Dele a half-full water-skin she'd been sequestering, carefully sipping. She'd made similar containers for all of them but Dele'd finished hers.

"Thanks." Dele started to gulp, then stopped herself before polishing it off. With an irritated grimace, she stoppered it and returned it to Bonden.

Shouma said, "A poor area is easier to hide in. Besides, I think that might be where my contact is."

"Really?" Yanda asked.

All their heads turned toward Shouma.

She shrugged. "Just a hunch."

"You haven't been to visit her?" Yanda asked, as she parried Zami's attempts to crawl off her lap.

"No. I've never met her."

Yanda wanted to ask, "Where did you go when you spirit traveled out of the compound?" But she had a feeling this line of questioning wouldn't be welcome at the moment.

In no time, it seemed, Tik returned, exclaiming excitedly, "Amazing gold underground city!" She shared an image with the others of the tile tunnel widening, giving onto a flagstone, subterranean street. Holes high above allowed rays of orange sun to strike cornices covered in yellow metal. "Buildings empty."

"Astounding. Thank you, Tik," Yanda said. "Did you see any roads leading north?"

Adjusting her black, sashed robe, Tik shook her head. "But it beautiful city, and empty. We stay there."

Yanda hated to damper the young Jejod's enthusiasm. "But we need to get to the north as directly as possible."

Tik's shoulders slumped. "I go back there. Explore."

At that moment, the other search party returned.

"I can get us into Sheffed," Vatu said, as they drew close. "I sensed it. But I think there must be another solid layer to get through, if these tunnels were lost from memory but Shouma's ally knows of another part of them."

"Then we should go to the west and we'll come out in Sheffed?"

"Not quite yet. We're still to the east of Dondar. But I have the feeling there may be a tunnel going north but we have to get through this wall. I thought I felt it."

They walked along the tunnel in the direction Jat, Chin and Vatu had just come from.

"Here!" Vatu said, struggling to get down. Chin set her on the ground. Vatu ran her hands along the wall. "I think I feel it. Yanda, come look. Do you see a tunnel through here?"

Yanda came forward and stood by Vatu. Closing off her eyesight, she let the other sight take hold. In the past, her skill had been for easy looking through walls, and body tissues. This was heavy lifting to extend her sight through layer upon layer of stone. It made her head ache.

"Not as thick as what we had to come through to get out of the Citadel," she said, leaning her back against the wall and facing the others. "But I do see a tunnel starting on the other side of a maybe eighteen- or twenty-foot barrier here." She adjusted Zami on her hip, suddenly tired.

"I take bebe." Tik reached for him.

"Let's get through this and then, yes, I'd love help carrying this big guy." She nuzzled her son's neck.

"Are you sure we have to go through that again?" Dele asked.

"We didn't see any others," Chin said.

"I didn't either," Tik agreed.

"Are you up to it?" Shouma asked Bonden.

"I'm starting to get the hang of it. I might be able to help."

"You just keep our hearts and lungs going," Yanda suggested. She wished she'd learned more of the others' skills—transformation, floating objects, disappearing—if possible, but maybe each of them had main proclivities.

"That must have been dawn light Tik saw," Shouma said. "Early morning may be a good time to arrive in the city."

So again they clustered, this time moving through sideways. It took more strength in ways than dropping for

Bonden and Dele to bring them along, but the good news was it was more like ten feet than twenty.

They pushed out on the other side as a mass, gasping in air.

After a decent rest, the started forward, at last directly north. Hope bloomed in the group at this sense of progress.

The way began to dip lower, then climbed and, sensing long-lingering toxic fumes, they covered their faces with their clothing.

"Do you think that means we're getting closer to Sheffed?" Yanda asked Shouma as she pulled her scarf over the sleeping Zami's face and tucked it in lightly as they started up another steep slope. She felt certain the older woman had traveled this far in spirit form.

"Could be," was all the elder responded.

At each branching, Vatu chose a tunnel that brought them slightly further northwest, until one angled steeply upward. This leveled, at last, into a hallway, black and closed off by a solid rock wall. Groans came from all of them, but especially Dele.

Vatu said, "I feel the city right past this. It doesn't feel solid. There's some sort of opening."

Bonden came forward and pushed her arm through. "It's illusion. These aren't stones, even though they feel real." She walked through.

The rest stepped up to the solid barrier, one at a time, pressed against it, and found themselves emerging on the opposite side.

From an archway, early sun turned their faces a smoldering rust-orange. They hurried to the end of the passage and clustered in the opening, looking out on an alley that stank of rotting vegetables.

Chapter 10

From the shadowed alcove, the Ten examined drab buildings patched together with metal and plaz scraps. Ragged children ran past in the early dawn light. A boy stared from an alcove across the alley, barely lit by a flickering overhead bulb.

"To the right is the city. Left dead-ends," Vatu said.

"Should we go out in small groups?" Dele asked. She stared eagerly toward noises coming from a nearby cross street.

Yanda hugged Zami's sleeping form. What were they getting into, once they stepped out. "Shouma, can you tell if there are sentients close by?" she asked the elder with the greatest mind powers.

"I don't sense any."

"Do you sense your contact?" Yanda asked. Weren't

they promised protection if they got themselves out of the Citadel? Yanda shifted her feet, tired, hungry, aching for coffee and shelter.

"I have the feeling she's close but our contacts have always been initiated by her," Shouma said, low voice sounding a tad self-conscious after all her promises of an ally.

I mean we shouldn't expect a red carpet or a greeting committee the instant we arrive, Yanda told herself. Still, a troubled lump formed in her throat. No Beri. Nothing reassuring. Just this stinking alley.

Chin bumped her, straightening. "We need to be together for Vatu and Shouma to hide us."

"Especially passing through the market that's starting up around the corner." Yanda put a shoulder to the archway's side, adjusting Zami and easing her aching back.

Chin gave a half-grin and shook her head. Clearly, she as well as others were still impressed by Yanda's ability to see through objects as large as buildings and as small as blood vessels. But they heard the early-morning shouts of something taking place past the alley.

"Maybe two groups? One with Shouma, the other with me?" Vatu suggested.

"Good idea," Yanda responded, wiggling to loosen lower back muscles.

"Chin, take Yanda, Zami, and Vatu. I can take the rest," Shouma said, worried, as they all were, about Vatu's dwindling energy.

Yanda studied the elder's face. "That many? To keep invisible," she asked, worry in her eyes.

Shouma patted Yanda's back. "Let Chin carry Zami a while." Then she whispered, "I do feel Merne closeby. I have no idea what she looks like but I'm sending out, trying to find her."

Yanda nodded. "Okay. Let's go first, and we'll send a message back when we find a place to hide," she said loud enough for the group.

They backed into the dark, out of sight of the small boy. His eyes widened when an unremarkable Terlondian family, with the features and clothing of the locals—Chin the man, Yanda a nondescript woman, toning down her amber eyes, Zami a baby with little change, and Vatu, a weak sister, skin a dusty brown, hood hiding her nubs—stepped out.

"I'm going to erase his memories of our images," Shouma thought to the whole group.

Chin strode ahead down the alley. When the others caught up, they turned right, entering the early morning setup of a rag-tag marketplace, booths lining both sides of the narrow road. "Shouldn't we avoid this?" Chin murmured to Yanda, jabbing her with an elbow and indicating another smaller alley as they passed.

"No, I think we should buy food. We don't know where we'll end up." Yanda's eyes lingered on a small pouch that hung at Chin's side, nearly concealed by her vest.

"Don't tell me you can see what's in my bag." Chin glared at Yanda, not very convincingly.

Yanda shrugged, with a grin.

"Fine." Chin counted coins into Yanda's hand.

"How'd you get these anyway. No, don't tell me." She turned back toward the market block, heart racing to encounter so much activity, so many new faces, any event outside of their single-room prison of the past year.

Their eyes darted around, as their minds scanned for mage spies or other hostile sentients.

Zami, having woken as market sounds grew louder,

stared with wonder at the sights. He reached for hanging grapes and sausages, scarves and treats.

Yanda carefully picked out dinner fare, with input from the others.

The last stalls bordered a busier street where vehicles swished by. A hovercraft, old and beaten up, buzzed past. Cycles of many sizes and styles wove through traffic. Yanda and her companions stopped at the corner to peer each way. Cafés served *kaffe* to eager patrons.

"Let's stay on this street," Chin urged, pointing to where it continued, across the busy thoroughfare. "It looks deserted on the next block."

In a pause between bicycles, motorbikes and *hintas*— single-person electric cars—they dashed across, slipping quickly into a deeply recessed doorway in a row of raunchy hotels and apartments. There was no telling who might look at them with suspicion.

Yanda'd detected no sentients examining her mind. "Wait here," she said. "I saw something I need at one of the last booths. And I could die for a *kaffe*. I've got enough left for all of us." She'd had a strange feeling about the woman in the last booth. Besides, there was a booth selling some kind of hot drink and pastry next to her.

Chin gripped her arm. "You're not going back alone."

"Fine, come on." Concerned about the amount of time Vatu had to keep them disguised, Yanda also knew Chin was right to want to hide them in a derelict block. But her pangs of hunger and longing for *kaffe* or *te* were pulling at her. Something else tugged as well, though she couldn't identify what it was; it lay back at that last booth across the road.

Vatu had squatted, resting her back against a wall dark with age and wear. Now she stood again, reluctant. Yanda scurried ahead, at a break in traffic, back the way they'd come, the others close behind.

As soon as they'd crossed, they spotted *fataq*, the soldiers of Dondar.

Not already, Yanda thought, heart pounding painfully. She eased her pace to avoid drawing attention and approached the booth on the end. She glanced behind. Chin had an arm around the sagging Vatu, supporting her.

The *fataq* had clustered at a vendor farther down the row.

Shouma mind-called, "What's happening?"

Yanda thought back, "Don't come quite yet."

Inside the booth, an old woman sat *fardling*—a form of Terlondian knitting. When Yanda greeted her, the elderly woman looked up with bleary eyes.

"Uh... as I passed by, I saw a..." she glanced around the table of wares for something, "... baby bottle," she concluded, spotting the only thing she could possibly imagine using. She realized it was made of silver and inwardly groaned, imagining the price.

"What the hell?" Chin's baffled thought shot into her mind and Yanda kicked the tall brawny woman-man in her shin. Chin cleared her throat in a low almost growl.

The merchant picked up the bottle. "Five sonder."

Yanda considered. It was a reasonable price. Easy to sterilize. But she had very little money left and still wanted *kaffe*. Sighing, she held out the coins. She'd settle with Chin when she could.

The old woman stepped into the light of a lantern that hung from the awning. Her eyes were now luminous, a radiant gold with velvety brown centers.

The bleary look must have been a glamour, Yanda thought.

Without taking Yanda's money, the woman lifted a drape at the back of her booth and waved Yanda through to a narrow, dimly lit stairway.

"What does this mean?" Yanda asked, wary, glancing to see if the soldiers had drawn closer.

She did not see them, which made her more nervous. Where were they?

The woman mind-spoke to her, "I'm friend, not foe." She pulled a pendant out, a symbol of Terlondian resistance they'd learned of among a few of the servants back at the Citadel. The woman tucked it away again. Yanda searched her mind, politely, only seeking the social entryway. Feeling she could trust her, she stepped past the woman. Chin and Vatu followed.

At the top of the stairs, she sat.

At the base of the stairs, Chin lifted the exhausted Vatu onto her hip like a child, and climbed, carrying both Zami and the Mingal. She sat by Yanda, Vatu resting between them, and they waited for further instructions from the mysterious seller.

Zami reached for his mama, and she drew him into her lap, where he turned, head to Yanda's collar bone, sucking a thumb and playing with Vatu's nubs.

Vatu seemed calmed by this and rested her head on Yanda's shoulder.

Yanda mind-spoke to Shouma. "There are soldiers. Be on guard. But I've met an ally. Maybe the one you found. The name on her booth is 'Once Bright'."

• ——— • • • ——— •

Shouma, Bonden, Dele and the three Jejod sisters slipped, invisible, from the archway into the alley. They had a clear picture of the market from Yanda's mind and ghosted along, avoiding bumping into buyers in the small crowd at this early hour.

"There," Tik clicked as she spotted the soldiers.

In their invisible state, most would not detect them. They had to hope no spy mages lurked there.

As they drew near Once Bright, *fataq* approached.

Quickly, the fugitives slipped between booths to their backs, off the street, hardly jostling canvas walls, hearts thumping. But the soldiers passed by, heading for the more raucous next street with its increasing activity. A siren wailed past.

They sighed in unison as they found the stairs and climbed. Once Bright's proprietor huffed behind them, carrying wares from her booth.

Bonden turned to her. "Can I help?"

"Yes. Thanks." The vendor handed her a load and went back for more, calling back up the stairs, "Turn right at the top. Straight ahead. The door's not locked."

The group on the stairs stood. Chin opened the door at the end of the dimly lit hallway and peeked inside, sending out sensors Yanda felt from the hall, then signaled that it was safe. The rest stepped into a long narrow room lit by street lights.

Their host pushed her way through, carrying a lantern and a last basket. Dele and Bonden followed with tables and awning.

"You're my ally," Shouma said.

The mysterious shapeshifter nodded. "Merne." She gave a slight bow, then crossed the room and closed curtains. She set the lantern on the single small table near a kitchen nook. Suddenly she was not old at all. Tall and fit, she appeared perhaps in her late thirties.

"Bring my things through." She signaled for Bonden

and Dele to follow her through a doorway to the side of the small kitchen as globe lights floated across the room, lighting their way.

When they returned, they were lugging enough bedding for all. The women went about lining the long walls with thick pads and blankets.

Their host said, "Let me fix you something to eat. Then you can tell me about yourselves." Chela moved toward the kitchen. "I'll help."

Yanda settled Zami on their bedding and brought the foods she'd bought in the marketplace to the kitchen counter. Others dug in their bags for their stashes to contribute to a meal.

Merne waved her hand. "I have fresh baked pastries." Soon the smell of *kaffe* filled the air.

Yanda grinned. "At last."

Chapter 11

Yanda said, "Merne, I'm grateful for your aid. I don't know where we would have ended up tonight if not for you." She wanted to get all cards on the table. She glanced over at Shouma who was delightedly picking at a tart with cherry-like fruits on top, savoring the rare treat.

Merne finished cutting pastries, arranged them on a platter, and turned her warm, unnerving eyes to Yanda. "You are not to worry. I am pleased to help you." Her glance went briefly to Zami who was rearing back on his knees, triumphantly holding up a hand-stitched ball he'd managed to take from the youngest Jejod.

"Yet I have to wonder." Yanda chose her words carefully. "You've been communicating with Shouma."

Shouma glanced up, expression wary.

"You knew there were tunnels but not how to help us

find them," Yanda pushed on, feeling she'd come across mean. Yet, why deny her anger? "It's been a year we've been imprisoned—"

"You want to know if I've known all along, how could I let you suffer for a year and not do more? Leave you to give birth to a child in that circumstance." Merne carried a tray of kaffe and pastries to the counter that divided the long room from the kitchen area, then set down a stack of plates and lined up mugs enough for all. "Please. Help yourselves." She took her own plate and mug to a small round table by the windows and sat.

"Well, exactly." Yanda looked at her son meaningfully, then got up to serve herself. Sitting again on her bed, she gratefully washed a mouth full of apple fritter down with kaffe, made light brown by *crema*. "Thank you for this, by the way. The fritter's incredible, and so's the kaffe. I haven't tasted anything like it in a long, long time. I do still have some coins, though. You don't need to feed us all."

Merne nodded acknowledgement of the thanks. "You're not to worry. It's not a burden."

She's just a seller of wares, though. Isn't she? Maybe her magical abilities bring in something more.

"You seem to know a lot about us," Yanda said. "Who else knows? And what are we looking at? Are you going to help us get a ship?"

"We have allies. My allies are yours." Merne glanced at Shouma and back at Yanda. "I have a strong system in place to shield all our minds. You're safe for now."

"How much were you reading in our minds while we were still captured? How did you know of us? How did you find Shouma?"

Shouma's brows held concern as she let Yanda ramble. The others listened closely.

As the fems settled around the room on their sleeping pads and bedding, holding their pastries and hot drink like gold, Merne went on. "To answer your first questions, my kind had lost track of the subterranean routes under the city."

As Merne spoke, a notion was building in Yanda. Her kind, she's said. She did not resemble the Elven woman who'd been in her mind as she gave birth to Zami. For starters, her ears did not taper up into points and her skin was not a cantaloupe hue. Yet Yanda felt suddenly certain she was the same woman.

"You were in my mind as I gave birth to Zami," Yanda said in a low, tremulous voice. "Weren't you?"

Merne swallowed. "I was."

"Why?" Yanda remembered their celebration, she and the Elf man, over the name she'd given her baby. "You were there and so was—"

"Can I hold off on explaining for now? I'm sorry to do that, and all *will* be revealed—"

"There's been too much mystery. Long months of it." Yanda shot a look at Shouma, impatience mingled with affection and respect. "And you're still shrouded in it. Why did I go to your booth? Was the silver baby bottle bespelled? Did you draw us?"

"I did feel you approaching. I knew you had escaped once you climbed closer to street level." Merne toyed with a scrap of pastry she'd torn apart, bit by bit. "I think sometimes objects and spirit, combined with our will, collide to draw elements toward a shared destiny." She laughed, just an out-breath. "I surmise that might have happened with the baby bottle."

"Did you feel us walk by?" Yanda didn't know why she felt so testy toward this woman. She made herself sip *kaffe* and nibble fritter. She felt she'd been played. Like a puppet on strings. Yes, they were being helped, but someone else held the cards. Why could she not be allowed to see her own hand?

"Yes. I felt you on the street. What do I know about you? For now, I'll just say I know you're escaped talents." Merne rose to put on more water, as the kaffe had run low.

"Do you know what's happening with the *fataq*?" Chin asked, wanting to get things back on track for the immediate situation.

"They never sensed you." Merne added ground kaffe to the urn.

Shouma made a sound of agreement.

"But the hunt has begun." Merne flipped a switch.

"What about the mage spies?" Yanda asked.

Shouma said, "They lost us in the tunnels. Krid is not at all happy."

"Beri told me there's a trans-system vessel leaving tomorrow," Yanda said.

Merne's hand jerked, splatting hot water. She seemed to measure her words. "There's only one ship at the port. And it's not one you want to get on." Her eyes again traveled to Zami with avid, unnerving intensity.

Yanda felt like covering him from that lion gaze. "Why not?"

"Cat-eye lady know Papa." Her baby sent the message clearly into Yanda's mind, startling her.

Papa? Did he mean Krid? Yanda shuddered and looked from Zami to Merne with new suspicion.

"Come with me." Their host signaled to Yanda who followed her into a small, simple bedroom as Chin and the Jejods again started up their dice game in the corner where they'd made a square of their four beds. Tik went back to playing with Zami. Chela called from the kitchenette that she'd fix the baby something to eat.

Through the wall of the bedroom, Yanda saw a narrow, doorless room with floor-to-ceiling shelves of merchandise.

Merne disappeared through wallpaper into this narrow, doorless storage. Yanda stepped after her.

"Look." Merne moved to the end, where a panel slid aside to reveal an array of advanced computer monitors and control panels. On one screen, a ship docked at the space port, displaying official space insignia. No nation or company Yanda was familiar with.

Yanda glanced at Merne. "That one seems okay. It's just a matter of finding a way on without alerting the authorities, or Krid. Isn't it?"

Merne gave her a long gaze, then entered data on a key pad. The screens showed the inside of the ship shifting from one level to another, and from room to room.

Merne made an adjustment to focus in on one man at a computer module.

Yanda took in the symbol on the wall behind him and her insides turned to ice. It was nothing like the insignia on the outside of the ship. "Blaz."

Merne nodded. "You got it. They've taken to disguising their ships. They have every detail down, even to the manifest and anything that can be scanned from outside, reading like a legitimate enterprise. They don't expect anyone to have access to the insides."

"Are you the only one who does?" Yanda asked.

"There are probably a few tech wizards who've found their way in." Merne shut down her system and closed the concealing panel. "I never keep the channels open long."

Yanda mind-sent the news to the others.

· ———··· ———— ·

That evening, after dinner, Merne passed around warm *kran*—a local grain drink with nut milk and honey added.

Yanda fed Zami nibbles of peas and a bright fruit called *aspar*. "Then we wait for another ship. Do you have information on arrivals?" Yanda asked Merne. "We have to get off planet. I need to take Zami away from Krid. And Vatu can't live in this atmosphere much longer. Plus, I have a young daughter I've been away from far too long." Her throat caught.

"I know," Merne said, sounding sorrowful.

Yanda's brow creased with that underlying suspicion. Why did Merne know so much about her? she wondered.

"Nothing is expected any time soon," Merne said.

"Where's the can?" Chin shoved a wedge of bread into her mouth and stood.

All grace and charm. Yanda suppressed a fond grin.

Merne pointed to a door next to the bedroom. Then she turned back to Yanda. "We can't stay here, though. As much as we're shielded, the search will close in."

"Where then?"

"There's a safe place. To the east."

"That's toxic swamp. I've seen it from Krid's tower."

"You have to trust me," Merne said.

It took great discipline for Yanda not to roll her eyes at that remark. She flopped onto her bed next to Zami and snuggled him, closing her eyes. "'Night, all. I'm beat."

· ———··· ———— ·

Next morning, early, Yanda watched Merne emerge from her tiny sleeping quarters. Loaded up with goods to sell, she left quietly and, Yanda surmised, descended to the marketplace. She pushed her blankets and sat up, looking around at their strange new digs. Bedding nearly covered the long, narrow main room of Merne's apartment.

Vatu already sat reading a plaz book, her back to the wall. Yanda noticed the Mingal's smooth breathing. Merne's state-of-the-art filtration system must have given Vatu a well-needed break from toxicity. She looked bright eyed and energetic compared to the day before.

Zami already sat playing. Some women sorted belongings on their beds. Yanda listened to them talking about purchases in the market with their meager funds, comparing stashes. She was only now discovering that most of the captive fems had earned small amounts by making craft items or using their skills for small amounts of change, mostly bartering with servants. How had she not known this?

"Go on. Take a turn in the market," Shouma said to Yanda. "A few of us have already been. We'll watch Zami." She slipped coins into Yanda's hand.

A rested Vatu transformed herself into a surly Terlondian teen, with tats, piercings and torn clothes. Yanda became the teen's angry girlfriend: two inches shorter, with a nose ring and thick black makeup.

"I haven't even washed up," Yanda protested, looking down at a tattooed arm.

Chin gave a whistle. "Look at you two." She and the Jejods gave cat-calls from their usual corner.

Tik came over and played the hidden object game with Zami.

Chela got up. "I'll make his vegetable mash."

Grateful, Yanda left with Vatu as they took their turn on the street, wandering the stalls.

Yanda glanced at Merne in her stall, busy with a

customer.

"Let me see what you made me into?" Yanda giggled, moving in front of a mirror. In the reflection, past Vatu, she saw the street behind them. "Beri," she whispered. Not daring to draw attention, she and Vatu turned and sauntered in his direction. "What can he be doing in Sheffed?" she whispered. "I never even had a chance to let him know we were escaping."

"Could he have sensed you?" Vatu suggested. "You've found each other's minds across the city. And didn't you tell him we might try to get to Sheffed?"

"Or he would guess, since it's closest to the spaceport."

As they approached, Yanda saw Beri study the two teens and smile, but he seemed uneasy. "What are you still doing here?" he hissed in mind-speak.

"We found refuge. Above the corner booth, 'Once Bright.' The merchant is Merne."

"I'll be there in a while." He ambled past them as if they'd never met.

Yanda stopped at a belt-and-sundries booth to watch his retreat in another mirror. Up the street, a soldier approached him and they walked off together.

Yanda's heart sank. Would he betray them? Would he accept money? Or a ride off the planet? If someone threatened those he loved back home, well, nearly anyone might...

Her stomach churned as she realized he may have been on this street hunting for her and the others, ready to give them up to that *fataq*. I told him where we're hiding, she thought. Full-throttle into paranoia, she pulled the Mingalian into the shadows between booths. At the back of a stall smelling temptingly of smoked meats, she stopped. I'm being absurd. Ask him. She sent a mental message to the man she'd considered her friend. "Why are you walking with a soldier?"

"He's a friend," Beri shot back. "We can trust him. Don't worry."

Yanda searched further into his mind. He could, of course, hide many thoughts from her, but she had finely tuned skills in detecting guilt. She found none. "Okay." Her heart rate steadied. "I'm glad you're finding allies. When can you update us?"

"I'll be in touch."

They parted minds. She and Vatu made their way to the stairs and climbed, having bought nothing.

They found Bonden, Dele and Shouma in the kitchen nook, preparing a complex rice dish with Qontaqian spices Yanda recognized from the few times Bonden or Dele had been able to obtain them while imprisoned in the Citadel. They parsed out cherished seasonings: *clarin, kodok* and *sweet satiyati.*

"Celebration?" Yanda asked, smelling the fragrances of Qontaq.

"Every safe respite is worth celebrating." Dele crumpled leaves into a pot. Even in hiding and after their harrowing escape through dusty, gritty tunnels, she looked elegant in her usual long skirt, blouse and vest, bronze hair held back by a patterned scarf. She wasn't often the one to expound wisdom. More likely, complaints.

Yanda's eyebrows rose and she shot a questioning look around to the others.

Chela, sitting against the wall, mending a filmy garment of indigo and teal *zarsh,* said, with a small smile, "That's so true."

Hm. Armistice. Had something brought it about? But her mind was in too much of a turmoil over Beri. She was relieved by his pronouncement that his presence on this street, with a fataq, did not represent danger. Nevertheless, how did he find them? And could others?

Yanda dropped to her mat and scooped Zami into her arms, rocking and humming to him, savoring the softness of his cheek against hers.

He murmured, "May-may"—his word for Mama—sounding sleepy. She put him to nurse.

Vatu sank onto her mattress by Yanda's, face drained, and lay her head down. Toxicity hung heavy on the streets of Sheffed.

"Did it take too much out of you, keeping our disguise?" Yanda whispered.

Vatu shook her head, delicate blue-green nubs dimmed almost to white.

"I'll make something." Chela went to work on one of the brews she'd been trying for Vatu's blood.

Yanda pressed a hand to the Mingal's back and searched. Finding the worst of the congestion, she cleared passages. Though it tired Yanda, she sent wellness through Vatu's circulatory system, a skill she and Shouma had discovered among her surprising abilities.

"I have to tell you all something," Yanda said, leery of the response. "We saw Beri in the street."

"Have you been in touch with him all along?" Dele snapped. "That was foolish, Yanda."

Good bye, happy philosopher, Yanda thought. "No, I didn't dare."

Now she hated to share the rest. "He's coming here."

Chin dropped the dice cup as all stared at Yanda.

Vatu chimed in, "He was with a *fataq*—"

The Jejods were on their feet, in warrior stance, by now, glancing at the door.

"But he assured Yanda the guy's an ally," Vatu hastened to add.

"You *belieff* him?" Aktat asked hotly with her Jejod accent pronounced.

"I tested his mind for sincerity. I do trust him." Yanda flushed with guilt and uncertainty.

"Of course, she did. She has no reason to distrust Beri," Shouma said, coming to her defense.

Yanda thought to her, "But what if someone threatened him, or offered escape?"

"I'll search for him and see what I see," Shouma said only to her, and closed her eyes.

Dele, still glaring at Yanda, sank onto her bed and brought her *zhoun-zhoun* to her lips to play an angry tune. The Jejods sat reluctantly, and returned to their dice game.

Soon, occasional spurts of laughter burst from them, along with their graphic, clicking profanities. As the game grew louder, Yanda lifted sleeping Zami, carried him to Merne's bedroom, and closed the door, sending a thought-question to Merne at her booth. "Can Zami sleep in your room?"

"Of course," came the quick reply.

It was fascinating to taste a new person's mind and spirit. Yanda only sipped the most open, shared areas of Merne's before giving a courteous farewell.

In the compact, tidy bed chamber, she spread Zami's quilt—lovingly stitched by the women in the slave quarters—and laid the sleeping infant down. She snuggled next to him, grateful for a moment alone. Her mind wandered to the computer in the next room, fingers itching to play with the console, to search for ships, but she had no idea how to work it.

Chapter 12

Toward dusk, Yanda and Zami returned to the common room, having both napped. The place was filled with the smells of dinner.

A tap came on the door to the outer hallway. Through the wall, Yanda saw Beri standing alone. She glanced at Shouma, who nodded. So she got up and opened.

"Come on in." Yanda stepped aside and the tall, ginger-haired man entered, ducking his head. He gazed around the room, nodding to everyone.

"You know Shouma can freeze you if we have *any* indication you've betrayed us?" Chin asked sweetly, cracking her large knuckles to show that Shouma wasn't the only one who might take action.

"I understand," Beri responded to the large woman he used to bring food to in her cell on Farn. "I promise, I'm still your friend. I cloaked myself all the way here. With Shouma's help."

"That's true. I only barely sensed him and my skill is beyond the military's," Shouma said.

Yanda snickered at the self-confidence, wishing she ever felt that sure of herself.

The Fugitives lined up to serve themselves the meal filling the air with complex, delectable scents.

"Sorry I didn't help," Yanda mumbled, scooping thick sauce, breathing in the steam appreciatively. She explained to Beri, "They've been working hard to prepare this. It's *soron*—a Qontaqian meal made for special occasions."

Bonden said, "We were never able to get all the spices to make it faithfully at the Citadel. Dip a rice ball in the sauce."

Beri said, "Lucky timing." With a tentative grin, he obediently dipped and took a bite. "Mm-mm-mm. Best thing I've tasted in a *sarfan*." He used the Terlondian word for a millennium.

Yanda mind-called to Merne to take a dinner break. She asked for help carrying wares and closed her booth early. Soon, she, Chin and Bonden came in the front door, lugging loads.

When she'd served herself and sat in a puffy chair, Yanda said to Merne, who was filling a plate for herself with appreciative sounds, "We have to find a ship. It seems like you can probably identify anything coming or going." It was part question.

"Nothing's on the charts. I told you." She took an appreciative bite of a Qontaqian dish with peanut sauce.

"Then there must be somewhere we can hide close by 'til the next one. You said we can't stay here. What about back in the tunnels? Tik found an intriguing—"

"I thought you were catching the ship leaving today,"

Beri grumbled, mouth full, a disapproving crease in his brow.

"If you thought that, why weren't you with us?" Yanda had to razz him.

He shrugged.

"As it turns out, that was a Blaz trader," she said triumphantly. Zami, on her lap, made a dive for a sticky rice ball. "Wait. Let me—"

Too late. He'd crammed it to his mouth and all over his face. She laughed as she picked rice from his cheeks. To Beri, she said, "Luckily, Merne detected it."

Loaded fork halfway to his mouth, Beri froze, looking astounded. "Blaz," he mouthed like he'd tasted battery acid. He turned to Merne. "How did you detect?" But then he remembered Gisli's telling him he'd discovered a woman with powers exploring secure networks with ease. "Oh, you must be—"

At the same time, Merne said, "Contraband surveillance equipment," before she bit into a sautéed *arda*-leaf roll.

Beri gave an admiring whistle. "Definitely want you on our side."

"Merne says we need to go east to hide," Yanda went on. "You're coming with us, right?"

"Into deadly swamps?" He looked from one woman to the other. "There's nowhere to hide there. We'd be nesting *squerbs*."

"Merne says we have to trust her." Yanda played with thick sauce over grains, dipped flat bread in and ate.

Beri turned his scrutiny toward Merne. "Gisli knows you. He discovered you in military networks, supposedly secure."

"Who's Gisli?" Yanda asked. "The *fataq* you were walking with?"

Beri nodded.

"But he didn't turn me in," Merne said with satisfaction. "Interesting mind powers the young man has."

It was Yanda's turn to stare from Merne to Beri. "You've met Beri's friend."

"I think I sense all mind talents on Terlond," Merne said, without arrogance.

Yanda's gaze bore into the cat-eyed woman. "With all this tech savvy, why couldn't you break us out?" A lump formed in her throat at the prospect that she might have gotten her son to freedom sooner and returned to her daughter on Alland. She hugged Zami to her. He reached for her plate and she quickly scooped a spoonful into his mouth.

"I watched," Merne said, sympathy in her voice. "Believe me, I wanted you out. Everyone did."

At this statement, there were small gasps around the room.

"Everyone?" Yanda voiced their puzzlement. Her mind went to the male who'd been watching her birth.

"There's an underground here." Merne pulled the symbol from under her shirt, a complicated design that looked like vines swirling around a central pyramid. "You aren't the only ones who've been unfairly held captive."

Yanda felt fairly sure Merne had done some quick thinking to veer from topics she wanted to avoid.

Merne went on, "I didn't want to put anyone in danger by crossing through the protections around the Citadel. Mine is a very distinctive vibration, much as I try to obscure or disguise it."

"But you did. You contacted Shouma." Yanda set her stubborn jaw.

Shouma finished her last bite of dessert and licked

syrup from a finger. "Different from anything I've known."

Merne smiled and Yanda detected an exchange the rest weren't included in. Is this a love thing? she suddenly wondered. There was a lot of mutual admiration in the air.

Zami crawled off Yanda's lap and perched by Beri, waiting for his attention.

Beri smiled at him. "Look at this chap."

The baby reached over and put a tiny hand on Yanda's chest. "Know him," he said in mind speak.

"You saw him from my belly, perhaps, son." …if you have your mom's ability to see through, she thought. She had no proof of that skill yet, though Tik tried to test him with her hidden-object games, hiding a new item under a cloth and asking him to show her in mind-speak what it was. So far, the result hadn't been clear—he might have read it in her mind.

Beri raised brows to Yanda. "Who's his father? Not Krid."

Yanda wasn't about to explain her theories on that. It was too odd. A man impregnated me in a dream? She shook her head, gave an infinitesimal shrug.

Beri pulled from his pocket a small animal he'd shaped from leather, carefully carving and dying it in several colors. "I snuck and made this at work. I've been waiting to give it to you."

Zami accepted the gift with bright, solemn eyes, turning it in his small hands before he broke out in a sunlit smile and put one corner in his mouth. Beri ruffled his strange-hued hair, lately becoming burnished magenta at the tips.

Beri looked up from the toddler and announced, "I'll go east with you."

Yanda stared at him. "Why the change of heart? Suddenly you're not afraid of radiation?"

"Not sudden. Gisli's mind powers have been discovered. I have to help him get away somewhere."

Yanda felt a moment's hurt. He would escape with them for Gisli? Was everyone lovers now? "Don't mindpowers make him part of an elite force?" she asked.

"Only if they were aware from the start. Now he knows too much."

"They want to control what's known, not have some rogue powers about?" Yanda suggested.

"Right. He's trying to make his way here."

Murmurs and scowls traveled around the room. Chin and the Jejods leaped to their feet.

"What if he's followed you?" Yanda voiced everyone's thought. "He doesn't have Shouma cloaking him."

Shouma held up a hand. "Slow down. We need to talk this through, make a plan."

"I agree," Merne said.

"He won't be followed," Beri defended. "He's specially trained to hide. And we've been working on concealing our minds from what you taught me."

Merne stood and paced, frowning in concentration.

Shouma looked with warning at Chin and the Jejod sisters, who remained standing, despite her asking them to sit. "How well is your surveillance set up around Sheffed?" she asked Merne.

"Very well. I'll go monitor it."

Chin and the Jejods readied themselves and within seconds, ducked under the low lintel, exiting, the sisters all the while clicking to each other in their Jejodian language.

Beri said, "Maybe I should go out there, too, and look."

"What you need to do is get in touch with him," Shouma said. "If you show me his location, I can bring him here."

"Would you take Zami?" Yanda held her boy out to Chela.

The healer put out her arms readily and crooned, "Want a snacky?" carrying him toward the kitchen nook.

Yanda blew him kisses as she followed Merne into the back room. She stepped easily through the wallpaper and joined Merne at her computer screens. The Sheffed borough was displayed as a light grid. Yanda could read more than was on the screen through Merne's thoughts; mind-powers showed as gold, orange or red spots. Or a gradation. The two women watched the dark orange dots of the Jejods and Chin fan out. They seemed to connect to each other and back to the apartment by a misty blue thread, as though the grid extended their thoughts into shared, graphic form.

On a second screen, the apartment shimmered with talents, glowing mostly orange-red. Shouma's was a deep maroon, like aged burgundy, the strongest that powers could register.

"There he is." Merne pointed and groaned. Beri's cool stream of thought, yellow-orange, touched a moving form, gold-orange, crossing into the perimeter the Jejods and Chin formed. The gold-orange one had some sort of data tag attached to it.

"What's this?" Yanda asked sharply, pointing.

"Gisli. He has an embedded chip."

"Oh, gods," Yanda gasped, as she realized the miniscule box near Gisli's dot contained tiny codes.

Merne tapped the senior Jejod's mind. "Jat, you need to guide Gisli into the tunnels. Quickly. We'll meet you there." She sent Gisli's location to Shouma. "Get him. Hide his chip."

Shouma's deep-red ball disappeared from the apartment, then reappeared next to Gisli.

At the same time, a dark gold dot passed into the perimeter at the very place Gisli had entered.

Merne and Yanda both hissed in breath.

"Is that a sentient following him?"

"I think so."

They watched as the eldest Jejod made her way toward Shouma and Gisli. All three blinked off the grid.

"Even your board can't register them when Shouma cloaks them?" Yanda asked.

"Nope. She's of the Sonda. I don't think Krid knows exactly what he snatched. There's no way he could have taken her unless she wanted to be taken."

"Sonda?" Yanda's brows creased.

"Of Elznap. It's a little-known star-system, difficult to get to. Asteroid belts, electric storms that throw instruments off."

"She's told you her story?" Yanda felt shocked and a tad jealous.

"No. I've guessed."

"But how—"

"Only the Xentu come close to their mind-powers. And they've not been seen for a very long time. Even their planet has gone missing." Merne stared at Yanda longer than felt comfortable.

Why is she staring at me? Yanda glanced away, back to the screens, then back to Merne's unnerving eyes. "How does a planet go missing?"

"Maybe a whole planet can be cloaked."

"What if someone went to its coordinates. Wouldn't they have to bump into it?"

"It could be shielded. Perhaps it can be moved." Merne shrugged. "Maybe they're made to forget what they were looking for."

Their eyes moved back to the grid. This woman knows an awful lot that I've never had an inkling of, Yanda thought, unnerved, admiring, curious as hell.

Without the elder's invisibility cloaking, Chin and the two younger Jejods had to depend on their fighting skills and keep to shadows. They let Yanda and Merne stay in their minds as they moved along back alleys. They were fast and soon joined Shouma and Gisli some feet inside the tunnel entry. They could not see this on the grid but in their minds.

They were blocked by a solid wall.

"This wasn't here when we escaped," Shouma said. "We're going to need Bonden to get us through."

"No, remember? We pushed through," Yanda thought to her.

Aktat paced the hallway, feathery head cocked to sense approaching soldiers. "*Fataqs* are likely following the transmitter."

"But it's not working this time," Shouma said, deliberately pressing her body against it. "Merne may know the secret of the wall." Watching the entrance in case the *fataqs* arrived, she kept them invisible, while keeping a shield around Gisli to obscure the data chip.

"She's hiding the chip. How would they still be following?" Yanda asked Merne.

"I guess their initial read on it. And probably the most powerful tech they have. I would try to read their minds but I don't think we have time."

Chapter 13

Yanda and Merne strode from the back room.

"Gather your things, quickly," Merne said.

The remaining fems crammed their few belongings into roughly stitched bags.

"What's going on?" Dele asked.

A tap came at the door. Merne opened without hesitation. Two Dondarians and a range of humanoids of varying heights and appearances entered, including a seven-foot primanoid, covered in hair of deep sienna tones, who ducked under the lintel. Even inside, he kept his chin tucked to avoid the ceiling.

Merne glanced down the hall behind them, then shut the door. "Joli," she greeted the last and the two chuck-chucked in a foreign tongue.

The Fugitives stopped their packing to gaze at the

newcomers who went straight to the kitchen and other room, stashing items in boxes and large storage bags.

"You're leaving, too?" Yanda asked Merne.

The lion-eyed woman nodded as she joined her friends in the kitchen, swiftly packing food and dishes in carryalls.

Bonden sat up straight in the midst of folding and stacking bedding. "Shouma's calling. Says they've encountered a stone wall that wasn't there before. One they can't pass through."

"We all hear," Dele snapped.

Uh-oh, Yanda thought. Nerves fraying again.

"I'm just saying, she wants Merne to come, and maybe me, to get them through the wall so they're safe to locate this fataq's chip and remove it," Bonden explained, conciliatory. "Soldiers are closing in on them."

"Ah." Merne's hands stilled. "I forgot about that wall. You came through it. It's harder to get past it entering the other way."

"I thought your kind lost track of the tunnels," Dele sniped.

"The parts going under Dondar," Merne corrected.

"But you might have told us there was a way. We just had to get through solid rock," Dele carefully packed her flute into layers of cloth. "Didn't Shouma tell you we can do that? I mean, she seems to have told you a lot about us."

Yanda glanced from one to the other as she prepared Zami for travel in the carrier fashioned by Chela's clever stitchery. She couldn't disagree with Dele. But this wasn't the time. She pursed her lips, gazing around the room at the seven escapees left in the apartment: Bonden, Chela, Vatu, Dele and Beri, besides herself.

She discussed storage of her belongings with the motley Allies, then scurried to her bedroom saying, "I just have to get one thing, then I'll go help Shouma."

Dele smirked at Bonden. "Guess you're not needed after all."

Yanda groaned inwardly at the friction between the two Qontaqs as she stood, ready, Zami in his sling, her bag shouldered. She watched Merne through the wall, crossing into the secret room where she grabbed a packed duffel.

Without any more warning, Yanda felt herself pulled by Shouma. In an instant, she stood ten feet into the tunnel. Merne arrived at the same time. The dark alcove was littered with trash and smelled of piss, a lot like subway terminals on her home world. She wrinkled her nose. "Homeless camp."

"Or party place," Aktat suggested as her long, steeply arched foot knocked an empty bottle of *Abat*, a local beer, which spun, spilling pungent stale fumes as she paced the width of the hallway,

Merne walked to the wall and an opening appeared next to her.

"It didn't do that for me," Shouma said as she started to hurry through.

Jat, with one long stride, blocked her way. "I go first." The elder Jejod stepped cautiously in, looked around, and signaled for the rest to follow, while Aktat moved toward the alley entrance, bird-head arched out, watching for intruders.

This side, thankfully, smelled only of earth and long-closed spaces. Once all had entered, Aktat brought up the rear and the hole snapped shut. Blackness engulfed them until Shouma floated globe-lights over their heads.

"How are the others coming?" she asked Shouma, who stood next to a wiry young man, skin a purplish brown tone, who sat against one wall with a serious expression.

This must be the *fataq* friend. He wore the uniform.

Beri squatted by him, talking in a low voice.

"I was going to get the chip out, then bring the rest," Shouma said.

At that moment, through the wall, Yanda saw *fataq* soldiers enter the tunnel's grimy entrance. "Shit," she said. "I guess the chip is a moot point now."

"I don't think so. They'll continue to get information from it," Merne said. "Luckily, Shouma's been shielding it so they've read no more since maybe entering the alley?" She turned questioning eyes to Shouma.

"I'm afraid that might be right. I didn't get enough of a shield up before that." She crouched and exchanged silent greetings with the young *fataq*. Then she said, "This is Gisli, of Tellot." She waved Yanda over.

Yanda knew from her exo-studies in schooling that the planet of Tellot had a fragile, semi-tropical climate and nonviolent culture. What was he doing in the military here she wondered as she slipped her arms out of the baby carrier and handed Zami to Chela, with a sound kiss to his cheek. Chin took her bag of belongings and hunkered to a squat in the middle of the hallway, staying close and watching avidly as Beri moved aside for Yanda.

She knelt by Gisli. "May I?" She indicated his arm.

He nodded consent, and she laid a hand on him, searching with her sight. Soon she located a tiny microchip embedded in his shoulder. "Can you pull these down to here?" She tugged lightly at his fatigues, indicating how far she needed his skin bared.

Gisli stared at her. "Are you a surgeon? Where's your equipment?" Clearly, he expected needles and scalpels, and grimaced in anticipation, yet her hands were empty. He looked around as if a tray of medical instruments might be held out by someone.

"Nothing is needed for this," she said, kindly.

"Just you," Chin said with laughter in her voice, and a touch of awe.

Gisli's eloquent brows lifted but he said nothing, just watched closely as Yanda scooted closer and stared at his flesh. After a moment, he winced, eyes growing wider as a miniscule polymer-coated cylinder poked from his skin, along with a tiny drop of blood.

Shouma, who'd been hovering nearby, plucked it out. Immediately, she vanished.

Gisli blinked, stared, looked around. "Did she just... disappear with the chip?"

Chela came forward and slicked a small plaster onto the bead of blood, Zami on her hip. "Yep."

"I could have just closed it," Yanda mumbled, quirking a smile up at the healer.

"Save your energy," Chala answered, bouncing Zami.

Shouma popped back into the space among them.

"Where'd you put it?" Beri asked.

"On the other side of Sheffed."

Jat whistled a high bird sound, long brows rising high.

Merne nodded. "Three *fataqs* are wandering around on the far side of this wall." She watched on a small hand-held device.

"Do they have mind-powers?" Yanda asked, looking through at them. "I don't sense any."

"A lot of devices. No powers that I can tell." Merne shifted settings on her device.

"They're leaving," Yanda watched as the soldiers exited back out into the alley. "Must have gotten a new reading on Gisli's chip." She grinned at Shouma.

Chin said, "When they find it without its host, they'll be

back."

"Do you think they'll blow up the wall to follow us?" asked Beri, offering Gisli a hand to standing.

"There's no longer an entrance," Merne said. "They'll only see a solid wall from the alley."

That was true. Yanda now saw through a second wall into the alley. Between was a dark, empty space, enclosed by four walls.

Gisli jumped to his feet in one lithe motion. He jerked his jacket back into place and said, "Thank you," to Yanda and Shouma.

Merne came over and carefully monitored Gisli's clothing, all over, with another hand-held instrument.

"Maybe I should dump these, just in case." Gisli looked down at his military garb. "Do you have extra clothes?" he asked.

Beri shook his head. "All I've got is on me." He lifted his arm to show a bag that lay nearly flat against his torso.

Gisli grimaced, misery on his face and in his slumped shoulders. "I hope I haven't brought danger on all of you."

Zami, now back in Yanda's arms, babbled to his small leather elephant-creature.

Merne finished her search. "I think you're safe, unless you want to lose the uniform anyway."

Gisli made a face. "Wouldn't mind."

"We can outfit you, if you can wait a bit," Merne said.

Gisli nodded. "Of course. Thank you, again." He made a small bow toward Merne.

She smiled at him and, pressing her long slender hand to the center of her chest, bowed back to him.

Shouma leaned against the wall, eyes shut. One by one, the others arrived from the apartment, holding their small bundles. They looked around, eyes taking in the scene, each studying Gisli briefly.

"Are we safe?" Dele asked.

"For the moment," Merne said, shoving her gadgets into pockets.

Everyone seemed ready to put distance between themselves and Sheffed. They moved restlessly east, glancing back toward the wall.

"So what about Beri's question?" Yanda asked after they'd gone a ways. "Can they start blasting holes through the walls? Surely, they'll remember the alleyway."

"No," Merne said. "They won't. It's an interesting type of stone, these walls. Also, there are actually quite a few of my kind around the city, monitoring. They'll have wiped clear the soldiers' memories of where that entrance was or even what alley they sensed him enter."

"Wow," Beri commented.

"What about a data log?" Gisli asked, coming up closer to Merne.

"My allies will have wiped that clean," Merne said calmly.

"Wait." Shouma took Gisli's arm. She hadn't made her floating seat yet. "One more thing." She put her hands on Gisli's head. She let Yanda follow as Shouma examined his mind for anything like a trap that would reveal their locations. "Seems clear. You next." Shouma did the same with Beri.

His brows went up as he felt her in his head.

After a moment, she said, "You've both worked on your shielding."

"Clearly not against someone like you." Beri winced with a half-smile. "But when would someone have had access to *my* brain?" He glanced at Gisli.

His friend shrugged.

"Any time you slept, or even waking, probably," Merne said.

Shouma nodded agreement. "There are those who can slip in without being noticed."

"And leave things?" Beri nodded, scratching his head wildly, as if he thought spy-lice might be in his hair.

"Oh, yes." Shouma nodded.

"Can you do things like that?" he asked her.

"I could, if so inclined. Hopefully only for a good cause." A hint of a smile was fleeting. "Keep up the shielding as long as we're near the city," she said to everyone. "Chin. Jejods. Fan out and check that no one's found another way in, will you? Vatu, can you also monitor for sentience? And Dele?"

Yanda felt happy that Shouma had included the flautist with a specific request. That might help reduce the tensions. Maybe she'd noticed the rivalry, too.

As the group moved forward, the three Jejods took off down the tunnels in long, avian strides. Chin trudged after them, tree-trunk legs eating up space, Vatu riding on her back.

Merne frequently took out her main device and checked readings on it. The woman with the strange gold-brown eyes now had a tall handsome otherness. Yanda had never again seen the bleary-eyed old woman, reserved apparently for the marketplace. She wore unusually cut garments, fitted yet flexible. Her blouse and vest, shades of moss and jade, draped cunningly over pants of a fabric Yanda couldn't identify; it looked strong yet soft.

Soon the Jejods returned.

Chin followed. "We saw no one. And I don't detect any wizard gaze." She looked to Shouma for confirmation.

"I'm afraid I do," Shouma responded. "Close by. But

not in here. Yet. Keep your shielding up."

All paused, trying to detect Krid's spies.

"They've joined forces in one of the Citadel's towers, putting all their energy into trying to find us," Shouma said.

Merne stared at the device in her hand. "There's a house-to-house search throughout the city. The military has sentients on every block, even in Sheffed."

At that moment, the sound of feet gritting on detritus doubled around them.

Chapter 14

Merne's Allies, including Joli, had arrived. Merne nodded to them and they fanned out around the group, stepping into pace with them as all moved on.

"We cleared your place," one of the Terlondian Allies reported to Merne, as they all walked east down the tunnel. "We made sure there's no trace left of any of you, not even thought-traces."

"Good," Merne said. "Thank you."

Joli bobbed his head which nearly scraped the roof of the side, tiled tunnels.

"If we're going to keep heading east," Shouma said pointedly to Merne, "won't we need protective gear? Masks, oxygen tanks? Hazmat suits?"

"All we need will be there," Merne said, mysterious as ever.

Shouma shrugged, giving tacit, though wary, agreement.

It was the first time Shouma seemed disenchanted with Merne's secretiveness. It was a bitter-sweet feeling to have Shouma finally join her in having information kept from her. Yanda wanted to relax and feel confident about what was coming.

"Isn't this the way we came?" Dele's long steps kicked out her shin-length skirt. "Seems familiar."

"This stretch of the tunnel, probably," Merne said.

A short way further, they filed into a massive cavern where light filtered from skylights high above onto golden buildings—an underground city street. Tik perched on a roof, scanning the enormous space that extended into darkness on all sides.

"I don't get it," Yanda said. "This looks like the golden city Tik came back and described to us. But we hadn't been blocked by the wall we had to get through to reach you. You said you didn't know how to get to the section that runs under the Citadel, but here we are, on the Citadel side."

Others made sounds of agreement.

Beri said, "You haven't even told me how you got away from Krid."

"There'll be time, I'm sure," Shouma said.

"Your allies had over a year to explore and find us a way out," Yanda went on, to Merne. She couldn't help herself. She'd been cheated out of more than a year of her daughter's life. Seiti was six and a half when she'd been pulled away from her planet.

She's nearly eight now, Yanda thought. Tears welled and she chuffed them away with a cuff.

"Leave it for now." Shouma put an arm around Yanda, who fought the urge to shake her off.

"But I want to know. How are we getting to this part that we reached from under the Citadel if Merne didn't know how to get to us?" Yanda pushed on.

Gisli stared at the Jejod crouching high above them, then around at shining walls rising on each side of the dusty street. "Did she fly up there? With no wings?" he whispered to Beri.

"Jumped, I think." Beri grinned, also sounding impressed.

The two went off exploring like kids.

Merne stepped close to Yanda and mind-spoke. "Some parts you can go through the wall one way but not the other. And... it's territorial. Not all the Elves in the City are friends to us."

Yanda stared at her. "You're kidding." She glanced around, then asked, in mind-speak, "There are warring Elf factions? Are we safe here?"

A few of the others stayed close to try to find out more. Dele eyed Merne and Yanda with suspicion, then stalked away down the dusty road of the golden city.

"I think so. They're more under the western parts of Dondar and Sheffed, but long ago, the walls were set up, and I think they still monitor any coming and going." Merne pursed her lips.

Yanda couldn't believe the mysterious woman was communicating so much with her.

Jat sniffed the air suspiciously, then stalked to an end building to peer in a dusty window. Others also took timid steps toward the abandoned city that shone gold.

"How has no one in Dondar discovered this place?" Yanda asked aloud, staring up at the filtered light falling on them. "Is that not daylight filtering in?"

"We are some distance past the edge of Sheffed," Merne

responded, "under an abandoned field. If anyone ventured out this far, they'd be guided away."

"And memories of it erased?" Gisli asked with a grin, back from his exploration.

"Most likely," Merne answered, giving him a level gaze and barely a smile.

Yanda's eyebrows rose but she only said, "I'd like to feed Zami. Let him out of his sling a while." Benches surrounded dead trees that formed a square. She propped her foot on one to ease her back, then brushed dirt and dead leaves off and sat, ignoring the dust coating. She crooked a leg on the seat to lift Zami out of his sling.

As soon as his feet touched the wood slats, Zami grabbed the back of the bench and stretched on his toes, staring at the play of shifting light from above with a crow of pleasure to be freed. Yanda grinned and glanced up, longing to take him outdoors in the wind that pushed clouds over, making moving shadows.

Vatu dropped beside Yanda, breath ragged.

Merne and Shouma settled on a nearby bench and pulled food from their bags.

"Does this place have a name?" Vatu asked Merne.

Merne shook her head. "It might be in the histories. My father may know it. It's from earlier folk."

"Oh." Vatu pulled out a pocket bread with some of last night's dinner tucked into it and bit.

Yanda dug around in her sack and found a small slice of soft pear which she tucked into her baby's fist, after hesitating at the grime on it. "How far to clean water?" she asked Merne. "Or is that not something we can hope for? What are we to expect ahead?" Yanda could barely contain her frustration. They'd escaped. Now all she wanted was to get on a ship back to Alland, to her daughter. Yet they kept heading east.

Suddenly she realized Merne's Allies were no longer with them. "Where are your friends?" She hadn't seen any of them since they reached the golden city.

"They've gone on ahead. And there will be clean water. Before the end of the day." Merne wrapped the rest of her lunch and shoved it into her pack. "We should push on." She stood.

Shouma mind-called the rest. Most had settled on the other benches around the square and munched on meager snacks. They gathered and left the strange subterranean city, entering a tunnel on the far side, globe-lights floating above them.

To relieve Yanda's back, the others took turns carrying Zami, as the group walked for three hours or more. A hole was wearing through the sole of one of her boots and the heel of the other sloped. She grimaced at blisters forming, knowing she could ask for a healing poultice or try to mend the tissues herself, but refusing to hold them up. She would endure.

Finally, they arrived at another solid stone wall. All glanced at each other.

"Is this another fake?" Bonden asked, feeling the surface.

Merne went to the side and triggered a disguised door; it seemed part of the rock wall until it slid to the side. They filed through before it closed again, meshing seamlessly with the sides.

"Wouldn't people wonder why there's a dead end?" Gisli asked.

"And start blasting?" Beri added.

"This can't be blasted," Merne said. "But you're right. There probably should be a better façade. The thing is, hardly anyone could get this far. These areas are monitored."

"By who?" Chin asked as she led on down the corridor. Float globes bobbed ahead of them and alongside, revealing a different type of tunnel, more rugged and round, with phosphorescence in some places. The floor sloped steeply down.

Now Yanda knew at least part of the answer. Merne had given it to her in secret, as she'd shown her the computer screens back in Sheffed on her own. Yanda wondered why. Why her? And what small part of the story would Merne feed them now?

Merne turned to face them all. "It will take time to give you more answers. And we need to... get farther."

Now that Merne had shared some information with her, Yanda felt like she couldn't get as snarky as she'd like.

After a short distance, Merne pressed against rough stones on the side until a panel glowed pale green and slid open.

"Whoa." Beri was right behind her and looked in over her shoulder. The group followed Merne into a bunker-like hall, rounded, sixty feet long, twenty wide. Even after the opening closed behind them, air seemed to flow freely. Along the sides, narrow hollows reached floor to ceiling and extended out of sight, burgeoning with lush green plants lit from above and other hidden sources.

Yanda gasped at brightly colored flowers and fruits cascading within these alcoves. "This is wondrous." She stepped into a recessed garden, a few feet deep, and stared up, trying to find what light would grow fruits this deep underground. "Where does the air and light come from?"

"A web of tubes," Merne answered as the group stared around in awe.

"Who maintains this?" Beri asked, peering up a ladder between arches.

Merne's eyes narrowed ever so slightly as Beri rested his hands on the rungs.

Voices rose in greeting from the far end of the long room with its arched ceiling, lit by glow-sconces. The Allies waved and gestured them forward.

"Come," Merne said, making sure Beri came with them.

Catching whiffs of a meal being prepared, the Fugitives approached the far end of the room eagerly, passing beds and small chests of drawers that lined each side.

The rounded end was lit brightly. Plants hung down. A long table heaped with a feast was lit by hanging lights that flickered like lanterns. Foods of every color, piled on long platters, smelled exquisite.

Joli towered above the rest, apron over his dark red fur, black at the tips. He lifted a long arm in greeting, grinning as he pointed at the table.

"Maybe we should wash up?" Yanda looked around for signs of water. As much as she longed to eat this tasty-looking meal, washing the grime from her seemed even more appealing.

"Toray will show you," Merne said.

A tiny being bustled to one side. It crouched slightly. Thin arms, a pale mushroom color, waved them over. With a flourish, Toray pressed a hand to a panel low to the ground and part of the wall slid open, revealing a small antechamber with several doors around the sides. "This way," came the piping voice of the gnomish creature.

"I'm eating." Chin dropped into a large sturdy chair at one end of the long table and started to serve herself. "Wash later," she added perfunctorily, mouth already full.

Yanda thought about those extra excursions they'd sent

Chin on and didn't blame her. Chin had also walked half the city while Yanda'd been popped right into the alley. Still, she chuckled, exiting with several others.

Toray held open another door and they entered a cave grotto glowing with pale green light. Verdant ferns festooned the walls. Warm water sprayed from a shelf in each recessed space, reentering the ground through crevices between stone slabs or splashing into deep pools. Shallow bowls carved into rock protrusions held soap bars. Benches lined the middle. The air was warm and steamy.

Those without compunction threw their clothes onto benches and ducked under hot sprays of water or sank gratefully into hot pools.

Vatu found a small hollow at the back where a rock partition hid her from sight.

Yanda peaked around the corner, naked, a chortling, equally bare Zami in her arms. "May we join you?"

"Come." Vatu grinned. She removed her vest and flexi-suit, neatly folding them onto a stone slab, then lowered herself onto mosses at the edge of the pool, slipping her feet in.

Yanda stepped into the water, bringing Zami with her. It was a perfect temperature, if you didn't have blisters on your feet. She gasped, then started to lower herself and Zami into deeper water. Her son, hands pressed to her collar bones, watched her face, reassured by her grin as first his feet, then his legs sank into the hot water. He scrambled down onto boulders to sit in a shallow dent within arm's reach, where he stacked, tasted, and clacked together small round stones while Yanda and Vatu sank down against curved sides, immersed to their chins.

Others found pools close by and the grotto filled with contented voices.

Beri and Gisli showered, then in a corner, climbed onto stacked, flat stones forming seats. They lay back on them with shouts and whistles.

"Are the rocks hot?" Yanda called to them.

"Yeah, it's like a sauna. You gotta try this," Beri called. "Something's heating the rocks and the air here."

Then came Dele's mind-call, "Towels. In a thermal warmer!"

When all had soaked and showered to their satisfaction, they wrapped themselves in warm towels, then dressed in clean, soft robes of varying sizes. They pulled on booties with reinforced soles, even ones small enough for Zami.

They gathered by the door, grinning at each other.

"We look like some secret order," Yanda said, laughing.

Gisli pressed a hand-sized pad on the wall and they returned to the large hall.

"Eat!" Merne said when she saw them. She must have gone to a different chamber to clean, for she wore a similar robe. She pulled out a large chair at the head of the table and sat.

Without ceremony, the rest sat around the table that accommodated all twenty-one of them.

Chin finished a bowl of crisped rice balls with gravy. "My turn for the baths!" She and the Jejods took their turn in the bathing grotto.

Yanda wondered if there were robes to fit them. She found a large leaf in front of her and saw others using theirs as plates. They dipped with flat breads. Curved bottles held fruity wine.

Zami on her lap, Yanda served them both, piling a couscous-like grain, a delectable eggplant dish called *pata*, and slivers of melon onto their leaf.

Zami reached for yellow melon. Yanda spooned grain

and *pata* into his mouth.

With Merne and Shouma at the head of the table, the Allies sprinkled in among the Escapees, chattering happily. Yanda would have liked to find out more about them but satisfied herself with watching. After a few bites, Zami drowsed on her arm. She tucked his head to her breast inside the robe's soft folds and leaned back, crooking a leg to settle her arm under him as he suckled, lids at half-mast.

Beri caught her eye and they smiled. They shared thoughts. What was next, they did not know, but for the moment, they were free. They thought how different this was from their past year: muscles tired from their long walk, surrounded by the comradely sounds, wearing soft clothes after magical baths, eating their fill of delectable foods.

Yanda anticipated getting into bed would be incredible, though maybe a bit too much like the Citadel, sleeping in rows. Her eyes traveled to Vatu, who curled sideways in the seat next to her, head-nubs upright and bright as she spoke animatedly to a slight, brown-skinned man, face delicately tattooed above a slim, dark beard. His arm rested on the table as he angled toward her, toying with fruit slices on his leaf-plate, listening, then speaking softly.

Yanda smiled, glad to see her Mingal friend so vibrant and healthy. The air here was good and the baths had done wonders for Vatu, originating as she did on a water world. Yanda's eyes moved back across the table to Beri. Gisli sat next to him, deep in conversation with his neighbor.

Beri's eyes stayed on her and she became aware of thoughts he wanted to share.

Chapter 15

Yanda found Beri's shields down, with two glasses of wine in him, and caught his memories in full view, going back to when they'd first been transported to Terlond. Separated from his only friends, he'd felt more alone than ever in his life.

His thoughts traveled to the day he first felt her mind-tap, from the Citadel two streets away.

"Shouma's teaching us to shield," she'd told him. "You have to learn, too."

"How do you do that?" he'd asked. He expressed to her how it had felt, after that, when she'd taught him to listen to others' minds, to hide his thoughts and to mind-speak from a distance, using any chance they got for him to concentrate on the lessons during work.

Then came the part she hadn't know. He'd had no one

to practice with until he met Gisli. The solemn purplish-brown Tellotian, a Dondarian soldier barracked closeby had one day walked into Café Selene where Beri sipped *kran*. Their eyes widened as they caught each other's thoughts. Surrounded by silent minds, they felt suddenly alive, as if music started up in a dead world. They practiced their mind skills whenever they both had time off, Gisli from the fataqs, Beri from leatherwork that stained his hands, over the eight or so months since.

Yanda let him know she was hearing what he recalled, and it became a mind-conversation. She shared how her strengths grew, working with Shouma, discovering more of her abilities, until she could communicate with him across town in the rooming house.

Yanda felt his emotion then, his elation at the connection with her.

"What relief, to be in touch not just at work," he thought to her. "I'd missed our talks at night on Farn, even if it was only for a week or so."

"I did, too," Yanda shared. "Unlike you, I had the women in the Citadel to talk to. I don't think I realized quite how lonely you must have been."

"I don't think I'd be here without your training."

She felt his gratitude. "I don't think we would have made it safely here if you hadn't."

"You've helped a lot of us," Beri said.

"It wouldn't have been fair for me to get training and not share it with you!" she responded.

Chin and the Jejods had returned from their baths and took their places again at the far end of the table. They started teaching Joli and a few other Allies their dice game. Shouts rose until conversation became difficult.

Yanda stood, lifting the sleeping Zami. Grinning toward

the lively warriors, she said, "Time to get this boy to bed."

Merne got up as well. "There's another sleeping chamber."

With that, the clearing of the long table began.

Yanda followed Merne from the main hall. As they passed the door to the subterranean grotto of heated falls and pools, she hoped she'd have another chance to enjoy them.

For the moment, they seemed safe, though Shouma'd detected Krid's mage spies unifying their efforts to find them, and Merne had seen an all-out search across the city for them. Entering through another doorway, they climbed steps carved in a narrow stairwell.

At the top, a small chamber held only six beds. Yanda settled Zami on one.

"I'll leave you," Merne said. "Don't hesitate to call for anything you need." She touched her temple, indicating mind-speak.

Yanda nodded. "Thank you." When Merne had left, Yanda put on the simple nightgown she found folded on the bed and slid herself and her sleeping baby under the covers.

Head gratefully resting on a soft pillow, she thought about the sharing of minds with Beri. It'd been nice to finally connect with him and connect more deeply. Maybe she'd send him a quick thought before sleeping.

• ———— • • • ———— •

Yanda woke, startled, thinking she'd heard Zami crying, but he slept soundly, cuddled into her. She squeezed her eyes shut, bringing back the last shreds of her dream. It was not him; it was her daughter, Seiti. Yanda pulled into a ball and shook with silent, wrenching sobs, wanting desperately to return to her girl.

A warm hand rested on her head. Through swollen eyes, Yanda saw Shouma's worried face in the light of a dim float-globe. The older woman gestured for her to come with her.

Vatu, in the next bed, scooped the sleeping baby and tucked him in with her.

Yanda put on slippers and robe and followed Shouma.

They sat by a pool, alone in the bathing cavern, voices mingling with the sound of a trickling waterfall.

Yanda spoke of the daughter she'd left. "I walked away, with nothing. Not even a photo of her."

"And Krid probably took any devices with pictures," Shouma guessed.

Though they'd spent time in mind-skills training, they had not shared all that much about their private pasts.

"Yep, before we landed on Farn, I imagine. I've never seen them since I left Alland."

Shouma bit her lip, her brow furrowed as she studied the younger woman.

"He's threatened to hurt my family if I contact them." Yanda splashed her hot face with scoops of water from the pool.

Shouma rested a hand on her arm. "We'll work this out. There must be a way to check on her."

"I just have to get off this planet, get back to her," Yanda muttered. "And we sure don't seem to be going the right direction for that. We need to go north." She stared toward the splashing fountain spouting from the rock wall, seeing nothing. Catching herself, she put her hand on Shouma's. "Thank you for coming to me and comforting me, though. Have you felt the mage spies while we've been in these caves?"

"Not since we entered the tunnel, past the first wall."

Shouma dabbled her hand in the pool, watching the water ripple out.

"Has Merne told you any more about what's coming?" Yanda asked.

Shouma shook her head. "Only that there will be an unprotected part of the journey that we have to plan for."

"So odd. Do you think we're headed for an underground world, beneath the toxic wasteland?" She shuddered at the idea of remaining in tunnels much longer. It'd been too long since she'd been free, in open air.

Shouma shrugged. "I don't know. There must be a reason for Merne's secrecy."

Yanda wanted to make an annoyed sound with her lips but pressed them together instead. Shouma seemed to not want to question their mysterious lion-eyed host.

Yanda yawned elaborately.

Shouma laughed. "Let's get you back to bed."

They climbed to the small sleeping room.

Yanda retrieved Zami from Vatu, kissing the Mingal's cheek. It was surprisingly soothing to settle into bed with only five other adults in the room. She lay trying to relax, breathing in the sweet scent of her sleeping baby's hair.

Even though air moved through freely, she felt the weight of mountains over and around her, sending her into closed-in panic if she thought too much about it. With shallow, quick breaths, she calmed herself, still hoping fervently they wouldn't stay much longer under there, though the only alternative seemed to be to don protective gear and enter toxic swamplands. For what? And if they headed east out of the tunnels, how would she get to the spaceport?

She needed to know what was happening, be able to make plans, for herself and her child.

Before she could spiral again into these circular, unhelpful thoughts, she reached out a tendril of thought to Beri. "Are you awake?"

"Yes. Things've just settled down in here." He conveyed happiness to hear from her. "You okay?"

"Yeah. Bad dream."

"I felt that."

"Did you?" She felt self-conscious, but also unaccountably pleased to know their connection remained strong, even when she slept. "I talked to Shouma for a while."

"That's good." He paused. "Did she tell you what happens tomorrow?"

"No. Sorry."

"What about the mage spies searching for us?"

"She hasn't felt them since we entered the tunnels. Hope you sleep well and that we get out of here soon. I feel like I'm being slowly smothered."

"Me, too. 'Night, Mirror."

•———•••—•

Though they could not tell morning from night in their underground caves, globe-lights floated as they gathered again at the long table, invited by a mind-call from Merne. Yanda'd found her clothes magically cleaned, next to her bed—ubiquitous cargo pants with lots of pockets, worn layers of shirts for any weather, a safari vest and army surplus jacket, covered in more pockets.

"Will we move on today?" she asked at the table, spooning hot cereal into a bowl made of a coconut-type husk.

"Definitely." Merne poured warmed plant milk into steaming roasted-grain drink. "High protein," she said, dipping into the cereal.

Yanda added nuts to hers, bits of fruit and date sugar to Zami's.

Once they'd eaten, they gathered their belongings and stood by the outer door, bags over shoulders, waiting.

"Ready?" Merne asked.

They gave eager nods. She opened the panel and they left the rounded Quonset, entering the phosphorescent-glowing hallway, again heading east. The Fugitives glanced at each other often, having no idea what they were walking into.

• ———— • • • ———— •

By mid-morning, the dirt-floored tunnel began to climb. They stopped to snack by a subterranean river, then continued.

At last, they all stood bunched at a barrier like the end of a mineshaft.

"Shield your minds," Merne instructed.

The rock barrier shifted, pushing outward. They looked upon a barren plain leading to far off swampland.

"Is this where we put on protective gear?" Chin asked, head ducking to clear the arch as she took in flat, scorched terrain.

"This is where we hide ourselves. Forget about toxicity. We need to have zero detectable mental presence and very little physical," Merne responded.

"Gnats," Shouma said.

Merne quirked quizzical brows at her.

"It might be best if Vatu makes us into gnats and I make us invisible. How far do we have to go?"

"About a mile," Merne said.

"We're going to fly?" Gisli asked. "Or our minds are

gnats and we run, invisible?" He looked around at the varied group, assessing ability to sprint a mile.

"Why doesn't Shouma just transport us from here to there?" Dele asked.

Shouma shook her head. "I don't think I can manage hiding twenty-two minds and transposing us in a new location. I wouldn't want to falter halfway."

"All the more reason to be quick about it," Beri grumbled. "Let's just follow Shouma's first plan. What about right now? Should we seal the opening back up while we talk?"

"There's no further tunnel under here?" Yanda asked. It seemed strange to have built an underground way out of the city and not finish the job.

"There's a kind of rock under here we can't penetrate," Merne explained. "Please, let's just get this done."

Bonden pushed forward. "I'll make us move fast. Let's link minds." She said to Merne, "You can guide. That will leave Shouma and Vatu's energy for hiding us."

"Beautiful," Merne said.

The ungainly group took hands in a closed spiral without speaking. Despite varied mind powers and degrees of training, the Fugitives formed their hive as they'd practiced. The Allies easily joined, having had long training. Already shielding, they felt themselves become tiny flying insects. As the small swarm soared from the cave mouth, they saw nothing of each other. It was strange to see no one else. Yanda felt the primitive brain of the gnat—mostly impulses. She understood nothing of the project they were endeavoring to accomplish—vague as that was, even in her human form—but she had some sense that the opening behind them was now a seamless wall again. No turning back.

After what may have been twenty minutes, their gnat bodies bumped against a barrier.

They responded with collective, tiny-insect dismay, flying erratically for just an instant, before they were through the barrier.

Their bodies expanded, lurching into full size. Back in their natural forms, they lay, a heap of twenty-one adults and one baby.

Staring around, disoriented, they took in a small clearing surrounded by lush forest.

Yanda gasped. No toxic wasteland in sight. Then she gripped her head as pain lanced through. She crouched, retching.

Chela swept Zami from the baby carrier strapped to his mother.

Shouma dropped to her knees by Yanda. "What is it?"

"Krid," Yanda said through gritted teeth. "He sensed me, attacked my mind, just before we came through." Her eyes watered with pain. "I've given us away—I didn't shield enough." Tears rose, along with more bile as she gave a dry heave.

"If he sensed you, he must know where we are." Tik paced, agitated.

"I think she's absorbed that possibility," Shouma snapped, scowling at the bird-woman.

Sitting up, Yanda dug the heels of her hands into her eyes, trying to clear her vision. She stared through the transparent barrier, back the way they'd come and made out Krid's tower, high in the distance. Or thought she could see it. Anyway, she felt it.

"If they don't know exactly where we are, they'll know something is out of sight here." Gisli chafed sweat-soaked hands down his pant legs.

Most were standing now. Yanda scrambled up, still woozy, swallowing back more bile.

Chapter 16

A deep, resounding voice came from the edge of the woods. "Let them wonder a while." A tall humanoid being with pointed ears and skin green-lichened in tone, stepped from the trees and approached. He walked straight to Yanda and pressed long hands to her head.

Immediately the pain lessened, then evaporated as she gazed into his strange eyes. They resembled Merne's, but with a pale green light, like sun penetrating a forest glade. In the next instant, she knew who this Elf-man was. He'd come into her dream on the Lark as they journeyed from Farn. "You're Zami's father," she blurted. A new turmoil came into her stomach while, from the touch of his hands, electricity zinged through her. The feeling of love from the dream swamped her mind with a complex turmoil of questions.

"Is that better?"

His rich voice sent tingles through her. She nodded, cleared her throat and croaked, "Much better."

"Good." He turned to Merne and they touched fingertips, eyes glowing. "Come." He swept his arm toward the forest, away from the transparent, domed membrane that held this alternate environment in place.

Yanda could perceive it now, with a new sense of the world.

"The toxic swamps are just an illusion?" Dele asked, following him.

"That's right," Merne said as they all walked toward the trees, following the tall Elf. "Well, there are some irradiated lands to the south, but we're protected from them in here."

"Why couldn't you tell us?" Bonden asked.

"In case the mage spies penetrated someone's mind before we reached here," Merne responded.

"Oh, yeah. Makes sense." Bonden sidled toward the edge of the invisible barrier, broadcasting curiosity around its structure.

Beri hurried with the others onto a path surrounded by dense forest. "How large an area is it?"

"There will be time for answers," Merne said. She directed her voice back to Bonden who was catching up behind the rest.

They stopped in a small meadow surrounded by tall, old-growth trees that towered, deeply shadowed beneath their canopy.

The Elf-man turned to them and said, "I'm Zamani." Hands pressed together in front of him, he bowed slightly toward them. "You've now entered the forest of Rotoul."

"Zamani?" Yanda thought, startled. She studied the Elf who seemed to be a leader.

It couldn't be a coincidence that she'd given her son the name Zami. Had that decision been imposed upon her? She loved the name, of course, because she loved her son. But now she was starting to wonder about the influences that might have played parts in all their journey.

Then she remembered, during her birthing of Zami, someone with Merne, in her mind, watching with avid eagerness. Was it him? It had been so vague, in that state of not quite here and not quite there she felt as she was giving birth.

Now it seemed like it was him with Merne. How much had they known all along? Worse, how much had they orchestrated? Her stomach churned. Just when she thought they were safe, or a little bit safe, receiving help, all the aid came into question in her mind.

She hugged Zami close, pressing her face to his, as he stared around at the leafy boughs above them. A knot rose in her throat. "He's mine. Not yours," she found herself whispering in her mind. All the while, she could not avoid seeing that the slight whirling in Zami's eyes echoed Zamani's and Merne's.

Zamani swept an arm around them. "Rotoul is our home. Be welcome."

But be safe? Yanda wondered. She felt Krid still, like a taint. What if he'd left something in her mind that none of them could detect? I have to ask Shouma to search, she thought. Sooner than later. I might be endangering us right now.

Another adult Elf stepped into the sun-dappled clearing. Adult Elves and a few shy children followed until the Fugitives and Allies were surrounded by Elven folk.

Merne took on her full Elven appearance then: tall, slender, pointed ears sinuously hugging the sides of her head; her skin color changed subtly to a peachy yellow-orange.

"You've met my daughter." Zamani laid a hand on Merne's shoulder. "She finally has a brother." He beckoned to Yanda, Zami on her hip.

Zami lifted his arms to the Man-Elf. "Comes in dreams," her baby relayed in mind-speak to Yanda.

She shivered, feeling a kind of deep, aching loss. "Are you sure it's him, sweet one?" she asked her son.

"Zami sure," he responded.

Zamani checked Yanda's face for acquiescence and, seeming to find it, lifted Zami into his arms.

"So, you two already know each other?" She gave him a wavering smile.

Zamani's echoing smile was wide and brilliant. His dark eyes crinkled. "Oh, yes, since his conception."

Conception. On board the Lark? Before they'd ever set foot on Terlond? She wanted to ask him in mind-speak but it felt too personal, and too tender, at this point. Despite Zamani's dazzling grin, Yanda felt uneasy with this newest revelation. Why had her son never told her? He'd said, at Merne's apartment, that Merne "knows Da." She'd thought he'd meant Krid and dreaded that the foul mage might have gotten into her son's head.

But Zami knew all along who his father was, his biological one. And they'd formed a relationship. Being so young, it probably just seemed normal to him and he never thought to ask. Zamani had been part of his world from the start.

Beri watched the exchange and Zamani's forward engagement with Zami with a puzzled, apprehensive expression.

Yanda noticed Gisli studying Beri's face. Gisli touched

Beri's arm and pointed.

Yanda looked, too. Vatu was climbing one of the rope ladders into a broad, lofty tree, disappearing up under the forest canopy. Gisli gestured with his head and he and Beri followed eagerly into the arboreal habitat.

"*Apat*," Zamani said to Yanda. *Come.*

She knew the meaning instantly, as if he put it in her mind. As her eyes acclimated to the darkness under the trees, Yanda detected rope ladders and bridges. Once she noticed these, a network took form.

Zamani soared nimbly to a rope ladder, Zami in the crook of his arm. Yanda gasped at the sight as he scrambled swiftly upward, but he appeared eminently capable. As if to prove that point, he swept down toward her holding a vine and caught her in his other arm. On the back swing, they landed nimbly on a ramp, as he set her down, keeping Zami firmly in his grip.

Zami reached up and felt his father's face and ear. His baby eyes seemed to show more signs of deep Elven swirling every moment they were there. Would his ears grow into points? Yanda wondered as she took a tentative step, testing the give of the woven ramp under their feet stretching from one huge tree to another.

Zamani began to climb and she followed, entering a wondrous world. As they climbed higher, she saw twinkling lights everywhere, like the fireflies in stories she'd read. After a time, they reached another bridge and hoisted onto it using the woven handrails. Easing into its sway, she hurried to catch up with the tall Elf-man carrying her son.

"Will you follow me this way?" His rich-toned voice hinted at pride and even excitement as he turned away. Along another ramp, he ascended a ladder, taking them even higher into the canopy.

I'll get in shape here, she thought, panting.

On a soft breeze, Zami's voice carried down to her, babbling words in an unfamiliar tongue. Unease trickled, sour, into her belly, even as she felt embraced in health and goodness in this magical place. Would she lose her son to the Elves? Was she delivering him to them at this very moment?

From a leafy tunnel, they emerged onto a splendid pavilion. Light cast in from many angles, spangling through small crystals that swung and cast rainbows. A firm, matted floor opened out into eating, sleeping and study areas on separate, raised levels. Books and a pleasing clutter of other objects were held onto shelves by ropes, like on a ship, or Traveler caravan.

"Look from here," Zamani said, stepping out onto a parapet surrounded by rails.

Yanda's breath caught as she eased out onto the platform, clinging to ropes. They stood perched over the forest, with views into the far distance: over a sea, and toward Dondar, where Krid's Citadel poked up above the city. She turned her head and saw the spaceport, far in the north.

Zami seemed unruffled by the dizzying height. Zamani drew her attention to a strange landmass northeast of them. A gash in the soil cut through trees, splitting on both sides as if peeled back.

Yanda turned to him. "What is it?"

"Look closely." He pressed his free hand, the one not enfolding Zami, along the side of her face. A barrage of images and noises threatened to unhinge her, then settled to a low, throbbing hum. Through it, a pounding voice came. Not one with vocal cords; another type of sound, but with thoughts and ideas. A mind.

She knew this sound. Her eyes widened. "That's what pulled me. That's the call." Her hands gripped the thick woven railing. "Made me leave…" her voice hiccoughed, "… leave my daughter. It took over my mind."

"Yanda." Zamani said her name on a breath. He ducked his head so his eyes locked on hers. "It is the Elf Stone of the Neyna. You are the one it called in all the universe. You have to save it. Save us."

The breeze on her face alerted her to tears she hadn't known coursed down her cheeks.

"Let's sit inside. Have something warm to drink." He put a hand on her shoulder and her entire body vibrated. *Is this just the Neyna touch or does he have something over me?* She remembered Kridenit taking over her mind and cringed, but followed as he led her back into the large living space. The woven mat felt cushiony under her booted feet.

"I'll take my boots off."

"You can if you wish. Your choice." Zamani set Zami on the covered flooring.

She dropped onto a woven bench and fumbled with fastenings, hands shaking. From emotions? The height? This latest encounter with the Elf-man she'd made love to in a dream? Maybe all of it. She glanced around the edges of the space. "Could he fall?"

"No, no. I've had toddlers in here before. It's protected on every edge. Like a bird's nest. Though I imagine he'd float if he dropped."

She yanked the second boot off and crawled to her son, scowling at Zamani. "Let's don't test the theory from this height." She sat cross-legged by her son.

Zamani's smile appeared indulgent, as if Yanda far underestimated their son. He stepped to a higher level and soon returned with steaming mugs.

"That was fast."

"The elements are willing," he commented cryptically. "Let's sit over here." He led the way to a small, comfortable, rounded cove circled by trees. Fluffy pillows adorned benches. Windows and walls formed an airy tapestry woven out of vines.

"It's like sitting inside a basket," she said as she chose a bench and leaned against a hammocking wall behind. Again, she tested her weight against it, finding it taut. She let Zami slip onto the softly matted flooring as Zamani set toys down for him, brightly painted, carved and shaped by she knew not what other means.

Animals, a banana, a star and moon. Zami examined them, then pulled up next to Zamani, who'd settled in a hammock that draped between thick branches. Zami squealed as they swung.

Yanda sipped the spiced drink, with a hint of spun honey. "Mmm…"

A companionable silence settled for a moment. Was the beverage having a calming effect?

Zami climbed down to examine a bird fashioned from light wood, with wings that moved when he pulled a cord.

"Yanda. The Stone."

Yanda gave him pained eye contact, reluctant to leave the brief respite.

He swung his legs around so he faced her, elbows on his knees, hands circling his cup. "The Stone is the heart of our people, our civilization. It has…" He seemed to search for adequate words, "most immense power."

At that moment, the Stone's thrumming penetrated her core. "I've noticed." Her natural instinct was to shut it out. By now, all she associated with it was her shame, her guilt and mounting self-doubt, connected as it was to deserting her daughter.

"But you don't understand. It's how we have the abilities we have; how we made this world. Others in the universe thought it was a power they could take. Possess. Use for themselves."

"You mean... the attacks on the planet? The nuclear waste?"

He nodded, staring down at his cup.

"You've managed to build a shield, though?" She indicated the invisible dome that encompassed the forest where they sat, tall enough to protect immense trees, powerful enough to elude all of Krid's efforts to find it. Until now.

Zami crawled to her leg and stood, holding onto her cargo pants. She set her cup, now half empty, on a side table and scooped him up. His little hand went to her shirt, and she undid it, tucking him under shirt and jacket to nurse. A lemony scent wafted up, reminding her that they'd been laundered just this past night. So much had happened since the cave in the mountain.

Zamani watched, a bright warmth illuminating his face.

Yanda felt herself pull back from that adoring look. "So, how did that work? You came to me in a dream, across space, and replaced Krid's seed with your own."

Chapter 17

She watched his expression grow somber. "Were you actually there, on the Lark?"

"Krid's seed *had* to be stopped," Zamani said. "He could not be allowed to sire a child with you."

Yanda remembered how she could not move the zygote out of her. She'd wondered then if it had some mage powers, even at such an early stage. "I tried," she said. "I tried to gently move the zygote out of me in its earliest stages, but I couldn't budge it."

Zamani nodded. "You have those powers, don't you? To look into a body, through the layers, and fix things. You've done that as a surgeon on your own planet? Or the planet you were raised on."

Yanda quirked a brow at the differentiation he made—her planet, or the one she was raised on—but let it go. "Only in small ways, clearing congestion. But I couldn't move Krid's seed."

"His mageness is potent, probably even in the first cells of his offspring," Zamani explained.

"How do you know that?" Yanda asked.

"We've studied his lineage. We know quite a lot." Zamani went on, "But I cannot end life. It is not my... it is not our way. Therefore…"

Yanda's mouth turned up, though the smile did not reach her eyes. "Therefore, you had to give me your baby. You can transform life but not end it. Is that right? Some might call that quibbling over semantics. That permanent transformation was also a death, an ending. His baby ended. Stopped existing."

"You would want to carry Krid's child?" Zamani looked surprised and confused.

"No. Not in any way." Yanda rubbed her baby's soft hair. Her eyes followed Zamani's gaze toward the ocean, seen in the distance, framed by a leafy window. "Now that I'm hearing your voice again, I feel sure it blended with the Stone's when I was called away from Alland. Did you help pull me here?"

Sorrow weighed Zamani's features down. He sighed. "I called, with the Stone. Many of us did."

Her brow creased. Wondering if she could trust anyone, she stroked her baby's back.

"We only want to return the Stone to its full strength."

She knew her look was stony now.

"There is much more to this story." His tone was pleading as he glanced again over the sea through the leafy gap,

"The planet is mostly sea, isn't it?" she asked, worn out and willing to change topic.

He nodded. Then he stood and moved to sit closer to her, setting his cup with hers.

Zami's lids had closed. His cherubic lips worked as if still on the breast in his dreams. Yanda gently pulled her shirt closed with one hand, resettling her baby's face against her.

Zamani studied her. "You're very bright. Special."

"Yet it didn't matter, did it? My intelligence. You pulled me here to make your stone whole, making me desert my young daughter, leave my responsibilities as a surgeon on my planet. With surgeries scheduled. I can probably never return to work at that hospital. I'm a flake now." Those had been thoughts that tormented her nights but she hadn't voiced them in all this time.

"I'm sorry." He touched her arm. "I did not know the specific target. We called, knowing our Stone suffered, thus we suffered. It was not how it was meant to be. The Stone was certain that the one who was meant to help, who *could* help, would come. It seemed like it would be by their free will. We did not know who... until I felt you approaching on the ship. Then I knew you were the one. But then I also felt... Krid's seed in you." He withdrew his hand from her to cover his face and rubbed, pressing the bridge of his nose.

"Have you transformed many others to be your children?" she asked.

His hand dropped and he stared at her. "Oh, Moons, no! Elves rarely procreate. I have only one child. Merne. And she has only one."

Yanda studied his face. He looked barely older than Merne. "I'm not even going to ask your age. So that means Zami will live... a long time?"

"He will live long. I assume. But then, you will, too, Yandawi."

Yanda frowned. "What do you mean *I'll* live long?" She had no pointed ears, no whirling eyes. How did longevity fit into *her* life? "And why do you call me that name?"

"You are of the Xentu. You did not know?" he asked earnestly.

Yanda had never known her parents. The family that raised her did not know either. Or so they said. She'd been a foundling, they'd told her. "How do you know what I am?" She felt dizzy. Zami had fallen sound asleep in her arms. She touched his cheek, a feather touch, searching for an anchor as tears smarted. "I... don't understand any of this."

"How do I know? How do I know that a *shifi* wind is blowing from the southwest? Xentu genes can be read in your spirit, your aura, your blood's rhythms." He pondered, studying her and Zami. "You may have been hidden on Alland as an infant."

"By whom?"

"We don't know that story. Yet. But I'm sure it can be read."

"Read?"

"In your unconscious memories."

"Oh."

"Would you like to lay him down?"

She hesitated.

"I'll have someone to tend to him," he assured her.

Deciding she had no choice but to trust them, since they had nowhere else to go and were kindly offering hospitality, besides Merne having helped them escape, she nodded.

They descended rope-slung, wood stairs to an airy room swathed in leaves and flowering vines. Like a nest, woven sides curved up a few feet from the base. A cradle swung gently from the reed-woven roof.

Two sprite Elves gamboled in, carrying art and writing

supplies. Giving greetings, they set their materials on a nearby table that appeared to be carved like a mushroom.

Zamani said, "Arsat. Bend. Meet Yanda. And this, in her arms, is our son, Zami."

Yanda's heart lurched at the "our." Protectiveness and suspicion warred with craving the sense of belonging and sharing it promised.

"I'm Arsat." One of the Elves, with green-tinged spiky hair, a buzz-cut pattern on one side, and sparkling eyes, bowed. It was hard to tell gender.

Both Elves' clothes were a blend of natural and synth fibers, with sewn-on bits of plaz and metals. They reminded her of teens, though age was impossible to read.

"And Bend." The other Elf was smaller, with hair as bright red as *aspar* fruit. "We'll watch over him." Bend stepped forward to take Zami and gently lowered him, still sleeping, into the cradle that swung from a large thick branch. "Show her around, Za."

Yanda was used to the Fems sharing in the care of her son so it was not completely foreign to relinquish him to the two bright eyed Elves. Yet, high in a tree, in a new place? How could she walk away?

"Oh. Okay." She moved toward the lightly swinging cradle and knelt, preparing her mind to leave him with strangers. She'd never done that.

"We'll call if he wakes," Arsat said.

Still hesitant, Yanda followed Zamani down the rope ladder.

First, he showed her to where the other Fugitives had been settled, in a neighboring tree platform that offered large rooms around the wide trunk—sleeping quarters and several pleasing sitting areas. They toured through, saying hello to her friends.

One of the sitting rooms faced the spaceport. Seeing this, Yanda turned to Zamani. "You can see when ships come and go from here. We need to get off-world."

"Merne keeps track of what's arriving and where they are headed," he answered readily enough but seemed guarded.

"That's good." Yanda searched his face with hope. Would he help them leave? Soon?

He gazed back with creased brow, then turned to stare out. Finally, he said, "Tomorrow I will show you something."

"Does it have to do with the gash in the ground?" she asked, hope dampening.

"The Stone. Yes."

She felt her heart sink as they climbed the final ladders to the ground and walked along a path lined with sweet-smelling *withum* bushes packed with tiny white flowers. At the end was a low, rounded building. They stepped down into another world—modern, with blinking lights, tech racks, swivel chairs tucked up to long counters packed with screens and keypads.

Down a narrow stairway, they found Merne tapping keys. The bank of screens she faced ran up the wall, showing what Yanda thought might be parts of Terlond and other planets.

Like in the underground caves they'd slept in, alcoves along the length of the long room rayed light through plants: tall terrariums that cast green light down to this underground level.

On Merne's shoulder, a small simian perched, tail wrapped across her shoulders. It turned large eyes on them under a gold forelock.

"Meet Tuk-Tuk," Merne said, scratching the tiny

primate's belly. "A Sandu freighter has a stop on Mingal on its manifest. It could get Vatu home."

Mingal was the most distant of all of the known planets. A knot formed in Yanda's throat as it struck her for the first time that she would have to part from Vatu. "And Alland?"

Merne spun around in her swivel chair to face them, eyes on her father. He pulled two seats from under consoles and offered Yanda one, sitting in the other. With high backs, they accommodated his tall frame. He crossed his long legs.

Picking her words carefully, eyes on her dad, Merne answered, "When the time comes, that's relatively easy."

"Are you sure about that?" Yanda challenged. "I got waylaid on the way here."

"That won't happen again," Merne assured her.

Yanda looked back and forth at the two Elves. Communication was happening out of her range of reception. Had one of them been angry? Were they both in with Kridenit? With what purpose?

She felt her trust pulling away from both of them. "I need to get off this planet." Yanda's jaw felt tight. "Is this dome impervious to anyone on the outside? Krid? His mage spies?"

Both shook their heads.

"We'd know if anyone even tried," Merne assured her.

"But Krid has his focus on the Dome now," Zamani stood. "We're going to need to deal with him. I must help with the Dome. I've been away too long." He rested a hand on Yanda's shoulder and said, "I'll see you at the evening gathering." Then he left.

Her shoulder tingled, unbidden, where he'd touched her. She was torn by the love she felt from their first encounter, and her suspicions. He'd been entangled in every tortured thought she had in the past year and a half.

"My father helps hold the sphere that protects us." Merne waved vaguely overhead.

"Oh." Yanda had no idea what that meant. A picture came into her mind of a number of Elves holding up a replica of a giant sphere.

"You'll see later. I'll show you the way back to Zami and we can bathe."

Yanda liked the idea of bathing. But she wanted many more answers.

As they climbed the stairs, she almost asked again about ships but heard laughter and familiar voices. As she and Merne stepped outside at ground level, they found the Fugitives and Allies gathered.

To Yanda's surprise, Chela held Zami on her hip. How had her baby gotten down there? She shrugged, grateful to see him in familiar arms and lifted him to join the rest.

They romped through the woods, coming out into a grotto of pools. The others had brought blankets they threw onto soft mossy knolls. Yanda stripped down to skivvies and waded in, shivering. She dove, letting out a screech from the cold water. Beri whooped and ran past her, launching himself like a missile, crossing to falls on the other side in one breath. When he came up spluttering, she called, "Impressive!" He came darting back, skimming so that a wave of water cascaded toward her.

Vatu shot out of the water, straight into the air like a dolphin, and came down with a cannonball splash that caught Beri just as he stood. Gisli, watching from shore, bent over laughing.

Shouma had Zami in a warm, shallow pool. Yanda joined them. The sun suddenly hid behind clouds, making Yanda shiver. Shouma sent glow-balls floating close over them, heating the area.

"Wow," Yanda gasped, holding her hands up to the warmth.

Vatu dropped into the shallow pool with them, paddled to the center, then crawled to shore like a salamander. Her skin was taking on a radiant blue tone in this fresh, clean air under the Elven dome.

Yanda patted the water next to her. Vatu wiggled closer and sat up, head-nubs dripping.

"There's a ship coming soon that will land on Mingal," Yanda informed her friend.

Vatu whirled around, eyes bright, cat-like pupils squeezing in and out. She put a hand on Yanda's knee. "What about you?"

"I guess I'll follow. There's... I seem to need to do something here. Help in some way."

"I'm not going without you. I'll go when you go."

Touched, tears welled in Yanda's eyes. Zami slapped cold little hands on her thigh, one full of mud, and chortled. She supported his chubby side as he reached for more and started coating her leg with it.

"Mud bath." Vatu's laugh had a sob in it.

"Ships don't go as far as Mingal often, Vatu. Are you sure you should miss it?"

Merne called, "We're heading back to help with dinner. Ready?"

"Hold onto him a sec," Yanda said and dove to the deeper pool to rinse off mud.

Chapter 18

They showed Yanda her sleeping area near Vatu, Chela and Shouma. Yanda was enraptured by the small details: shelving with carved figurines, books, notepads, and pens, flowering plants growing everywhere, soft Elven lounging clothes laid out. Yanda was tempted to push pillows against the thick trunk shoving up through the decking, and do some reflective writing on one of the notepads. Such a luxury after the Citadel's deprivations.

With a silent sigh, she dressed for dinner and put Zami in Elven infant clothing like bark and lichens, with an acorn hat. With him secured in his carrier on her back, she scrambled down the rope ladder, muscles aching from their first day living in trees.

All the Escapees wore Elven wraps and expressed pleasure in the break from their meager supplies of clothing, admiring each other's mauve and taupe hues.

They'd all pitched in on preparations, Tik taking the opportunity to play with Zami. The Jejods had hardly been seen since the groups had ascended into trees. But now could be seen perching most anywhere in the lofty branches.

As evening fell, Elf-fires hung from trees. Globe lights floated. Long tables held food and flowers.

Musicians played from a grassy knoll and walked out among them. The instruments looked ancient to Yanda, like mandolins, harps, lutes. She sat at one of the long tables, surrounded by her friends. A golden drink poured for her tasted like late harvest wine and made her glow inside. For a while, she stopped worrying about the future.

Merne sat next to a tall Elf with tangerine hair cocatieled into a crest. She'd been introduced as Tlalit. On Merne's shoulder clung the tiny primate Tuk-Tuk. She was a *sadthis*, Merne told them.

Zami ate a little, then wanted to get down. He crawled on clover grass with two toddlers; there were few children, as Zamani had indicated. Tuk-Tuk caught Yanda's attention and sent a mind message: "want to play with children."

Yanda checked with Merne who put up a hand and let the long haired, long-tailed creature scamper onto the table, then to the ground.

Zami squealed as the minuscule climber ran past and grabbed the spongy *snook*—a ball-shaped toy formed from mosses that was floating and bouncing around the lawn—and trotted to a tree where she climbed.

Yanda felt Zami call the *sadthis* down. The orange-brown creature darted out on a branch that dipped low, and dropped by the baby's knee. Zami held out chubby arms and Tuk-Tuk sprung into his lap, holding out the ball. Their

154

eyes locked. Carefully touching the primate, Zami pulled her into a light hug and kissed her small head.

Yanda and many others watched closely. Merne gave her companion Elf a smiling glance and they laughed, sharing a secret moment.

When it grew dark, some stayed around an Elf-fire that burned no wood, fed by energy pulled from the rich forest atmosphere. They listened to the musicians and talked. Yanda held Zami in a hammock chair, nursing him until his eyes drooped. Hers were starting to, too. She picked him up and found Merne. "Can you point me to our tree?" If there were markers indicating which tree was whose home, she hadn't spotted them.

Zamani appeared at her shoulder. "I'll show you."

Her heart pounded. Was she expected to be his lover here? She hardly knew him, though she could still feel the bonding of lovers with him from that night on the Lark.

Beri walked toward them. "I'm tired, too. Are you heading up?" he asked.

Gisli joined them. Soon there was a small trail of Fugitives following as they climbed. Yanda was relieved. She wasn't sure how she felt about Zamani. She was aware that he'd been part of calling her away from her daughter. It was a lot to process. She could use a night on her own. Or several.

• ———— ••• ———— •

Kridenit stood at his high window, looking out to the east at murky swamplands. Poisonous gases collected over pools of discolored sludge. His face cracked into a grin that never made it to his calculating eyes.

"Nice illusion you've created. But you've revealed yourselves and your invisible protective sphere. Now it's just a matter of getting through to you."

Of course, he knew of the Stone. Hadn't his father obsessed over it? Led forays against the Neyna Elves? Kridenit had bided his time on Farn, had his own small domes built, installed living systems on a lifeless planet. And then... the Lark appeared on his ubiquitous surveillance system. A surgeon drawn across the Universe headed for Terlond. Didn't he have a chunk of the Stone there on Farn, being tested in every imaginable way? He'd detected its call—combined with the infernal Neyna talents —without any trouble at all. But had not detected the source.

The mage pushed away from his view and paced, long sumptuous robes kicking out as he strode over plush carpet.

Digging under had proved futile; that unseemly stone layer surrounding the area chewed up the most powerful drill bits and proved impervious to blasts. Nuclear war had eventually decimated the last dome fashioned by the Neyna.

Terlondian ministers were being tedious about his proposal of repeating that approach. For decades they'd believed the Stone decimated. No sensors picked it up. But there must be a considerable amount of the Stone remaining or the Neyna could not sustain the impermeable dome, he reasoned, passing back across the rug.

He moved to the expansive polished-wood desk, dropped into his stately chair with its myriad adjustments, and began to tap proposals for presentation to his grand counsel.

· ———···——— ·

Merne watched her father and Yanda pass by her long low windows.

Tlalit landed in the adjustable chair next to hers and flung the back to a protracted slope with one practiced flip. Her purple eyes darted back and forth between her lover and the tall Elf escorting the mysteriously important surgeon along the path.

"Dad hasn't taken a *fajan* for a long time." Merne tapped a key, then swung her legs around, landing them on Tlalit's lap.

"Are they lovers or did he just impregnate her?" Tlalit picked up a remote and switched scenes on the screens covering the wall in front of them.

"Sstt. Crude." Merne studied the new visuals. A lively street scene populated one com unit. Buildings replicated old Europe. "Erzon again?"

"With your mission almost accomplished, we can get off this world for a while, can't we?" Tlalit adjusted the view to focus on the musicians, high on a raised stage in a packed, grassy square. The performers, a variety of species with daring piercings and tats, danced, defying gravity, spiky hair unlikely shades of purple, orange and green. They wore colorful, torn clothing under draping overcoats.

Merne rolled her eyes and grinned indulgently at her partner. "Prokit's moon, again?"

• ———— • • • ———— •

Yanda and Vatu lay on a sun-warmed patch of moss beside the pools.

"I could come to Mingal after I get my daughter." Yanda tried to envision settling back into her life as a surgeon on Alland. With inner turmoil, she realized the life she'd worked so hard to build seemed suddenly lonely, sterile, even meaningless after all she'd been through—the closeness formed with the other fems, discovery of an Elven world, even her apparent role in saving the planet, though she had yet to discover what that was.

"There are still the others to get off planet and away from Krid," Vatu pointed out, as she watched a bright blue and gold beetle climb a stalk. "I can't imagine this'll be quick. Besides, this Elven haven is about to be attacked." She turned on her side to face Yanda. "I can't really imagine you on my world." Her skin was bright as a peacock in the sun after swimming.

"Why not?"

"Well… we don't get many visitors because... You see, I'm suited to it there."

"It's a protected world?"

"Yes." Vatu nodded.

They both glanced toward shouts and loud splashing. Chela held Zami up squealing with delight as Bonden sent a ball of water over the largest pool to burst on those lying in the sun.

They laughed.

Yanda said, "Describe Mingal. I know almost nothing about it."

Chin on her fist, Vatu began. "It's a dim, dark place, like constant dusk. My eyes are suited to it. Everything appears blue on the surface."

"Like you," Yanda said.

"Like me. We live in cave systems above and below the sea. Most creatures on my world swim as easily as they walk, or climb, or fly. Plants on land resemble sea kelp. Low gravity allows children to bound easily up rock structures or eight-foot fronds from an early age."

"Sounds fun." Yanda watched the others play in the swimming hole, listening to Vatu.

"But could you stand constant dark?"

"Hmmm... I wonder. Can you see in the dark?" Yanda had noticed the cat-like iridescence of Vatu's eyes.

"Yes. Of course. Though there are species that glow in many of the caves."

"What are your living spaces like? Do you... sleep in beds?"

Vatu grinned. "We've been influenced by other worlds in some of our comforts. But we try to form a lot from the natural world." Vatu sat up and pressed a cerulean-blue hand to her chest. "I'm of the Seron. We're slightly built, agile. Our sister humanoids, the Chechons," Vatu ducked her head with a fluting giggle, "...are big. Very big. Like they were carved out of stone. They do most of the building, even chisel out caves with their massive teeth."

"Whoa."

"You have to understand, we try not to use disruptive machinery. The eco-systems are delicate."

"Sounds amazing. So, it's low tech?"

"In ways. Environmental scientists abound among the Seron. We're like the priests." Vatu wrinkled her noise. "It's hard to explain."

"Makes sense to me, more than most worlds. There's a pagan underground on Alland that talks about Old Earth as Gaia, a goddess. Seems similar, I mean respecting what the planet needs in all your decisions. Now I really want to see it. I wonder if my sight—being able to see through—would help. I'd probably have to wear a goofy headlamp on my forehead. Are you wet all the time, like salamanders?"

"There are cave areas that descend toward the warmer core of the planet. We have university libraries there and advanced technologies. My body can adjust to cold and damp, but some have become more adjusted to being dry."

"I'm definitely going there." Yanda rose and waded into

the water to fetch her son.

• ——• • • •—— •

The Fugitives lounged in the common area of their tree, Yanda in a low-slung hammock, Zami sleeping draped over her. A breeze played through, ruffling the leaves that surrounded them.

"Should we be expecting imminent attack?" Gisli asked, sprawled on an immense cushion by a window woven of willow.

Yanda knew none of them had forgotten the sight of menacing hovercrafts seen through the transparent sphere.

Merne's head popped up. She hoisted herself onto the platform with the help of a draping vine, nearly as agile as Tuk-Tuk, who clung to her neck. Settling against the tree's massive trunk, she said, "I heard your question, Gisli. We're safe for the moment. Vatu, you'll need to make up your mind swiftly. Getting you to the star-base will take engineering."

The escapees glanced at each other. That was a rather cool dismissal of their fears. Gisli shrugged.

Vatu lay curled above them in a cubby of the tree, reading. She leaned her blue-nubbed head over the edge to peer at Merne. "I thank you for your efforts on my behalf. But I'll find my way back to my world. I want to help Yanda get home."

What is the deal? Yanda felt almost angry. Vatu had already said no. It seemed as though they wanted to separate them. What was this job, this task, that required her to be isolated from a friend. She studied Merne, staying out of her mind but longing to climb in and search.

Merne brought her gaze around to Yanda's.

Yanda asked, in mind-speak tuned only for Merne's

reception, "When's an Alland carrier coming? And when do I learn more of this mission you want me to perform?"

"Peace, Xentu-wizardess. Tonight." Merne sent back to her, also privately. Then she got to her feet which were covered in soft, gripping slip-on boots. She dropped over the edge. Several steps down the ladder, she jumped onto vines and descended quickly to the forest floor.

· —— · · · —— ·

With Zami settled for the night in a cradle next to Chela in their tree-loft, Yanda followed Merne and Tlalit along a path. Soon it climbed. Glowing spheres lit their way in otherwise total darkness. They skirted a hill and arrived at a sheer cliff. At the base, a panel slid open at Tlalit's touch. They entered a small vestibule and Yanda felt the floor rise. Moonlight penetrated thin marble walls, providing suffuse gold-brown light.

"We're on one side of a pyramid within the hill," Merne explained, seeing Yanda's wide-eyed wonderment

The lift stopped and one wall moved aside, giving onto a large hall smelling of earth. Floor, walls and ceiling were covered in complex symbols Yanda longed to study. The three climbed narrow stairs until they arrived at a tall door of strange material, radiating energy. Merne pressed her long-fingered hand to the center and it opened inward.

Within, a round room formed a peak above like an acorn. Twelve Elves sat in a circle of mossy thrones. A moss carpet swept under them to a dark pool at the center.

Yanda stood transfixed as sensations rushed up and down her. She gazed above at indefinable beams, curved and shaped with figures, overgrown with mosses and twinkling with evanescent life.

Merne tapped Zamani's mind. His eyes opened. He

nodded once and Tlalit stepped into his place, slipping into the seat as he moved out without interrupting the connection.

Chapter 19

Merne and Zamani—daughter and father—brought Yanda into a foyer to one side, sealed off by a covered archway. They sat on soft cushions, offering Yanda one. She accepted, but declined refreshment, too nervous to eat. They surrounded a tiny, blackwater pool.

Zamani spread his long hands over the water. "We will go here tomorrow." The gash in the ground appeared on the surface, but now they saw it as if they hovered above. Torn earth gave way to a trail delving deep underground. Their view shifted to a massive cavern; a black hole took up much of the center.

Yanda squeezed her eyes shut and swayed as power engulfed her. This was not a new sensation. Its source was the power that had gripped her on Alland when she'd left her life as a surgeon and crossed the universe to its call. Her fists pressed to her gut as she lurched forward as the overpowering mind communicated deeply only to her. It conveyed that a rounded stone should have risen up, curving like a small world, into the hole at the center of the cavern. Instead, only a black maw with jagged edges stretched there.

Yanda took a few long breaths, then opened her eyes. An understanding with the Stone had formed in her. She felt tears brimming.

Zamani and Merne watched her, holding her gaze. Yanda nodded. They would begin the work tomorrow.

"But what about Krid?" she asked.

"We've planned this. We have loyals among his mage force."

That threw Yanda into a chaos of thoughts. "You have Allies in the citadel?"

Merne rested a hand on her arm. "You're wondering why we didn't help you escape sooner."

"Yes, indeed." Yanda twisted the pull strings of her jacket, caught between a shout and a sob. Being the person she was, carefully schooled in her emotions, she only said quietly, "My son spent nearly his first year in captivity. I haven't seen my daughter in all this time." She searched the Elven faces for understanding, even apology.

Zamani adjusted his long, green-clad legs on the cushions. "It's taken careful maneuverings to build to this moment. So much is at stake. A world. More."

Merne pressed Yanda's arm again. "We were going to start training you for the Circle tonight, but maybe it's too much. Go. Rest. Get a good night's sleep. Tomorrow we will begin."

"And soon after I've done... the task I'm needed for, there will be a ship to take me to Alland?"

The two Elves unfolded their long limbs in a lithe rise to standing. Zamani reached down to Yanda, offering her a hand up.

She wished she could imitate their motions but accepted the help.

There was sadness in Zamani's eyes as he said, "There will be a ship."

• ———— • • • ———— •

Light seeped in through layered boughs in myriad shades of green. Yanda snuffled into her pillow, squeezed Zami and he puckered his lips in his sleep. She gave them a kiss, then gently disentangled herself from him and the covers. Quietly she dressed and unlatched the netted child guard, she lowered herself onto the ladder, re-latched the gate and descended.

Merne met her at the base with a warm cup of *chala*. Yanda blew, hands wrapped around it, bringing the rich beverage to her mouth.

Merne looked her over and pursed her lips. "This is going to be a long day. I can't anticipate all it will entail, but let's get you geared." She took Yanda's hand and they walked together along the path.

What was this physical contact about? Yanda wondered, even though she liked Merne's touch. She admired the woman and sometimes felt protected by her. At other times, the Elf woman seemed closed off, keeping secrets. Last night, Zamani'd given her puppy eyes about leaving. Maybe he didn't want his son to go. Were they closing ranks, with a plot to enfold her as family in order to keep Zami? Yanda put up her usual barriers, suspicions forming a chess game in her mind. If they tried to keep Zami... her stomach churned. She imagined the arguments they might raise. "It's too dangerous for him to come with you." "He'll never be understood anywhere else."

Alone. She was always alone, battling the universe.

At the long, low, tech quarters, Merne led her to a third level, underground. The tube-like terrariums continued down through the subterranean layers, letting in natural light at intervals.

They passed a gym filled with large, bright plubber balls and climbing ropes. Other apparatuses were unfamiliar to Yanda but had clear purpose. She longed to play in there, get herself back in shape, though the trees were providing more exercise than she'd had in the past eighteen months.

They walked by long indoor pools and a sauna. Yanda's favorite workout on Alland had been swimming laps, two floors down in her apartment building.

The door at the end of the corridor opened onto an attractive chamber.

"Is this where you stay?" Yanda asked her host.

"Rarely. Sleeping in trees is definitely my top pick. This is here when I need it."

"Does everyone in your clan have underground quarters?"

"Yes, all can fit. We have gardens, everything we need."

"Have you spent a lot of time down here?"

Merne picked through a closet and drawers, the silence stretching. "Too much," she said at last. "Here." She tossed a few garments to Yanda.

The feel of *zarsh* pleased Yanda, soft yet durable. Seeing Merne's, she'd longed to try some. She peeled off her clothes on the spot and tried on stretchy draw-string pants the crimson of santu fruit, gathered at the ankles, and a tunic made of the same material. Then she pulled on an intriguing saffron-colored jacket with roomy inner and outer pockets. She pressed it closed at the front, delighting at the quiet shushing sound.

"All plant-based. Try these." Merne handed her the type of slip-on shoes she herself wore that gripped any surface. These were dark forest green.

The booties snugged onto Yanda's feet. "Aren't we hiking down into caves on rugged terrain?"

"Oh, yes. They're very tough. They also climb trees well." Merne came close and turned the jacket lapel outward. "Run your opposing digit down this strip to make it cooler. Up for warmer."

Yanda slid her thumb as shown. The coat felt lighter, then heavier, thicker. "Whoo. Tricky."

"Take this." Merne pulled a beanie from a hook and tucked it in Yanda's pocket. "The caves get cold."

Grinning, Yanda tugged the sky-blue woven hat down over her ears and trailed behind Merne into a spacious kitchen. Two packs sat, full and ready, on the counter. Merne held one out to Yanda.

The tunnel they left through came out on the far side of the underground fortress, wending upward to an exit point under a mound. A panel slid shut behind them, hidden by vines.

Stepping away, Yanda looked back. They were some distance from the wooded Elven home. The land ahead lay bleak and bare of natural growth. They started forward over rough ground, churned up by something. Yanda could already feel the Stone. After last night, the feel in her heart and body was becoming more familiar. The very ground seemed to vibrate and hum with it under her feet, sending bone-deep reverberations through her. She heaved a sigh.

Merne turned to her and nodded. "I know. I feel it, too."

Yanda studied her companion with side glances as they navigated huge dirt clods. Merne seemed to almost float over them, as Yanda barely avoided twisted ankles and wished for her more stompy boots. Merne held a grace now, strong, tempered. Her face had strength. Yanda admired the lines of her peachy-orange face and neck. She wore her hair in braids on each side that curved around the sinuous pointed ears, like leaves.

The air here was slightly more glowering, like Dondar. She imagined it tinged her own skin with red. Lifting a hand, she saw that it did indeed put rose on her complexion. The team of Elves in the high reach of the pyramid must put more energy on the forest home. Was this area more vulnerable? She gazed up, trying to detect the dome that supposedly shielded them, and saw nothing. From here, Krid's towers were blocked from view.

Climbing over a small rise, the wide gash in the earth that she'd seen from the treetops appeared before them. The thrumming increased three-fold. She gripped her head, dropping to her knees.

Merne knelt by her and put a cool, soothing hand on the back of her neck.

Slowly, the energy Yanda had absorbed at the pool with the Elves melded with this more powerful close presence. She let it settle into her bones, first with gritted teeth, but then with acceptance. She knew this feeling in an ancient way—something far beyond her current lifetime.

When she was ready, she got up, Merne helping her.

"Shouma and the others should be here," Yanda said. "Shouma helps my mind. And Vatu... she helps my spirit. Can we call them?"

"Tlalit is bringing them."

At the bottom of the trail, they stepped into the immense

cavern's floor and approached a thirty-foot gaping hole at the center. No stone was apparent.

They sat on a rough bench, a natural formation. Silence grew.

Then Merne said, "This was under forest. The Stone was perfectly round and smooth. A chunk was blown from its surface, then more pieces knocked out. Shards have been stolen, sold, and scattered across the universe, robbing It of Its power." She took a water bottle from her backpack and drank. "The Neyna were peaceful for centuries. We had no idea how to handle such aggression. What would have worked among Elves held no sway on these invaders. We depended on the Stone for a lot of our power."

"It still feels strong to me." Yanda shivered with the effort of holding the energy still zinging through her blood.

Merne turned swirling eyes on her. "Then you can only imagine, when the Stone is whole." Tears glistened in the light from the float-globe. She inhaled, sitting up straighter. "We've had to bring our minds together in new ways."

"The pyramid in the hill? Do those seats channel power from down here, through the pool?"

Merne grinned a broad, pleased smile. "Right. That pool connects to the Stone by a subterranean river, far below us. And the seats are carved from sister stones that lie under here." Merne waved toward the chasm. "We did all this with the Stone's guidance, of course."

"But you couldn't put your mind powers together to help the Stone heal itself, become whole again?"

Merne shook her head. "At last, the Stone located you. You *are* the necessary resonance. Father helped call you."

Tears finally poured down Yanda's face. With a sob, she croaked, "Why couldn't he have just come and asked me?"

Merne whirled toward her, staring. "You thought Father

knew who, where you were, all this time?" Her eyes darted over Yanda's face. "No! He and the Stone sent out a call, over and over. You were the only one who sensed it. When you approached Terlond on the Lark—that's when he knew. Oh, Yanda." Tears filled Merne's eyes as well.

Yanda studied her, wanting to believe.

• —— • • • —— • •

Kridenit again stared out his high tower window. This time the Lark captain stood beside him, mop of dark, curly hair to his shoulders, outfit typical star-fare—worn vest, frayed at the sleeve-holes, military-issue shirt rolled to the elbows, no particular allegiance, rugged pants with rivets and patches, calf-high studded boots.

"You can see it, can't you?" Krid snarled.

"See what?" Tenali asked, bored-sounding.

"Don't be obtuse. The land of the Neyna. You've seen it all along."

"I see nothing but toxic swamplands."

"You'd have me believe that?" Krid glanced over at this enigma of a star captain, with his surprising level of resistance to mind control and decided on a different tactic. "We both know you can be bought. What's your price this time? Improvements to your precious Lark?"

Tenali resisted pressing a palm to his temple as he felt the headache that sometimes plagued him coming on. "I'm done with your riddles for today." He turned to leave.

"Not so fast. How many fighters do you have access to?"

"I provide transport." Tenali did not turn back as he strode toward the door.

Krid made a farting sound through his lips. "My ass. You provide whatever pays."

• ———— • • • ———— •

Voices alerted Yanda that the others had arrived in the caves, Tlalit in the lead, her tangerine, peaked hair like a flaming beacon. Behind Tlalit, Yanda saw Chin—tall as the Elves but broader—peering into the massive darkness underground. The rest, lit dimly by float globes, gazed around as they descended the trail into the endless-seeming caverns.

Yanda sent mind-calls to Shouma and Bonden to come close. Vatu slipped up beside her and sat, leaning into her, her eyes luminous saucers as she studied the roof and walls that were mostly obscure to Yanda. She imagined Vatu might see the entire subterranean chamber in detail though it stretched hundreds of meters away from them.

Vatu assured her, "Zami is in good hands, in the nursery with the youngest Elves and tenders."

"Thank you." Yanda slipped an arm around her friend. Colors—orange, chartreuse, pale yellow—rippled across Vatu's skin. Yanda'd never seen that and wondered if it was the good health, the blackness of the chamber, or her touch. "Can you show me what you see?" she asked.

The two shared minds. As she'd guessed, Vatu saw far more than she: areas of luminescent stone in the walls, the tones of rocks in crevices.

"Whoo. Thank you," Yanda said with fervor. "That's a whole new view of these caves."

Shouma and Bonden had come to stand near them in time to share in the vision.

"Awesome," Bonden said on an out breath.

Yanda reached a hand to Shouma. "I need your help. The Stone's energy is overwhelming. Will you support my mind?"

Shouma nodded. "Of course, Love."

Chapter 20

Merne approached, tugging a thick rubbery mat from her backpack. She dropped it to the cave floor, letting it roll out. Yanda and Shouma took the cue and knelt.

They spent an hour, Merne guiding them, as they acclimated to the vibrations of the Stone. Yanda's head began to ache and they broke for a snack and respite. Scooting back to lean against the rock formation behind, they ate fruit and drank fresh crystalline spring water.

"We should include all in a circle for your first contact," Shouma said, mouth half-full, dripping the juice of the reddish-purple *coos* fruit.

"That would be wise." A deep voice came from a distance. Zamani, accompanied by several Elves, descended the path into the massive cavern.

"How did he hear us?" Yanda asked Merne.

"He will have amplified our voices the minute he saw us down here." Merne chuckled.

"Handy skill," Yanda mumbled.

"I think he's polite with it, most of the time." The Elf woman stood, laughing.

Tlalit came into their minds. "Most of the time? I wouldn't say so." The orange-haired Elf stood twenty feet from them, fiddling with a device that seemed built into the wall.

Break over, Shouma sent a call to the other Fugitives, while Merne summoned the Allies and Elves. They all gathered near the hole, cautious of friable edges. Nineteen in all, they circled and held hands, increasing bonded potency.

Yanda's first thought was that the Stone loved this energy, and soaked it in. Then came the clearest communication she'd ever received from It.

"I am Shalt."

"The stone's name is Shalt?" Yanda turned, sending a questioning look around the circle.

Zamani's eyes widened.

In that moment, Yanda knew the Neyna had never known the Stone's name.

Shalt spoke to her again and she gently broke free of the circle. "I must go to The Stone's surface." Her words came out fierce. A compelling sensation filled her. This time it did not feel mindless. She had her faculties.

Bonden brought the mat onto a promontory that hung out over the hole. "Do you think this is safe?"

"Oh, yes, we've been using it for centuries," Tlalit said.

And so it was that Yanda stepped out over the abyss and saw Shalt's surface for the first time.

Far below them, stretching out into blackness, was an

almost flat, frosty green surface.

Staring down, Yanda called, "Vatu, will you sit next to me and show me what's in the darkness?"

Vatu dropped cross-legged by Bonden and they shared the narrow space, as Yanda stepped to the end of the protruding rock ledge.

Bonden nodded to signal. Yanda felt herself lifted.

Dele sidled over and Bonden made room for her.

Yanda's heart jolted as she floated out and away from the solid cave floor, hanging over black nothingness. Vatu's mind joined with hers and, as she lowered, Yanda saw a place of wonder: crystals flickering with myriad rainbow hues, stalactites and glow worms beneath the ledge.

Bonden slowly lowered her, checking at intervals. "Am I going too fast?"

"No."

"Do you feel okay?" Shouma asked.

Yanda answered "Yes," though Shalt's force grew to a crescendo as she neared the surface and her heart thundered.

She felt Shouma's and Chela's soothing words in her head as they helped soften the impact within her.

As her feet neared the pearlescent green expanse, it began to glow. Her feet touched and she stood on the vast stone. It was then that she saw where enormous chunks had been brutally blasted out. Sensing Shalt's pain, she felt the marred areas like wounds and wrapped her arms around her middle, tears welling as she fought to ease waves of hurt.

Chela, Shouma and Vatu, as well as some of the Elves, joined her in her mind, sharing the ache and then easing the burden of it.

Slowly she became aware of warmth growing under her

feet. Shalt turned rosy where she stepped. Following an urge, she lay her full length against the Stone. It was as though she were naked but she couldn't tell if she was. She felt elation, pressing her temple to the marbled surface to make further connection.

The Stone's history poured into her mind. She watched the planet develop, the Elves evolving over millions of years, others eventually landing there. Shalt had felt motherly toward the colonizers at first and provided all the energy they needed. They lived well and wanted for nothing. Crops grew, water was abundant. But an immense starship arrived, having heard of the prosperity. They searched for its source and found nothing in the cities to explain it. People could only say it was their god who cared for them. Angered, the invaders blasted the cities, leaving Dondar the sole, bedraggled settlement near the spaceport.

As they were leaving, one commander noticed the forest area and sent surveillance teams in. Having no weapons to match those of the invaders, the Elves fled into caves. Shalt tried to expel the men but had no idea how. These beings brought poisons and destruction. The Stone tried to go cold and hide Its power, bringing all sources of energy to a halt in what was left of the city.

This chamber was discovered and the energy was felt, despite Shalt's efforts to hide it. Blasters broke pieces out.

The shock of any damage to the Stone caused it to grow red and hot. The entire planet shook violently. Parts of the cavern fell on the invaders as a piercing sound filled the air. The men ran holding their heads in pain. The noise grew until the men had nightmare visions that would never leave them. They scrambled for their flyers to reach their ships, crashing into each other. The fleet left with chunks of the Stone. Those who made it off the planet were forever insane.

But the shards of Stone began to make their way across the universe. Each piece carried a bit of Shalt's energy, but never *right* energy, when not in wholeness.

• ——— • • • ——— •

Yanda shakily pushed to sitting. As she stood, her clothes reappeared on her body. Was this a quality of the garments Merne had loaned her? Aware that her first session with Shalt was at an end, she mind-called to Bonden to bring her up.

• ——— • • • ——— •

The Fugitives had never before been brought to the Neyna's community tree. Yanda had thought Zamani's might be the tallest when they looked out from his crow's nest. But hiking deeper into the forest, they'd climbed one with an immense trunk that seemed to rise forever. Yanda's muscles were shaking at the mid-point when Merne swung toward her laughing, sitting in a sling.

"Or you can take the fun way." Merne reached a hand upward and a loop of vine dropped next to Yanda, who climbed gratefully in.

Testing the tautness, she let her weight, and Zami's, in his sling on her back, down into it.

"Don't worry. I won't let you drop. Neither will Zami."

That was the second time the Elves had referred to her son's ability. It still irked her. But for now, she tentatively swung out and began rising through the branches. "You could have said sooner," she called to Merne, who laughed a peel of sound only Elves managed, one-third bird, another flute, the rest... all Elf.

Leafy strands seemed to part for them to pass. Zami reached out, chortling in glee as they rose higher and higher. Float globes bobbed over platforms and walkways woven throughout the canopy.

At last, they stopped by a landing leading onto platforms scaffolding outward and upward from an impressive central stage against the still-broad trunk of the *sarwil*—that was the name of this gargantuan tree. *World Tree,* Yanda thought it might mean.

She grabbed hold of ropes as hands reached and pulled her and Zami onto the wood decking. Unsteadily at first, she walked forward, thanking the Elves who greeted her and joined the others who'd also arrived on slings.

"How far'd you climb before they let you in on the elevator secret?" she asked, a tad testy, coming up beside Beri. Her muscles still ached.

"Oh, right away. From the ground," he said, puzzled, then took in the grimace on her face. "They made you climb, with Zami?" he asked, rust brows rose into a crinkled forehead. "Hey, little buddy." He touched Zami's cheek with a knuckle.

Chela took hold of the Elven child-pack provided to Yanda and lifted so Yanda could unbuckle it as the Fugitive group settled into one of the scallop-shaped sections that cascaded in layers toward the stage like a vast lotus flower. Cushioned benches with soft blankets stretched alongside small tables that looked like flat mushrooms poking up. Multi-colored globes cast light of every hue onto the gathering.

Small humanoids like the one in the caves on their journey here scuttled among the growing crowd, carrying trays but also joining in with the rest in eating and drinking.

Gisli strode over to them. "Quite a sight, isn't it?" He slapped Beri's shoulder.

"That it is." Beri grinned up at his friend. "Join us." He

scooted over, closer to Yanda.

She smiled at him, then watched as his gaze scoured the crowd and stopped on the stage below them where Zamani had stepped out.

She'd noticed he sometimes seemed uneasy about the lead Elf. She saw his brow crease now as Zamani took a bow to thunderous applause. She wished she and Beri had had more time together. It hadn't been her design. When would there be enough time for so many things?

Yet time ate at her, too. It seemed to race by as her daughter grew older. Seiti'd had her seventh birthday while Yanda languished there.

A male Elf pulled Beri and Gisli to be seated at a different table, where Allies and Elves mixed. She felt a twinge of regret that she'd not had a chance to get to know those outside the circle of Fugitives. Much as she loved them, she craved new contacts as well.

Zamani's voice drew Yanda's attention. Tall, strong, he was a picture of elegance and uniqueness far below on the round stage.

"—trying to find a force," he was saying. "He's having trouble locating enough fighters. He'd depended on... certain sources which haven't come through for him."

Yanda heard chuckles throughout the crowd of varied humanoids and Elves, a scintillating sound, like rain on leaves, chattering and hoots.

"So, we have some time. I invite you to enjoy your meal. Tomorrow, we plan an excursion to the sea, an area protected by our dome. Please. Eat. Talk. Be merry."

As he left the stage, musicians climbed on, a blend of beings with instruments Yanda'd never seen, though she'd been to many concerts on Alland. She watched Zamani climb the long, shallow steps, skirting several layers of platform, heading toward theirs. Her companions made room for him next to her. After a few moments, Merne joined them.

She felt heat as Zamani sat next to her, legs stretched under one of the mushroom tables.

Zami, on her lap, had discovered a plate of filled cups made of some edible plant resembling sweet cheese and ground almonds. She'd tasted it. Not a nut. Perhaps fungi. She'd gently pushed it aside until she could ask, instead encouraging him toward some fruits she recognized.

"Is it nuts?" she asked Zamani, pointing to the little stuffed cups.

"No nuts. A mushroom we dry and make into meal. It tastes very much like nut, though. We can grow many varieties of edible fungi under the forest canopy."

"I bet you can." She brought the desired plate back into her son's reach. "So, we're safe for a bit?" she asked Zamani, turning her face toward him. His eyes were dizzying this close up. The memory of their long-ago lovemaking melted through her flesh, into her bones. She felt confused, wanting to draw away, or sink deeply into him. She let her breath trickle slowly, searching for anchor. She longed to pull on Shouma's strength but felt unwilling to share the panoply of feelings that washed through her insides, terrifying and heating her at the same time. Until she knew the whole truth of that night on the Lark, and even her being drawn here—until they could fully discuss it—anger and suspicion would still move inexorably along her insides at every contact with him.

He nodded and began to speak when his eyes jerked away from hers, widening in amazement. Her head whipped around to see what drew his attention. A man stood by Merne. Was it a man? In all appearances, yes. In mind vibrations, no. He wore the rugged clothes of many star-captains. Yes. Now she recognized the Lark captain.

Merne scrambled to her feet, letting out a cry. She launched into him, body shaking. Sobs and laughs cascaded from her.

Tlalit reached up to hold her hand and she gripped it, still clinging to Tenali. He kissed Merne's head, brought her face up with gentle hands. Tears formed like jewels in his eyes.

Much of the crowd watched this reunion. Music stopped and then started up again as Zamani got to his feet. Yanda felt cold as he moved away from her, stepping around the carved wood banister backing their section to enfold Merne and Tenali in a great embrace.

Chapter 21

Yanda relaxed on a settee in Zamani's quarters, fingers absently rubbing the satiny fabric of the luxurious couch.

The Elf lounged on pillows near her so that their eyes were on a level.

After settling Zami with her companions, she'd come at his invitation to his quarters in the leafy canopy, insides and nerves warmed by the dinner's sweet fruity wine. They'd exchanged small talk about the tree village, the roles of elders, the plants they liked to grow and eat. Now they held cups of herbal tea, touched with honey.

Yanda pushed to sitting and crossed her legs. "I need to know each part." She enunciated carefully, wanting to get the complete story and nothing less this time. She held a finger. "I felt the huge voice. Of Shalt. And boarded the Lark. That was captained by none other than your grandson, Tenali."

Zamani had straightened, keeping his eyes level with hers, seeing where the conversation was going. "Wait." He held up a long, shapely hand. "We had not had contact with Tenali for years."

"So it was just happenstance that you wanted me here and I was brought on your grandson's ship."

"Yes. No." Zamani shook his head. "I don't know." He glanced down at his hands in his lap.

Yanda was amazed to see the composed Elf flustered.

He shook his head. "I don't understand it either. I'll need to talk with Tenali but wanted to make time for us to talk first. I've seen it in your eyes that you hold unease about my role in your coming here."

Yanda nodded. "I do."

"Okay. I'll tell you. I called and called and called with Shalt. I know not why our call finally reached you, and had such an effect when it did. I never would have made you leave your precious daughter." His voice choked.

She stared at him, wanting to believe him, hesitant to do so. "And when you came to me, on the Lark? It seemed like a dream. Yet you had in fact changed my embryo." She felt vulnerable, tears stinging her eyes.

He scooted to her, closing the distance, and took her hands in his. His voice sounded insistent, almost pleading. "You knew, at the time. We talked about it. I said I could not destroy life, I could not allow Krid to procreate with you, with your..." He faltered, but seemed almost frightened to not finish. "You agreed."

"But we were dreaming," she said.

"It's a dream state. But it's spirit travel." His face had been close enough to kiss her, but he pulled back to study whether she was with him.

She wasn't.

"In spirit travel," he explained, "you might still, in essence, be there. The scene is happening. We entered a plane of existence where our bodies were in spirit travel yet this is also a reality. We manifested this dimension's reality while on that plane. Do you see?" He asked this but could not let himself stop there. "You agreed. I know your mind was fully there. Yanda." His lip trembled and he let her—almost pulled her, gently—into his mind. "The words are too hard and hold so little of the full emotion outside the body," he said in mind-speak. "You loved me and I loved you. It's not a new love. It's an old love. We've loved before. I don't know of it consciously but I know it's true. Not here. Not on any of these planets. Elsewhere. Do you know it too?"

It was as though they still sat in Zamani's aerie, yet Yanda was also inside Zamani's mind, and he in hers. It was the most comprehensive connection with another being Yanda had ever felt.

She reached out and touched his face. "Could we right now travel anywhere, in our spirit bodies? Could we fly?" She felt sure they could.

"Of course. We could fly." He drew closer to her. "If that's what you felt like doing right this moment." His arms went around her.

She could feel him physically, and emotionally, and mentally. She kissed him. She kissed his mind. She kissed him everywhere. He kissed her back and it was all-encompassing. They floated, merged, were one.

• ———— • • • ———— •

Next morning, all talk was about Withum.

"We're going to waltz off to the seashore with Krid

about to attack?" Yanda asked at breakfast, an array of sweat breads and creamy or dark hot chala. "How? What about the circle? They're not going to leave their posts, are they?"

"Everyone takes part at some point," Merne explained. "They'll be able to hold the Withum while in the Circle, too, though."

"What is it?" Gisli asked.

"It's... a festival." Tlalit seemed thrown by having to explain. She and Merne shared eye contact.

It must be very ingrained in Elven culture, Yanda thought.

"It's when the Withum blooms." Merne shrugged. She and Tlalit held a dreamy gaze and small smiles. "You have to experience it."

"Oh. So this With-Them is pretty special?" Beri quirked his brow into a question mark.

Elves turned toward each other, faces unreadable.

"Is that expression good or bad?" Gisli murmured, *sotto voce*.

As the morning meal was ending, dishes were deposited in tubs, and those on the clean-up crew carted them toward the kitchens a short distance down forest paths. The others began leaving the tables. Yanda stood, one foot on a bench, fastening Zami into his carrier.

"You can get to the festival by sea," Merne said, coming up beside her and helping lift Zami onto her back.

Go by sea. See an ocean. Yanda gazed at her. As she climbed, using the rope-gliders that lifted into the lofty home spaces above, she thought about it.

"I might go see the ocean, Bits," she said, turning her head to her son. They communicated in mind-speak. "Would you want to stay a while with the other children while Mommy takes a little journey of her own?"

"Yes. They take me in sky-bird. Daddy told me."

Sky-bird? Like a plane? She wondered. "Okay." When they pulled onto the platform, she knelt and brought the toddler around to face her, kissing his soft cheek. "We'll do it this way. And go to a festival! I don't know what it'll be like." *Maybe he knows better than I do. His father might have put images in his head.* This bothered her less now.

She brought Zami to the care Elves, then tried to figure out what to wear to go on the sea. "A jacket?"

Flashes of guilt kept flitting through. "I'll show Zami the ocean soon, but this first time of ever seeing a truly big water, I'll have it on my own."

• ———•••——— •

Yanda walked into the forest with Merne and Tlalit. Without warning, they teleported her. Instantly, she stood on the deck of an Elf-craft, swaying on the Terlondian seas that had an orange cast like perpetual sunset from the planet's rusty sun. *Were they trying to throw her off at every possible chance?* It sometimes felt like it.

There wasn't time to dwell on these strange tricks Merne and Tlalit seemed to play as she stared around her with wonder. Every inch of the boat was carved in a relief of laughing, cavorting creatures among tossing waves, making the polished wood vessel seem like a delicate toy though it felt sturdy enough under foot.

They slipped across the sea with ease, seeming to leap from wave to wave as easily the Neyla—Sea Elves—hopped to rigging, exalting in the cool spray that lashed their faces. She saw land become a thin line in the distance. For the first time in a year and a half, she'd left the land of her captivity. For the first time in her life, she felt salty sea air on her face.

She breathed in the tangy scent, marveling at the vast distances, nothing but sea and sea birds.

She explored the length of the fairy-boat and returned to the bow, puzzled. "Where are the sails? Is the boat powered by your minds?" It moved along with no indication of what propelled it.

Mnenu, a tall dark-haired Neyla Elf who eyed her often with intense curiosity, pointed out at the water.

Yanda noticed, then, creatures leaping to the front and side. They looked like art she'd seen of ancient dolphins on Old Earth. "They're pulling us?"

Asborn, a female Neyla, leaned over the side and held out her hand. One of the blue-grey creatures came to nuzzle her, making soft chattering noises. Asborn chattered back. Then it dove and came up, head in a ring attached to a rope.

"Our friends, the *tesu*." Asborn climbed to a perch and gazed out to sea.

Yanda found a similar seat near the edge of the boat, and swung her legs over the water.

"So they work for you? Serve you?" Yanda asked, surprised. Maybe that was a difference between the Neyna and the Neyla.

"Not really. It's great fun to them. They take turns pulling, then swim away to play or find food."

After a while, the boat changed direction toward the shoreline. As they drew closer to land, Yanda watched forest and sandy coves slip by.

A vibration ran through her mind. She jerked her head around.

Mnenu gazed at her, winding a rope, his eyes teasing. "Come swim with me." He stood on the next level up, long legs easily absorbing the movements of the boat. Neyla lacked the velvety skin of the Neyna, their woodland cousins. Instead, their skin seemed almost layered, shadows under light. Mnenu was exquisite, with eyes that sparkled, the colors of the sea.

Yanda laughed, not thinking him serious. "My planet had no ocean. I've only swum in lap-lanes. I'd be afraid." She looked down into the dark depths of the sea.

"I'll keep hold of you," he said.

As he spoke, she felt a force coming from him, as though he compelled her. She was about to snap a final refusal when he landed lightly in front of her. She looked into his jewel eyes that swirled with teal, green and gold. Then they shot over the side, skimming the water's surface, his arm firmly gripping her. He dove, swam under with her, then legs pumping in smooth thrusts, they shot up above the water.

By now, Yanda was choking and spluttering, nearly crying. "Enough!" she shouted.

His powerful legs pumped as he shot them up over the boat's railing. They landed light-footed on the decking. She bent over, coughing.

He started to pat her back, then drew back as she straightened up, glaring at him through watering eyes.

His grin fell away. "I'm sorry. I thought you'd like it."

Asborn started clapping slow applause. "Brilliant, Mnenu. You think she's a Neyla youth? Try asking."

Yanda could not understand their language but the meaning was clear in their minds.

Dripping wet, she shivered uncontrollably. He put his hands on her shoulders and she dried instantly, even her hair. He, too, was dry, and his clothes relaxed, fitted but not skin-tight.

She was still heaving deep, shaky breaths as the boat pulled into a small lagoon. Elves waded out from shore and pulled the barque onto sand. Mnenu raced away to help. Yanda wondered if she should, too, and searched for a rope ladder or other way down. A plank appeared and she disembarked with several Neyla, a few she hadn't seen on board 'til now. She walked off with Asborn and spotted her friends on shore.

"Did you come on other boats?" she asked as they came to meet her.

Vatu rested her fingers lightly on Zami's shoulders; he was now standing though not yet taking steps. Grinning, he said, "Bird-thing." He reached for her.

She dropped to her knees on the sand. Eye-level to him, she caught a glimpse from his mind of a silent bird-apparatus carrying him through the forest to this cove. "Wow, sweetie. You coasted through the forest while I came by sea."

"Want ride boat too," Zami squealed and pointed toward tidepools, giving her a picture in her mind. She swung him to her hip and walked with him across the sand to rocks shaped by time, full of colorful pools.

Chapter 22

That evening, they sat around fires that burned no wood.

Merne settled cross-legged next to Yanda. "Did you enjoy your boat ride?"

Yanda turned to the Elf woman who relaxed against Tlalit's shins. Tlalit leaned against a tree in animated conversation with several Neyla and a couple of the Allies. The ocean waves carried on a steady shushing and lapping.

"I did," Yanda said after a moment. "It was magical. Only..."

Merne's eyebrows raised as Yanda gave her a picture of being swept overboard by Mnenu. She was tempted to laugh because it seemed innocent enough. She looked up into Merne's eyes, ready to add, "But it was fun."

Merne wasn't smiling. In fact, Yanda thought Merne was angry about Mnenu's actions.

Yanda was glad she didn't have to lighten the weight of what she'd shared because she hadn't felt amused when she thought she might drown. "I want to be able to stop something like that, unless I choose it."

Merne said, "I have a small cottage up the hill from here. Why don't you stay the night and tomorrow we can work on your defenses. There are flowers there that we need for the festival anyway. You can help pick and make garlands."

"For the Withum Festival?" Yanda asked.

Merne responded, "Withum. As orange as this world's sun," as if she chanted something from a ritual, or children's rhyme.

At that moment, Mnenu walked over and sat next to Yanda. Zamani settled on her other side. It was the first Yanda had seen him since they'd come to this shore. Yanda greeted Zamani, edging slightly away from Mnenu.

Maybe it was the recent intimacy but she felt memories of her day release to Zamani unbidden.

His eyes turned toward Mnenu, who grinned, teeth glinting in the firelight. An exchange ran between Neyna and Neyla, private mind-speak, but Yanda could feel angry sparks in Zamani's mind at her memory of choking and fear.

Asborn, who sat a little off from them, said, "Mnenu's a fool." Yanda could feel herself the topic of a barrage of mind-gossip all around the fire. She focused on Mnenu's feet, stretched toward the fire. Rather than fin-like, the Neyla's feet were quite beautiful. In the firelight, Mnenu's appeared to be made of glass, vein colors running through with brilliant translucence. She glanced up at his face as at last the conversation drifted off into other topics.

His eyes rested on hers. "I'm sorry. Truly," he thought

to her.

She felt emotion behind his words, an intensity that came across powerfully to her. He wasn't grinning now.

Her eyes dropped to Zami, who droused in her lap, and suddenly she longed to have something she called home—her own home—to go to.

Merne tapped her shoulder. "Time to retire?"

Vatu got up with them. They said good night and followed Tlalit and Merne up off the beach, onto a path lit by float-globes, winding through thin woods. They came out into a clearing and lights glowed in the windows of a small cottage nestled between two hills.

Yanda heard a brook burbling. They crossed a bridge and entered a gate. She could just make out flowering vines and smelled something sweet in the air. Back on her home planet, there were vines, but few hills and no trees. It enchanted her, like a storybook illustration.

Merne opened the front door to welcome them in. Shouma, Chela and other Fugitives were already enjoying themselves inside. The place was filled with laughter and the smell of late dinner cooking. It seemed larger once she stepped in; high, angular ceilings held spangled windows catching a bit of moonlight.

She greeted the others before Merne led her, with Vatu and Zami, to a cozy bedroom on the second floor.

* ———— ··· ——— ·

In the morning, light streamed in and Yanda could see their room was tucked into a crevice of the hills; she could have stepped outside from their room, but instead she stretched, contented in the warm quilts and soft nightgown Merne had provided. From bed, she gazed across a meadow of flowers like small suns, bobbing in a breeze.

Zami stirred next to her and sat up. "Play Tuk-Tuk?"

The little creature had been on Merne's shoulder the night before.

"Let's go see," Yanda said and scooped him from bed. "First we should probably clean up a bit and get dressed." Her hair felt sticky from salt air. She sent a mental feeler downstairs and found Shouma's mind open to her. "Are there showers?" Shouma and several of the other fugitives arrived upstairs with Merne, carrying towels and they paraded out the back door to a hidden row of falls that formed natural showers from a warm pool above.

"We keep it warm when we stay here," Merne explained.

Tuk-Tuk, on Merne's shoulder, held Zami's attention. Yanda got him suds'ed before he pulled free.

"I'll take him and let you bathe," Merne offered.

"Thanks." Yanda gratefully stuck her head under the heated falls and rubbed scented soaps into her hair.

Clean and dressed, Yanda and Vatu stepped into the steamy kitchen from a back door. Smells of baking assailed them from twisted bread loaves, freshly baked and golden, steam rising from them in pans on the long central table. Others sat ready for the oven.

Spotting Merne heading out the front door with Zami, holding gloves and snippers, Yanda called, "Can I help?" and hurried to pull on boots.

"How about some breakfast for you two?" Chela asked from the kitchen doorway. She called to Merne, "I made Zami's favorite," and held up a banana mash. "I'll bring him out after. Let him eat." She turned to Yanda and Vatu. "What would you like?"

"I'll just have *chala* for now." Yanda held up a full cup

she'd snagged on her way through.

"I'm going to explore." Vatu left through the front door, a warm steaming roll in her hand.

Merne returned and sat Zami in a beautifully carved high chair, enjoying hot cereal and banana mash. Tuk-Tuk jumped vines to a high window. Zami looked like he'd like to follow.

"Where did the others sleep?" Yanda asked Merne.

"Some camped near the beach, and there are treehouses that way." She sat with Yanda and Zami and nibbled currants.

After, the three made their way around the house, into a mountain meadow filled with the sunny flowers and their delicious scent. Yanda crouched to look closer at the fragrant blooms.

Merne was crouching, cutting long-stemmed flowers and laying them in her basket. "The Neyla stay close to the sea. They have caves near here." She pulled a second pair of shears from her basket and handed them to Yanda.

"That doesn't sound very comfy." Yanda clipped flowers low on the stem as she saw Merne do, and added them carefully to the basket.

"They live in an underwater city. They sort of transform to part sea animal so they're comfortable on kelp beds."

"I think I've seen signs of transforming." Yanda remembered Mnenu's amazing feet, and the way his clothes became a sort of skin.

As she worked with the plants, Yanda felt euphoria creeping in. She turned to Merne, eyes wide.

"Uh-oh," Merne said. "You need to take Withum in small amounts at first. I should have given you gloves against their pollen. I'll get Tlalit out here to help me instead."

A moment later, the tall Elf with tangerine hair walked toward them in long strides, swinging more baskets.

Yanda wandered toward the house with two filled baskets, listening ecstatically to bird song, noting every leaf on branches swaying overhead as she neared the Elven abode. What made it Elven? She asked herself and got her answer. The Elves had shaped it, without any cutting, with their minds and their hands. Parts were earthen. It was a living edifice, with flowering plants growing over the top. Birds flitted into the moss and sod and nested there.

Yanda opened the front door and was struck again by the warm, yeasty smells. Several Elves sat in the living room area now, including Zamani. Where nature had felt perfect, the house, filled with sounds, minds, smells and activity assailed her senses. She could even sense the Allies in tree houses near the beach: unfamiliar interplanetary mindsets tumbled in with the rest and she felt chaos. Standing in the doorway, she swayed, barely noticing Zamani watching her.

Finally closing the door, she walked unsteadily toward the kitchen to offer help with food prep, but overwhelm swamped her faculties. Shouma sat beside her, where she tried to peel and cut fruits.

"I know how to wash the extra-sensory input away. Shall I help you?"

Yanda tried to speak but words came out in gibberish, in languages she could not understand. Zamani came in and spoke with Shouma.

After a short exchange, he led Yanda out into the open air and she sighed with relief, still under the influence but at least able to draw on nature to ground her. They walked up the hill, away from the withum fields and she was barely aware as they climbed into a tree house that was very small compared with those of Rotoul.

They sat in a a cushioned swing on a veranda overlooking the slope down to the coastline.

Yanda could see that Merne's festival cottage spilled up into the crevices of the hills, with tiny cottages beyond.

Zamani took Yanda's hand and, turning to her, peered into her eyes. Tendrils of his thoughts drifted in among hers. The noise of the many minds fell into place. She still heard voices in myriad languages but they became soft, leaving a feeling of one mind, the hive-mind of the Fugitives strongest. She could pick out a single voice and bring it into focus, or leave all as a comforting hum.

She sighed with relief. "That's better. When do the festivities start?" She became more aware of his hand holding hers. It felt comforting.

"All of this is the festival," he answered. "But at sunset, there will be a special time, a ritual of sorts. For now, we can enjoy this quiet."

And they did. Yanda's head came to rest on the Elf-man's shoulder. Birds flitted in the eaves near them. Yanda felt their tiny avian minds and, through them, knew the sense of flight, the feeling of weightlessness as they flitted between branches and alighted on the smallest twig. "But shouldn't I be helping?" she mumbled, not really wanting to move.

"You're helping," he answered, resting his cheek on her hair.

"How?"

"Your mind gives to the whole," he answered.

• ———••• ——— •

After a long while, and no time at all, they walked hand in hand down the hillside, others joining them on the path until they became a throng. Zami rode his father's shoulders. The cove came into view. Then they slipped into forest. The woods were filled with twinkling lights. Soon they stepped onto the beach, where flower garlands draped driftwood stands, lit by tiny encrusted mollusks of crimson, gold and azure. The state of their minds as they gathered together seemed heightened, as one, not in a jumble as Yanda had experienced earlier, but with clear shared thought.

To one side, the Neyla stood looking out to sea. Theirs was a different thought pattern: vibrations like ocean waves and deep-sea emanations.

Zami reached for Yanda and slid into her arms, gazing wide eyed as an immense sea turtle dragged itself out of the waves and up the shore. Other giant turtles followed.

● ———● ● ● ●—— ●

Sometime in the wee hours—Yanda had no sense of time passing—they rode back to the Elven forest home in what Zami had called "flying birds"—apparatuses that winged above the treetops. To Yanda, it felt like a theme park ride. Soaring in the mysteriously powered mechanical birds, she had a sudden pang to take Zami to the large theme park in Skarth, and smaller ones in the countryside near her hometown of Balyou.

● ———● ● ● ●—— ●

Now, in bed on a fluffy mat near Vatu and the other Fugitives, she felt unsure what had really taken place and just how much they'd all shared. It seemed as though she'd been undersea some of the time, with ocean creatures, and learned that there was another stone of equal power to Shalt's, in the depths of the ocean. Was it true? Sometimes it felt like the sea turtles were talking to her alone.

As life-changing as those moments had been, she felt happy to be back in their treehouse quarters. Home was taking on a variety of meanings: a fairytale cottage out of a childhood synth-book; an abode containing her familiar compatriots; or merely this bed where Zami snuggled into her. She nuzzled his cheek and smelled his hair, now tinged with the aromatic blossom oil made by Elves, and smiled to herself.

She needed that sweet moment before the weight of what lay ahead descended.

They had had the festival. What came next?

Chapter 23

Light grew around the tree branches and music drifted from below. Zami stretched and pushed up. He was growing less interested in her milk in the mornings, gravitating toward what he could consume on the run, or on the crawl, as it were: a bottle, finger foods. He'd had experiences she wasn't part of, like his first ride on the "flying birds." What if someone else saw his first steps? She panicked. What was today? How soon was his first birthday? Where would they be for it? Would they be safe?

Not wanting to miss anything important in his young life, she decided to spend the day with him, focused on his activities.

Their favorite place to bathe was the hot springs in the grotto. She pulled a sweatshirt on over pajamas and strapped Zami into his backpack, stuffing clothes in next to him, then swung off the platform, grasping a vine and swinging out, landing only once on a ramp before reaching the ground. Zami squealed with glee. Her hands, a mass of blisters the first couple of days, were callousing nicely, reminding her of playing on the bars as a girl.

As she stepped into the grotto holding Zami, green walls of moss rose up around them, creating shelter and steaming from the hot pools. Shouma already soaked in the hottest one, submerged to the chin. In the air warm like a sauna, Yanda stripped down, slipping Zami's nightie off as well. She stepped to the edge of the first, more tepid pool and lowered herself and Zami in.

"What did you think of the festival?" Shouma asked across two intervening pools.

"Did you get the full effect of the withum flowers?" Yanda called. "The one-mind feeling?"

Shouma nodded, blowing bubbles. "I did. It was beautiful."

"Did we go under the sea in spirit travel?" Yanda asked the older mentor as she scooted deeper, finding warmer water while Zami splashed ecstatically.

Dele pushed into the middle pool with a deep, happy sigh and sent several bubbles onto the water for Zami to swat.

Merne approached and sat, dangling her feet in.

Yanda studied her face. "You need me."

Merne nodded, flashing an apology.

Shouma put her arms out for Zami.

Yanda climbed reluctantly out, carried her son to Shouma, then dried and dressed. So much for a day with her little guy.

"I'll share my sight with you whenever anything new happens," Shouma promised.

"Thanks."

As Yanda and Merne started up the path, Chela was climbing down their tree, Beri close behind her. Zami would soon be fed, Yanda thought, and she waved.

They did not go to the underground bunkers, as Yanda had expected. Instead, they made their way to the crystal pyramid in the mountain. In daylight, the views from the top were exquisite, over the Elven woods and even across the sea.

"Lucky you to see through." Merne stood at her elbow, staring at marble as they rose in the lift.

"Oh." Yanda had forgotten about the wall.

Merne opened to the chamber of stone seats. Tlalit was among those who had held the energy through the night. Had she missed the festival? Yanda tried to remember seeing her since two nights before, but couldn't.

"We're going to try something," Merne said quietly. "With the collective mind strong after our Withum Festival, we're going to raise power."

"With the other stone?" Yanda asked.

Merne gaped at her. Yanda felt the eyes of the dozen Elves. A conversation ensued which she was kept out of.

Rude, she thought.

"Yanda is right," said a male Elf with his seat's back to her. "When will she be privy to our councils? She is, after all, half-Xentu."

"Half-Xentu, half Erlon," Tlalit put in.

Xentu, Erlon? Yanda wanted to ask. But she was sure she'd learn eventually.

In fact, she would not for a very long time.

Discussion continued. Though this time they did not shut Yanda out, she found it dizzying and incomprehensible.

"I don't know what any of this means," she said in a soft voice to Merne. "What did you want to try? And what about the other stone? The one deep under the sea? Did I imagine it?"

Merne stepped to the man-Elf who'd spoken on Yanda's behalf. He leaned around to look at them.

Yanda bristled, recognizing the Lark captain who had ferried her away from her daughter almost two years ago. Tenali, they'd called him in Sarwil, their World Tree. How could they trust the Lark captain, who made deliveries for Krid, such as transporting talented fems, marked for his collection, to sit in the Circle that maintained the dome protecting their land?

"Wha… why…" Yanda stammered.

Instead of answering, Merne slid into the seat to release Tenali from his role in the Circle.

He stepped to Yanda. "Shall we?" and he walked past her, arm wide as the door slid open, inviting her outside.

Yanda glanced back at Tlalit across the circle, since Merne's back was to her. The rest were relative strangers, though she'd seen many at meals.

Tenali touched her arm lightly and gestured for her to come with him, as the Elven guardians' eyes slid shut with their energy-holding.

Why had Merne put her in this position? She glowered, remaining in the doorway.

His mouth quirked. Not a smile, or if it was, it was a sad, crooked one.

Finally, she stepped through, but backed immediately away from him in the hallway, still scowling.

"Can we walk?" He pointed to the lift. "Wherever you'd like."

"I don't think so." The door snicked shut and they were

alone together, no sound but their boots gritting on stone flagging. "You kidnapped me."

Tenali did not respond at first. "There's a nice wood three levels down." He walked toward the lift.

Staying put, she glanced the other way, trying to suss out an escape route. She wished she could disappear, like Shouma, briefly considered asking Shouma to pull her away, but that was childish. When would she feel powerful? She and Merne had planned to work on her abilities, her strength, to repel powerful thoughts like Mnenu's, to sense others' intentions before they acted. But withum had swept her away.

Situations like these threw her into escape mode with no real defense. Suspicion began a slow drip-feed: was there a plot among the Elves to get rid of her, keep Zami?

A warm tendril of thought slipped into her mind, ever so gently, like a tap at the door. She recognized Zamani in her mind: "We love you. We'd do nothing to harm you, or your son, or to separate you from him. Please talk with my grandson. There are answers we need."

"That's creepy, you reading my fearful mind," she sent back in mind-speak.

"I'm sorry if it felt that way. Your fear broadcast into my thoughts as a cry for help, starting with 'Why did you all desert me with a traitor?!'"

Yanda gasped. She thought she'd learned better control from Shouma. Contrite, she replied, "Fine, I'll talk to him." She did feel better with his pronouncement of love, though that was dampened by the "we." Who all was he including in that? All the Elves? He and Merne?

She scuffed her boots along the corridor and stepped past Tenali into the elevator. Tenali moved his hand over lighted buttons and they lowered, both silent, minds closed, looking in different directions.

They exited the pyramid through a smooth, tubular tunnel onto a wooded path. Tenali led the way to benches by a rushing stream and sat.

She stopped nearby and gazed down the mountainside, then further, over hills into the distance.

There was another stone bench across the path. She paced to it, sat, got up and paced some more. Finally, she stood facing him, arms crossed. "Your grandfather thinks I should talk to you."

Tenali seemed in a quandary whether to stand like her or stay seated. "Will you... sit?" He patted the bench. When she remained silent and standing, he said, "I know you blame me for your precipitous departure from your home planet."

"Of course, I blame you!" she spluttered. "How do they even trust you with their protective dome? You're a..." she pressed her lips together, trying to think of the most despicable word she could find. Finally, she spat out, "trafficker!"

He opened his mouth to protest, "I…"

"You work for *Krid*!" she hissed, hate filling her eyes as she thought not just of the injuries to her life, but all the Fugitives. Shouma's kids and grandkids, all their families and lives, broken apart.

Tenali sat up straight, a dark flush creeping into his cheeks. "Work for... I don't work for Krid. I have a starship for hire."

"Come on. How did that all happen? I was pulled to the spaceport and then a voice compelled me to board the Lark. What voice was that? You were ordered by Krid. He probably compelled me."

He took in a deep breath. "Will you sit so we can talk?"

She whirled as if she'd stride away but, instead, she dropped onto the bench opposite, chest heaving with fury.

Tenali sat forward, elbows on his knees, and studied her.

Against her better judgment, Yanda noticed he had a strong face, with large deep-set eyes that seemed troubled.

Finally, he asked, "A call? To board the Lark?" He spoke slowly, as if it were the first he'd known of this.

Yanda made an exasperated sound. "You delivered me to Krid. What are you talking about?" She got up and walked away down the path, considering trying to find her way across the hills back to Rotoul. But she remembered Zamani's words: we need answers.

"Gah," she snarled to herself and came back. This time she perched on a boulder near him. The stream burbled past.

He waited for her eye contact, spread his hands palm up, and, with a helpless shrug, said, "My manifold told me your destination was Farn. That's all."

"What about those things put on me by your staff? You had to know they were dampers."

He looked uncomfortable then. "Krid's reps got on after you. I was told to 'leave it to them.'"

"i…" she made a disgusted sound.

His face was unreadable now, maybe defensive. Closed.

"You had no idea the Stone was calling me?" She tried to read him for truthfulness. What did he feel?

"None," he said. "Would you like to come into my mind and see for yourself?"

She reared back. "No, thank you." How could she know what traps might lie in wait? What were his abilities? She knew nothing about him. "I think we'll just talk. You didn't know your grandfather was helping the Stone call?"

"I was out of touch with my family for many turns." The sides of his mouth pressed in a deep frown.

"You just happened to renew your acquaintance at this moment?" She leveled her gaze at him, frown lines deepening. A question struck. "Where's the Lark?" Maybe he could get her back to Alland. Should she befriend him? Or hold his past deeds over him? If he had a conscience, that is.

He didn't answer right away, but stared into the distance. "Hidden," he said at last.

"Hidden from whom?" she asked.

"Everyone. But I would show you."

"Why?"

He pulled in a breath that shuddered. "I want you to trust me."

"Why do you care?" Despite the vulnerability he seemed to be displaying, he could be acting. She was basically a kind person but losing almost two years of her daughter's life, and giving birth to her son in captivity, constantly feeling threatened, had hardened her.

He crossed one leg on a knee and pulled at his lower lip. His wide, shapely eyes darted to her, away, back again.

To her surprise, he scrambled to his feet, closed the distance between them, and sat on a tuft of grass at her feet, cross-legged. "No one here knows," he said, gazing up at her earnestly. This close, she could see his inner eyes whirl, until he turned his head away. He pulled a blade of grass and as he slid his fingers over it, it split into six tiny threads that curled back, forming a miniscule lantern shape.

She gasped, and he handed it to her, almost shyly.

When she took it, a bloom of light filled the center, first azure, then flame-color.

He leaned his shoulder to the boulder she sat on. "I left

here feeling rowdy, rebellious. I felt nothing ever changed. We were insulated from the worlds and no one was solving anything. I stowed away on a ship, worked my way around the universe, learned to fly."

Half-reluctant, Yanda scooted down onto the grass, too, still holding the wispy toy he'd made as it continued to shift hue. She leaned her back to the rock, eye level with him. "Maybe you could have helped things to change. There was so much to fix here. Bad air, power stone blown apart, invaders and corruption..."

"Exactly! No one doing anything," he responded. "How could I? No one was including me. I was young, and... half human."

"They were prejudiced of that?"

He shrugged.

"But what did you want them to do?" she asked.

He was silent a moment. "They could have tried to learn more." His voice had grown quieter. "Actually, I think things did start to happen after I left." His face creased in disgust. "I said mean things to Mom and my grandfather. To everyone really. I was kind of an ass."

Yanda suppressed a smile. "They've built the stone seats and all since you left? The dome?"

"Some of it was already in place. But there was fear. There had been rumors that a broken stone would be worse than no stone. They'd seen what it did to the invaders, heard rumors of the madness it caused."

"They were afraid of the Stone?" It was Yanda's turn to twist her lower lip with this new information. She'd seen only confidence in the Elves, never fear.

Telani nodded.

"I asked Merne about another stone, equal in power, under the sea." She gestured out over the hills, though she was unsure where the sea was from where they sat. "She wouldn't answer me."

He stared at her. "How did you learn of it?"

"During Withum."

"I think it may have even more for you than the rest of us. How did you become aware of it?"

"I'm not sure if it spoke to me or what."

"They just... won't acknowledge it," he said. "Or won't talk to me about it."

"Why, do you think?"

Tenali shook his head. "I don't know."

Chapter 24

Yanda still felt torn as they walked down the mountain path toward Rotoul. Skepticism seemed safer. She wasn't ready to let go of anger. She didn't yet have all the answers. But a subtle shift was working in her.

Interesting that he'd been kept in the dark by his people. Was that aimed at garnering her sympathy?

As the trail narrowed between tall grasses, she followed his footsteps, thinking through what she'd learned. He'd left there, a rebel. Yet, clearly, he cared about his Elven folk. She thought about the homecoming—Merne's surprised yelp as she threw her arms around him in the *Sarwil* amphitheater. It did seem to be the first she'd seen him in years.

Maybe he *didn't* feel the Stone's call.

"Are there snakes?" she asked, eyeing the brush on either side of the path.

"I would sense any being, friend or foe," he remarked over his shoulder.

"What if I came out here alone?"

"Ah. You need to be taught."

She might have bridled at that, but he was matter of fact, not censuring, so she said, "I'd like to learn."

He stopped and turned. Though a foot shorter than most Elves, he was taller than her. He looked down with his serious eyes. "I meant it, that I would show you my ship. Do you want to see where it is?"

"Would you take me home in it?" Her whole being awaited the answer.

He looked regretful. "I believe our world needs you a bit longer."

"But after that?" Her heart ached at the idea of waiting any longer to see Seiti, to hold her in her arms, but she'd made it this long.

"After that, certainly. Would you spirit-travel with me?" He held out his hand to her. It felt warm, broader than Zamani's, rougher, but very pleasant.

She felt contrite. Her most recent spirit travel with Zamani had been very intimate. "You mean to show me your ship?"

He nodded.

"Should I trust you?" She allowed a small smile to creep up.

"Yes," he said, with little-boy candor, yet all their history lurked behind, in his eyes. "But I understand if you don't."

"If you weren't trustworthy, I could be in trouble entering your mind," she said.

"I think you're strong," he said.

"Because I'm Xentu? Because I can see through?" She

thought about Mnenu leaping with her into the deep seas. "Maybe somewhere in me I'm strong, by nature, by blood, but my training has been very brief."

"Then how will I prove myself to you as trustworthy?"

They'd entered the edge of thin woods. He leaned against a tree trunk.

She squinted up into his eyes. The orange sun made her blink and she shaded with one hand. "Do you have an Elven way of doing that?"

A crooked smile touched Tenali's lips. "I'm half-human, you know. Here." He took her other hand and pulled her a few feet into shadow among straight, white-trunked trees, then dropped to his knees on soft loam and gently pulled for her to kneel, too.

They faced each other, hands forming a bridge.

He closed his eyes. "I'm in your mind, just at the threshold."

She could hardly tell, so light was his presence.

"I'll show you something from my childhood. Then you show me something from yours. We'll make a pact of secrecy." He opened his eyes. They shone with moisture.

This meant something to him, she thought. Her stomach butterflied. She checked to make sure no one was eavesdropping in her mind-space—something she had been taught and felt sure about, regarding most beings—then nodded.

His eyes dropped shut again and she closed hers. Her knees ached from kneeling but she was unwilling to break the moment.

A vision came into her mind, of a man. Tenali loved him, admired him. All those feelings were conveyed in their mind-connection. The man hugged Tenali, then turned away and strode onto a ramp, disappearing into the bowels of a spaceship without a backward glance. Tenali's stomach churned.

Yanda's eyes flew open. Tenali's were brimming with tears.

She wanted to hug him but it was her turn. She wondered what memory she should choose. What could possibly be equal to his? Then, unbidden, one came bursting into her mind, so sharp, so poignant, she let out a cry. This image had haunted her all her conscious life, vague, at the periphery of her mind... until now. It suddenly took on clarity: A woman sobbing. She was gorgeous, unusual. Black hair in a smooth cut, her eyes a strange purple-sunset hue. Then the woman was gone. Was she taken? Did she walk away?

Yanda's heart felt on the point of breaking as low-grade frustration crystalized in sharp pain, with the face so clear, so dear to her, again gone. She let go of Tenali's hands and dropped from her knees onto her side, curling into a ball, arms around her middle, trying to quash the ache. "I don't want to remember this much, if I can't remember more," she whispered, unsure if that was true.

After a moment, she opened stinging eyes. Tenali's face was inches away, resting on his hand, on the forest floor, expression supremely sad.

They both sat.

"Was that your mother?" he asked.

"I don't know. Was that your father?"

He shrugged. "Yeah. No one told me but I'm pretty sure." He rubbed his face, arms resting on bent knees. "I didn't know that's the memory I'd show you."

"I didn't know about mine, either. I don't think I really chose it. It was as if your memory triggered mine." She pulled her knees up, back to a narrow tree. "All my life, that vision has floated just out of reach. I never saw that face so clearly. But I know it's the memory that's haunted me." A tear escaped down her cheek and hovered on her chin. She back-hand swiped it. "I don't know where that was, or what happened before or after." She snuffled, took in a shaky breath. "I'll go on a spirit journey with you." Truth be told, she wanted to go anywhere but here, think about anything but that image and the heartache it had brought.

"Okay then." His expression was eager as he scooted his back to a neighboring tree and took her hand.

Yanda and Tenali sank into the sea, down, down. She knew it was spirit-travel and didn't try to breathe, just gazed out at sea life, thinking how Vatu would love to be there. She faced outward, feeling Tenali at her back.

A strange sight came into view. Tall, sinewy buildings. Yanda turned to look at Tenali, see his expression, asking, "Is this where the Neyla live?" Then behind him, she saw, over his shoulder, the Lark, deep underwater.

"You keep your ship here?"

"I do."

"Why do you hide it?" she asked.

He shook his head. "Not now."

"I want to show Vatu this."

"We can do that. Do you want to go back, or explore further?"

"I want to go back. For now." She slipped under his arm, feeling his warmth as she pressed to his chest.

That's how they sat when their conscious minds returned to the woods, his arm around her.

Yanda pulled away. All was not forgiven.

Tenali sighed a small huff, and clambered to his feet.

"Yeah. Better get back."

As they walked along a little-used path toward the Neyna tree homes, their hands found each other. They walked in silence but for a few bouts of conversation.

"I do want to return. Soon," she said.

"With Vatu," he responded.

"Yes. And to see more of the Neyla city myself. What's it called?"

"Zotoul," he said.

"How many Neyla are there?"

They heard voices and then came into view of midday meal in full swing.

Yanda had forgotten their held hands.

Beri and Zamani both took in the sight, as did many others.

Yanda was the one to release Tenali's grip, pushing her hair back and striding ahead, flummoxed.

Yet she wondered why she felt embarrassed. She held no allegiance to any partner here. Any lover even. Her gaze scanned for Zami. She found him with Vatu and the other Fugitives at a far table and made her way there.

As she lowered onto the bench, she felt Tenali's eyes on her from the next table, where he sat between Merne and Zamani, his mother and grandfather, one a few hundred years old, the other... older. Yanda wondered how old Tenali himself might be.

He asked her in mind-speak, "Why did you walk away from me?"

"I don't know. I'm sorry," was her lame reply.

Of course, hiding their recent sudden connection made sense in some ways. But she could feel the rejection in his eyes, the puzzlement after their deep sharing, and hated herself, a bit.

Zami turned to her, standing on her thighs, and put his hands on her face. He crowed and thought to her what fun he'd had that morning.

"Shall we see what's to eat?" she asked aloud, noticing enticing edibles on trays: clever mushroom formations, shapes carved from fruits and vegetables, cheeses and unknowns.

"I ate," he said, also voicing.

"It's true," Chela chimed in. "He likes the *mantazos*." These were a banana-like fruit that the Elves fixed in myriad ways. At this meal, they were formed into small towers with a creamy filling.

"I hope he ate something reasonably sustaining as well," Yanda said over his shoulder, then kissed his nose, while she wetted a cloth napkin to wipe his sticky fingers.

"There are *tafag* rolls." Vatu held up something like a veggie corndog. These were a Terlondian bean-curd dish.

"Mm, you love that," Yanda said to her boy, cleaning his cheeks, too, for good measure.

Sweeka, one of the Elves with piercings and tats who'd watched Zami before, stood at her elbow, holding the Elf boy Arkut's hand. "Can Zami play?"

Tuk-Tuk bounded from Merne's shoulder and with one glance off the table edge, landed lightly on Zami's shoulder; its several bright orange inches must have weighed only a few ounces.

Zami lit up and stroked the bright orange head, speaking in sounds just like the tiny simian.

The other child's eyes grew wide, glowing with admiration and desire. Sweeka held out a hand to Zami.

Yanda stared as her son walked away with almost sure steps, holding Sweeka's long fingers. He'd started walking without her. An ache started in her sternum and traveled a live wire into her bowels.

She became aware of a number of minds trying to soothe her: Tenali, Zamani, Beri, Shouma, Vatu, Chela. Giving a tremulous smile, she grabbed a small mushroom architecture from a tray, pretending to study it carefully. It was amazing to be surrounded by so much empathy, but at times also... intimate.

Gisli detected the emotions and decided on distraction. "I'm working on something that might help... the Stone." His eyes were on Yanda's face, eager.

Chapter 25

Merne stood and signaled to Dele. Suddenly everyone stood and backed away from where they'd been sitting. Yanda stumbled off the bench to follow the mental imperative. With one swift motion, the tables reformed in a square that could seat all, benches moving with them.

They took seats again. Yanda retrieved her mycelium masterpiece before someone cleared it away, and bit. It was even tastier than she'd anticipated.

A strategy discussion ensued. Gisli took the lead, now sitting at Yanda's right. Though distance was mostly irrelevant with mind-speak, he liked to draw diagrams.

"I joined the Circle briefly," he said excitedly. "Those seats are remarkable. You have to sit on one."

"I want to," Yanda said. "Almost did this morning, but Tenali and I got... sidetracked." Too late, she realized how that might sound.

Sure enough, Beri's brows shot up. "Tenali, captain of the Lark?" He shot the thought, only to her, "Kidnapper for Krid!"

Yanda nodded. "I know. We've talked. There's a lot to share."

It was awkward with Zamani and Merne at the table.

Merne took the helm. "Gisli was brought into the dome circle since he was military security in Dondar."

"Not just security," Beri put in.

There was a special bond between Beri and Gisli. Yanda noticed it often. Beri'd been very lonely before he discovered Gisli. It might be like her and Vatu, the closeness. But Gisli'd been very involved with Tlalit and Merne lately, with the tech side of things. What had Beri been up to? She was always being pulled away.

"You're right. Much more," Merne agreed. "That's why he's also been brought into Tlalit's work with the rogue mages."

Yanda thought about how Tenali had come into her mind, so quietly, so softly she hadn't known he was there. "Couldn't there also be someone here spying both ways?" she asked, bluntly.

This seemed like the time when all gloves were tossed onto the table.

"No, there couldn't," Zamani said with assurance.

Shouma shook her head. "I'm monitoring as well."

"Okay. That's good. So, what is this new plan for the dome?" Yanda asked.

"Well," Gisli shifted, body electric with impatience to explain. "Shalt has to be able to call all the stone fragments back. And, naturally, Krid is going to try to stop that, or snag them to keep power until he can militarily control a complete Power Stone. He has hired mercenaries who are traveling here now."

Tenali blurted out, "Krid has a piece of the Stone in a vault." He winced—that look Yanda'd seen before, as if he'd felt searing pain.

"What the hell? Why are you wincing?" Merne asked him.

Tenali's eyes watered. He backhanded tears. "Just something I picked up."

"Something, alright." Shouma looked at Yanda and tilted her head toward Tenali. "We need to know what." To Yanda alone, she mind-spoke, "You need to look."

Yanda gazed at Tenali. He shrugged, eyes hooded.

He's defensive, she thought. He suspects... what? That he had a part in what's happened to us? Is happening? She stepped over the bench, walked to his side and put a knee on the bench next to him. "Can I?" she asked him.

"Can you…?"

"Look? See what's in your skull?"

"You... don't need equipment? Oh, yeah. That's what you do. That's your superpower." He flipped his hand, as if to say "have at it," but his brows pinched, expectant, fearful.

Resting a hand on his shoulder, she let her vision sink through the layers, knowing whether each tissue, bone, blood vessel, was healthy, and whether it should be there. Her sight came to a sliver of stone. Definitely should not be there.

She could sense what stone it was. An echoing response raced from Shalt's cave to her in the form of a rumbling murmur. Zamani placed startled hands on the table and leaned forward, brows creased, staring at his grandson.

"You have a Shalt chip in your head," Yanda said, then asked, "Were you there for the explosion?"

Merne shook her head. "No, he wasn't." To her son, "We need to retrieve this memory, how it got there." She placed her hands on his head.

"Do we have to make a public display of it?" Tenali growled to her, voice low, face a mask of misery. His eyes met Yanda's.

She gave him a look of apology before taking her seat again, across the far side of the tables.

"Peace, daughter." Zamani reached for her.

Merne swept her arm around the group. "We're all friends here, aren't we?"

Through gritted teeth, he said to his mother, "You're retrieving a memory I don't even know about. That's... uncomfortable."

Yanda knew Merne had kept things from him, like who his father was. Maybe this felt like further wounding. She sent that thought to Shouma.

Shouma said, "Chela and I are healers. Might we try?"

"Just get it done," he said, and he wouldn't look at Yanda now.

Shouma and Chela sat on either side of him. Yanda went with their minds into Tenali's. Shouma frowned with concentration as the half-Elf, half-man closed his eyes. His hands gripped the edge of the table so tightly the knuckles whitened as he allowed the uncovering of deeply buried memories.

Shouma's frown deepened. "Krid had this chip placed in your brain."

"Barbaric," Beri snarled. "And not at all surprising."

"Thinking you'd lead him to the stone?" Tlalit suggested.

"He couldn't control you with it, could he?" Beri asked, looking around at Zamani and those who'd lived with the

Stone's energy all their lives.

Tenali shook his head vehemently. "No, he never learned to use the Stone except—" He stopped, glancing at Yanda.

"Except?" Vatu finally entered the conversation, eyes drilling into him, head-nubs flushing an angry rose.

Tenali's eyes moved back to Yanda. "It seems he felt the Stone's call. He traced its connection with Yanda in Alland and used it to direct her to board the Lark. Then it was no problem for him to put her on my manifest to Farn."

"How did you resist being pulled by the Stone to Terlond?" Zamani asked.

"From what you've said," Tenali directed himself toward his grandfather, "you didn't know the call had been received until you felt Yanda approaching Terlond. So Shalt must not have, either."

"True." Zamani looked at his hands folded in his lap. "If only we'd been in contact. All these years." There was great sadness in his voice, and eyes.

Tenali leaned toward the Elder Elf. "We should use the Stone of the Neyla to bring Shalt back to wholeness," he said, urgency in his voice.

Zemani sat back. "That's not possible."

Tenali's fists came down on the table, startling everyone. "Why not!?"

Merne put a hand on Tenali's arm.

Zamani's eyes dropped again. "The Neyla have cut ties with us, except for at Withum."

"That's... not true." Tenali looked to Merne for confirmation.

Zamani went on, "They thought we were foolish to allow the colonizers so much access to the Stone, to our world." He shrugged. "Turns out they were right. They've put up barriers against any invasion to their zones, even toward us."

"Not entirely," Tenali said.

Yanda thought about his ship, submerged near their city under water.

"I could ask them for help."

Zamani slapped the table. "They won't help. They shouldn't. I want them safe. They don't deserve what we brought on ourselves."

Merne looked back and forth at them, undecided, as did a number of the Elves at the tables.

Tenali pressed his temple, pain clear on his face. This time, a look of disgust suffused his features. "Get it out," he said to Yanda through gritted teeth.

"Okay," Yanda said, throat tight. "Shalt wants to be part of the... removal."

•———···———•

Only those necessary to the operation filed in the night toward Shalt's cavern: Chela, Shouma, Merne and Zamani, Yanda and Tenali. Vatu accompanied them, as did Tlalit, as support. Globe lights bobbed overhead.

Tenali reached for Yanda's hand. Surprised, she returned his grip. His thoughts trickled into her mind: fear, but also eagerness to no longer suffer the pain of the stone fragment.

Questions circled through them. Had Krid in fact ever controlled him?

Merne held back to walk next to them. "Do you think he did?"

"That's rude, Mom," Tenali said without rancor. "I don't think so. But how can I know."

Leaving the woods, they soon descended into the

massive cavern that was Shalt's home.

"You and I will go to Shalt's surface." Yanda spoke as oracle of the Stone.

Tenali nodded.

Shouma said, "You need to be prepared for the strength of the Stone's energy."

The elders gathered around Tenali, touching his head, shoulders, sides. Yanda felt a surge of electricity that smoldered, distributing through his cells. She remembered this preparation. It was exhilarating as well as frightening. She'd thought her heart might not survive but, just as the amplification seemed to reach the brink of destruction, a transformative strength manifested. She saw it in Tenali's eyes.

Everyone stepped away as Yanda took Tenali's hand. Dele and Shouma lifted them off the ground and floated them slowly above the cave floor, then lowered them into the immense hole, surrounded by blackness.

• ———• • •—— •

Zamani watched as his grandson and the mother of his only son descended toward the immense surface of the Stone that had produced a beloved vibration throughout his long life.

He'd raised Tenali as his own, had loved him always, though his pride had let hurt and anger supplant some of his affection in recent years. He was not proud of that. Now he gazed, filled only with adoring and concern as the two lay face down on the glowing stone surface as he braced himself to feel his grandson's pain.

Chapter 26

Yanda's fingertips touched Tenali's as they faced each other on an unblemished part of the massive Stone, smooth, unmarred by explosives. The surface warmed, turning deep rose under them.

Tenali, head resting against Shalt, felt a tug. He winced and slid his hand over Yanda's, bracing himself.

Yanda called to Shouma and Chela. "Numb the area. I'll do the moving so there's little tissue damage."

Then she spoke with Shalt. "You know Tenali holds a part of you through no fault of his own."

"I know of Kridenit's crime," the Stone boomed into her mind. The Stone's thought-communication thrummed in Yanda, reminding her of the first time she'd felt it, just after completing her last surgery. Her stomach felt the familiar pounding, bone-deep, now part of her.

"He cut a piece of me with a diamond saw," Shalt went on. "I felt it. Then he inserted it in one of my Elf children."

"You've been aware all along." Yanda said it as a statement. "And now you would take it back. I want to help."

"I want you to help. I might pull too hard and injure him."

"We'll go slow and I'll repair as we go."

Tenali's eyes watched Yanda's. "Are you speaking with the Stone?" he asked, lips barely moving as he whispered.

She nodded. "Are you ready?" She said this to all the team. Team Shalt. Team Tenali.

"Yes," came four responses. No, five. She felt Vatu's loving embrace in her mind and heart. Zamani, Merne and Dele kept in the background, not wanting to disturb the operation, but holding the energy.

As Yanda let her sight tunnel benignly down through Tenali's tissue layers, she felt Shouma and Chela numbing just ahead of her, watching with her vision. As she came to the Stone, she checked for the safest route out. She showed this to Chela and Shouma who numbed that path.

As Shalt began to draw the sliver, Yanda slowed it and directed the movement.

Tenali's expression went from anxiety to surprise as he watched Yanda's face, his fingers incrementally relaxing.

The Stone shaving emerged from his scalp and floated through the air and slipped out of sight, into one of the exploded areas. Shalt gave a sigh.

Yanda felt Tenali relax. Fairly sure it had been painless, she reached and caressed his cheek. "There should be little recovery needed since I repaired along the way. It was lodged in a fairly safe place."

"Thank you." Tenali squeezed her hand.

They stood.

"Are you okay?" Yanda slipped a hand around his wrist to check his pulse.

"I feel... good."

This time they shot up out of the hole. Tenali let out a bubble of laughter as they landed back with the others.

Yanda answered with a short chuckle, happy that he seemed to be already recovering, in spirit especially.

She felt Shalt lovingly incorporating its long-lost sliver and knew the satisfaction of bringing healing and reunion, all at once.

As they walked back through the woods, Tenali asked her, in mind-speak, "Will you stay with me?"

Yanda felt a burst of sweet sensation in her groin. "Let me check on Zami," she thought to him, conveying a scrap of the eager longing that sat in her belly.

Zamani glanced back at them, sharing no thoughts.

Tenali gave her a sideways smile.

Zamani, Tlalit and Merne left for their trees. Tenali stayed with the Fugitives, climbing up into the guest tree after them. Yanda briefly wondered where he usually stayed. He accompanied her to the children's playroom. Zami slept in one of the cradles. Yanda scooped him up, still sleeping, and crossed into their quarters in the next tree, along swaying ramps, resettling him in his own bed next to hers.

Yanda and Tenali sat side by side on a hammock outside their sleeping area, quiet talk interspersed with mind-speak.

"You upset Zamani tonight," she said with a small smile, but with questions in her eyes.

"They need upsetting. It's stupid to reject help they need."

"But... it sounds like there's been some history, since

you left," she said. She brought a knee up so she could turn sideways facing the half-Elf man. "Even with the Stone out... maybe it would build more trust if..." she thought about it. Where was she going with this? "If Shouma did a deep-memory sweep to check any activity Krid might have had in your mind. I mean, what if we could know for sure he's had no access to your thoughts up to this point, while the shard was in you?"

Tenali heaved a breath. "You mean tonight?"

She searched his face. "If she's awake. It really is rather urgent."

Tenali reached for a strand of her hair and lightly slid his fingers down it, letting the curl bounce back up. "Not exactly what I had in mind for just now."

Yanda felt a tendril of amorous thought sidle in, but gently escorted it to the side. Every time her thoughts drifted, dire possibilities entered as she reviewed pathologically how Krid might have influenced him over the past two years. "Please. For me? For everyone."

Tenali sighed gustily and shifted away. "Fine."

"You're mad at me."

"No, I'm not."

"Disappointed."

"Sure. Yes." He tipped his head toward her. "I know you're right. Just don't want to deal with it now."

"I can understand. You've been through a lot. But... I can't relax." She pushed his hair back to see his eyes. "And I want to relax with you."

He nodded. "Go ahead. Call her."

Yanda sent a mental message to the Elder. "Are you awake?"

"Very much so. Let's go to a small conference room Merne showed me yesterday. We won't be disturbed there."

Yanda and Tenali vanished from the hammock and appeared instantly in a room full of comforts—soft carpet, thick cushions, warm tapestries, side tables holding refreshments—in Vashal, the pyramid within the mountain.

Shouma stood looking out at stars and one of the planet's three moons—this one pale blue—shining in a long narrow window that slanted inward toward the top following the pyramid's shape. She wore a long saffron-colored robe. It must be new. Yanda had never seen it among their spare items in captivity in the Citadel.

"You have an interesting skill there," Tenali said to Shouma. "Bringing us in here instantly. I'm not sure who among the Elves could do it with such ease."

Shouma laughed as she moved to a cushioned chair, her robe shushing with each step. "How do you know it was easy?"

"Oh, she can do so much more," Yanda said, smiling. She pulled a sumptuous seating module-for-two near Shouma and dropped into it, propping her feet onto a poofy stool.

Tenali started to join her on the small couch, but Shouma said, "I prefer this for you." She gestured and a flat divan slid from the wall to extend in front of her. "Put your head at my end."

Tenali glanced warily from one woman to the other, but he crawled gamely onto the cushioned length and stretched out, face up.

The lighting in the room came from low-lit strings of globes stretching along ribbed seams of the curved walls.

"Lighter? Darker?" Shouma waved her hand and the brightness shifted.

"Dark is good," Tenali said.

Did any light bother him? Was his head hurting after all,

from the surgery? Yanda wondered. Or did he want to obscure himself, as they perused his recent entanglements with Kridenit? Alarms returned, clambering in her head. She did not want to learn this man had purposely colluded with the foul mage.

Did he have the ability to hide memories even from Shouma? Would the powerful elder know?

Shouma left the lights low and spread her hands at his temples, closing her eyes.

Yanda sank lower until her head rested on the back of her seat. Her lids drifted shut and she felt the journey begin, back through Tenali's memories, starting with his leaving this planet, stowed away on a spaceship headed for he knew not where. "Lucky it wasn't Blaz traders," she thought.

What followed was a fast-track review of his encounters with Kridenit. Tenali knew Krid's father had been one of those who'd blasted Shalt, taking parts of the Stone off-planet and subsequently going mad.

Tenali had intended to be the Elves' hero, tracking down the chips of stone from the far reaches of the universe. Krid had been one of his first targets; he knew a slice of their Power Stone was likely to be in his possession. And so they had become acquainted.

After years of investigation, fit in between paid contracts, he had little to show for his efforts.

On one mission, he lay sleeping on board a satellite where his ship had docked.

Krid hovered over him.

Shouma spoke suddenly, jolting both Yanda and Tenali. "Even what has occurred during sleep may remain as an unconscious memory."

"Jeez, pick your moments," Yanda thought.

But Shouma knew what she was doing. "Do you need a

break?" she asked Tenali, letting the image slip away.

"What?" Yanda opened her eyes. "Good god. We've got to see what that asshole did!"

"Patience, young acolyte. We do this right or we don't do it at all." Shouma bent her face over Tenali's. "We can stop now. Go back in later."

With obvious effort, Tenali opened his eyes. "Please complete the scene." His teeth sounded gritted. He reached up to Yanda.

She knelt by him and held his hand. He closed his eyes. "Go on."

Their three minds slipped back to the scene they'd left off, with Krid hovering over Tenali's sleeping form. "So, you'd spy on me," Krid said as he leaned close to the half-Elf's face. "I'll go you one better." He sounded sinister. "You'll lead me to the Stone that killed my father. I haven't decided if I'll try to build it back to its full power, or decimate it."

Tenali grimaced, gripping Yanda's hand.

"You must have been drugged," Yanda whispered. "Otherwise, he wouldn't be talking so close to you."

"Shall we go on?" Shouma asked.

"Yes!" Tenali hissed.

"For now..." Krid gestured to a man who pushed a tray full of instruments close. "Find a safe way to insert this." He held a familiar piece of stone, flat, the size and shape of a thin coin.

Shouma said, "Should we stop?"

Tenali's eyes flew open, his face a tableau of shock and dismay shifting swiftly toward smoldering anger. "Go ahead. I want to know all."

Yanda suspected Tenali felt murderous at this point, fueling revenge in his heart. She glanced at Shouma, dreading seeing Tenali walk forth from this scene a Zombie, under Krid's control.

"Let's see what's happened since." Shouma kept a calm voice.

She skimmed over the years, searching for signs of manipulation.

At last, when they finished the most recent scene, where Tenali stood in Krid's fortress looking over toward Elven land, invisible from view, she brought them out of his memory.

Tenali turned on his side, forehead against Yanda's shoulder. She rested an arm over him.

"I didn't find any indication of his influencing your thoughts or actions through the embedded Stone," she said. "Even when you steered your ship off course to take Yanda to Farn, you seemed to follow the manifest without being controlled by Krid's thoughts."

Tenali slowly sat up, rubbing his head where the incision still healed. He heaved a sigh, then looked from one woman to the other. "But I knew what Krid was." Not looking again at Yanda, he said, "I…" His throat caught. "I could have guessed he'd do what he did. It was a contract to me. I'm… not a good man. Not a good Elf either."

Yanda's heart dropped. What did he mean? Could she bear to hear more confessions?

He laced his fingers in his lap, knee arched, pulling away from her. "I'll kill him," he murmured.

She pushed hair off his forehead to let him know she didn't hate him.

He still didn't look at her. Did he want to confess something that hadn't shown up in his memories?

She knew the next steps would be a thorough data examination by Gisli and Merne, of his past destinations and how they coincided with Krid's doings. But for now, she wanted him to leave thoughts of vengeance. Again, she glanced at the elder healer. What was the best course?

Shouma took his hand and Yanda's and sent soothing waves through Tenali's mind. Yanda felt them, too, as a fresh breeze or a pool of healing waters.

After a moment, Tenali turned to Yanda, half-smiling, then swiveled toward Shouma. "Thank you. I know you did it for everyone, but I appreciate it. I needed to know."

"Shall I bring us all back to our sleeping quarters?" Shouma asked.

Tenali started toward the door. "No thanks." He kept his face averted as he abruptly exited the room.

Chapter 27

Yanda gave Shouma a backward shake of her head as she followed Tenali.

He had reached the lift when Yanda caught up.

"I think I need to clear my head," he said, turning away and pressing a finger to the light panel.

"I was thinking of a soak in the pools." Yanda was reluctant to let him go off on his own with his thoughts.

He leaned against the open door, arms crossed. "I don't think I'd be good company just now."

"You don't have to be company at all. Just lay in the pool. Or a different pool, even."

He flinched.

"How's your head?" she asked.

"Worse than earlier."

"Maybe too much jostling for the repaired tissues. I

could check, you could relax in the warm waters. It would do you good." When he didn't answer, she added, "I am a physician, after all. I could prescribe it."

"Is that the capacity in which you extended the invitation to the pools in the first place?" The corners of his mouth twitched, though his dark eyes remained grave.

"Well, not initially. But I don't like to see you in pain." She meant that on several levels.

He bowed, acquiescing, and stepped out again, letting the doors close. "Then let's float down."

A foliage arch gave onto a path that skirted the mountain at its highest point. Draped in vines, it was mostly hidden from sight. Dawn was just touching distant hills.

They swept down the mountainside in near dark, starting from higher than before, and landed unfailingly, close to the hot springs.

"That's accurate!" Yanda said, stripping and lowering herself into the middle pool.

Tenali dropped to a bench carved from the cavern, near the water's edge.

"Come in. It's nice."

"You go ahead," he said, resting his head back against the rock wall.

The day began to weigh on Yanda. She didn't know why he was hesitating but wasn't sure she had the energy to coax.

She swam up close to where he sat. A rock shelf below the surface held her in a soft curve, and she relaxed, gentle waves lulling her. The surgery had taken more out of her than she realized and exhaustion suddenly hit her. Stretching an arm along the pool rim, warm water lapping, she rested her head and closed her eyes.

A body sleek as a seal slid up behind her. Her eyes

popped open. She hadn't heard Tenali enter the water. The two snuggled into the curved dish formed by the rock pool. After a sweet moment like this, Yanda turned around. Looping her arms around his shoulders, she pressed her cheek to his and let her thoughts slide to the area of the Stone sliver's removal. She'd been careful to mend after the shard's passage, but she saw that subsequent movement had caused inflammation.

He said nothing but held her close as, face against his neck, she grew still and let her power-sight find microscopic details. This was the most beautiful her skill could feel— having time and intimacy to mend even the tiniest of ruptures, until she felt satisfied.

She pushed away and studied his face. "Better?"

He nodded. "Better."

Filled with elation from this most personal and satisfying manifestation of her abilities, she slid away into deep waters and did a somersault at the center of the pool. As she came up, Tenali swept under her and they tumbled together, bobbing up laughing.

Merne faced them, sitting at the edge of the pool, lapping her hand in the warm waters. "The Circle tried bringing a single stone, drawn by Shalt, safely from Erlot," she said without preamble.

Yanda swam to the side, wiping water from her eyes. "That's a fairly close moon, isn't it?"

Tenali had come to her side. "Yes. It's in the Mendor system." He blew water.

Merne went on, "We discovered Krid has sensors set all around the perimeter of the planet to detect any stone of Shalt's vibration traveling in this planet's direction."

"Of course he does." Tenali climbed out, held a hand down to Yanda.

She scrambled up and pulled on clothes.

Tenali did the same. "How'd you find out?

"Gisli detected the signals," Merne answered. "He's been monitoring Krid's incoming and outgoing messages."

"Then we're smoking Krid out." Tenali slapped the stone wall.

"The single shard has made Krid speed things up," said Merne. "He detected the trajectory and thinks he calculated Shalt's location."

"We have to get aggressive then, shut him down, not wait for his next move." Tenali started up the path, face fierce.

"You two should join the Circle. We're going to need fresh energy." Merne glanced from one to the other.

Yanda, though soothed by their soak, felt a lack of sleep keenly. "I've spent so much time away from Zami. I'll just lie with him a bit. Then come join you?" Her breasts were heavy with milk, even though he was slowly weaning himself from needing her.

Merne nodded. Tenali gave Yanda a last, lingering glance before he and his mother—tech-wizard, shapeshifting, centuries-old Elf—rose into the sky, drawing energy from the plants and stones of the mountain, and disappeared over the tree tops.

Yanda made her way from the pools up their tree, and snuggled with her sleeping son. He woke and nursed. When he'd fallen back to sleep, she strapped him into the Elven baby carrier she'd been gifted and sent a mind-tap to Shouma, giving her Merne's news.

By the time Yanda walked fully dressed into the communal area in their lofty tree quarters, others were stirring, pulling on clothes.

Elves, Escapees and Allies together made quick progress

through the woods to Vashal. Some took the elevator. Others floated to the top level. Yanda was too tired to consider that.

The rooms below the Power Circle had become a hive of support: beds made for resting, foods prepped for easy snacking, towels put next to pools for soaking. An Elf held out her arms for the sleeping Zami and Yanda reluctantly passed him over, sling and all. She watched the mature, kind-looking Elf carry Zami into a room nearby.

Merne, Tlalit and Shouma prepared Yanda to enter the One Mind of the Circle, a new hive-mind for her. She would sit on the seats carved from Shalt's sister stones. Her heart thumped as she entered the dramatic chamber, with its circle of tall stone seats, each like a monument, and pictured climbing onto the hard, cold chair. Strings of globe lights followed the curves of the walls upward to a sharp point far above, like an onion. Still dark, tall windows allowed diffuse starlight in. The green moon, Talal, was a small smudge in the low corner of one.

Could she do this when she was so tired?

Tlalit signaled Yanda to a seat and touched the arm of the Elven woman sitting perched atop it, indicating for Yanda to take her place. The female Elf named Wondu gestured to Yanda and she climbed up. Scooting over, she told Yanda to slide one leg on, to keep the connection.

As soon as Yanda's leg touched the stone seat's surface, she felt a surge of energy, from the stone beneath her and from the combined minds in the Circle. It took her a moment to be able to breathe properly in and out; it was all she could do to maintain her equilibrium. As her heart settled, she opened her mind to the brilliant, and daunting, web of minds that held the protective sphere over this land.

After a while, she found she could wiggle deeper into

the contours of the seat; a subtle cushion had formed under her so that no point put too much pressure on her body. It felt almost soft.

Slowly, she came to a point where the momentous job became a background effort and she glanced around the Circle. With concentration, she felt certain she could mind-tap an individual without disturbing the overall power of the dozen who held the dome.

She sensed, then, Gisli speaking to her from the tech bunker at the base of the mountain.

"There you are," he said. "I've got a direct tether to Shalt and we want to plan our next move with you."

Panic rose. Holding the protective sphere within this mind-meld of epic proportion already felt taxing. How could she divert her focus to a different job? "I don't think I can plan while holding this," she managed to convey to Gisli. "It's too new to me. Can you wait 'til after my first shift?"

Yet Shalt awaited.

A moment of silence followed, in which she again took in the enormity of her fellows' minds. The full immensity seemed to come and go in waves. Maybe it had to. It was now clear to her that all of the area—this part of the planet, the trees, stones, ocean—helped build and maintain the interstices of the powerful dome. The meld was with plants and animals as well. Birds were drawn to the vibrations and easily gave small bits of their energy. Even their songs increased the strength. Their flight was a give-and-take that strengthened with time. She knew this merely by being part of the Circle's web.

She also noticed that all in the Circle were Elves except her.

Gisli returned to her mind and agreed to hold off the

planning with Shalt until the end of her shift. She mind-tapped Merne and Tlalit within the Circle. It was settled that, at midday, they'd convene in the bunker so that tech was also at hand.

· ——— · · · ——— ·

When the tap came for her to switch out, Yanda was surprised that her energy was not drained. In fact, she felt energized, as though she'd received as much as she'd given, or more. She felt the mountain's strength around her and that she could draw on it at any time.

She walked with buoyancy out the door to partake in refreshments before heading down the hill.

· ——— · · · ——— ·

"We could catch the wind." Tenali came up behind her as she approached the lift.

"That's true."

This time she understood what energies held her as they shot out from the mountainside into the open air.

It was a feeling she'd had in dreams. Winds swept them as they drew energy effortlessly from plants and rocks and the air itself. Tenali guided their direction as he had to the hot springs. They entered the forest and, in moments, landed lightly on their feet next to the long, low building that housed miraculous technologies and a layered, underground refuge.

Yanda started down the stairs, Tenali behind her. At the second level, they found Gisli, appearing very much at home in front of a bank of screens, his legs propped in a chair of ergonomic wizardry.

Seeing them, he snapped the extensions of his seat to upright position and stood. "They're this way."

"They?" Yanda figured he meant Merne and Tlalit.

He led them out through tall clear doors to a patio with surrounding vine-covered walls rising thirty feet. A long conference table stretched through the middle of a flower garden with paths, surrounded by at least thirty beings: Elves, Fugitives, Allies.

Chapter 28

Yanda had expected to meet mainly with Gisli and Shalt, not nearly the entire community, minus those who came and went, taking shifts in the Circle or elsewhere.

Tenali and Yanda had walked into the middle of a discussion.

Chin sat straddling a large chair toward one end of the table. "So, there are three rogue mages who are our Allies. How many are loyal to Krid?"

The Jejods, never far from her, perched on backless benches, their long gangly legs stretching across paths; sometimes Yanda had the feeling they bore a winged consciousness despite appearing physically wingless.

Tlalit answered, "Five. Krid has other allies, though, as well as enemies, around town. Sentients for hire. Some in the military."

"So do we," Merne put in.

"No one loves Krid." Gisli said. Responding to questioning looks, he went on, "I've poked around Dondar and Sheffed in my capacity as fataq."

"He's a valuable asset, knowing of a lot of factions," Merne said.

"I think many would come to our side with any incentive at all," he said.

"If we had the time," Tlalit pointed out.

Zamani wandered through the arched doorway; he'd been in the Power Circle when Yanda left. At the head of the table, next to Merne, he manifested a magnificent chair for himself, resembling both wood and cushions, and sat.

Joli entered after him, bending nearly double under the archway, and set a tray of nibblies on the table, then hunted for a seat large enough to accommodate him. The others scooted over to make a wider space and a chair sufficiently commodious appeared.

Yanda felt that familiar thrumming in the ground beneath her and in her heart. "Shalt is agitated, wants to know how Its pieces can come through safely."

"I know. That's why we're holding this meeting," Merne said.

Yanda wondered if Shalt spoke to Gisli. How had he gotten that communique that Shalt wanted them to meet?

"What happened to the shard you tried to bring in?" Tenali asked.

"Shouma and Bonden hopped it out of reach, out in the universe." Merne moved her hand over a portion of the table and a screen lit up. "Among us, we have strategists of the highest degree, Tlalit being one." She glanced at her mate, who made a silly face.

Yanda felt new fascination with the peach-haired Elf

woman.

Tlalit took over. "Krid only identifies shards of Shalt if they're approaching this planet. Therefore, they can be hidden. Shalt, of course, feels where they all are."

Yanda wondered how they knew that. She'd been Shalt's voice. Now it seemed others could communicate with the Stone.

"Before we go any further, I have a suggestion that might make some of your planning a waste of time." Tenali hunched forward, elbows on the table.

Zamani shifted uneasily.

Yanda cringed, remembering the tension that had built at the last gathering around the topic of Neyla sea Elves accusing their cousins, the Neyna, forest Elves, of courting disaster from colonizers. She anticipated another abrupt ending to the talks, with both sides glowering.

Merne's eyes flitted from father to son and narrowed.

"That's right. Neyla," Tenali said crisply, as if explaining what should already be known. He went on, "Their Stone is Ash-don. With them, we could extend the shield much farther and protect Shalt's pieces."

"What about before they reach this atmosphere?" Yanda asked.

"Ah." Gisli wiggled up taller in his seat, eager as a puppy; he was among the smaller humanoids here. "That's where you come in, Yanda. I'm thinking Shouma and Bonden, too. When you and Shalt draw the shards, you'll be able to sense them, I'm sure—of course we'll have to test that—and you three can give each a skin that makes it untouchable. Shouma can also bring them closer, by hopping them, so they don't get fiery with speed."

Bonden hunched forward over a plaz-pad, sketching notes and designs.

"If we took Krid out, we wouldn't have to worry. We could just bring the Stone to wholeness." Tenali pushed a salt shaker back and forth, clearly agitated.

"There are far more than Krid involved now." Zamani reached for grapes and popped one in his mouth, chewing hard, agitated.

"That's true," Tlalit said. "Krid would have kept it to himself, but he needed local cooperation. Probably plans to dispose of city council members he's corrupted the minute he has control of the Power Stone."

"Unless he decides to destroy It out of revenge for what happened to his father," Shouma put in, based on their recent perusal of Tenali's memories.

Eyes turned to her, wanting explanation.

"Do you know something?" Tlalit asked her.

Shouma checked with Tenali.

A thought passed between, then he nodded.

"I checked Tenali's mind last night after the surgery. Yanda and I thought it'd be better to see exactly what occurred with Krid in his brain."

Many around the table straightened or leaned forward with interest.

"What did you find?" Merne asked, trepidation in her gaze that was glued to her son.

"We went clear back through, every memory that involved Krid, even when Tenali was drugged and unconscious."

A murmur went around the table. Tenali shifted, crossed his arms and stared out into the trees.

"There is still residual memory even in such a case," Shouma explained.

Some nodded.

"Krid did intend that the Stone shard lead him to Shalt.

If Tenali's mind powers had been less strong, Krid might have worked it out. He's worked out the resonance, followed it when it reached for Yanda, but couldn't locate the source."

An Elf spoke. "Well, now it has."

Yanda had never seen this Elf in the Circle, only caught glimpses of him at meals. He had an unnerving stare and used it now, sending his gaze around the table.

Tlalit straightened as if something alerted her. "I have our mage allies on standby to join us, if we're ready."

"We haven't decided anything," Gisli said, frustration in his tone.

Yanda suspected he wanted to get the tech infrastructure out on the table first, establish a clear direction before involving the mages.

Those mages, ally or not, had stared at her, listened to her thoughts, examined their movements for over a year. She felt some hesitation herself.

Tenali shoved the shaker aside and it fell, spraying coral salt crystals across the tabletop as he turned away, arms crossed. "You'll bring in Krid's spies before consulting our own Elven cousins?"

Dawn was turning to full daylight and sunrays suddenly filtered down on them.

Beri stepped into a ray of sun just outside the shadowy threshold. "Can I join?"

Merne signaled for him to approach. "Of course. We might have need of a master-thief busy-body journalist." She smirked at him fondly.

He took a bow before squeezing onto a bench next to two of the Allies. They seemed well-acquainted and Yanda again felt distanced from her friend. The sun caught his chestnut-red hair, grown out from its cropped cut to form a mass of curls on top.

Yanda decided to take up Tenali's cause. No one had stood with him. Probably no one dared, with Zamani glowering. And she was curious. "What about Tenali's suggestion of extending the dome, getting Neyla help returning the Stone pieces?"

Zamani's gaze skewered her as he pronounced tightly, "They will have nothing to do with us. My grandson refuses to believe me."

"Because it's not true." Tenali sat straighter. "Yes, it was once true. But it's been years."

"And you've what? Been softening them with off-world gifts?" Zemani's tone held unworthy rancor.

Tenali pulled back as if struck. Yanda felt disappointed in the Neyna leader.

Zemani softened. "Son, it's a matter of principle. We won't beg."

"Principle! We're about to lose everything. Nuclear waste again. We might lose Shalt altogether and then the Neyla *will* be endangered. We could lose our forest. The seas could be poisoned by fallout—more than they were before. It's to the Neyla's interest to help and they know that."

Merne watched her father and son, clearly reluctant to be in the middle. At last, she rested a hand on her father's. "It might be time," she said quietly.

Yanda watched to see what the dignified elder Elf might do. Would he stalk away as he'd done before? But no. He gave one slow nod.

"We're all tired," Merne said. "Let's take a break, wait on our conversation with the mages." She shot Tlalit an apology.

Yanda felt relieved. She'd tired of the tensions. Shalt had long since taken to rumbling unhappily until her sternum vibrated.

She stood and sought Zami. She found him in a tucked away alcove of the garden, curled on a bed of *jallis* moss filling a reed basket like a small cloud around him, under a colorful quilt. The soft fiber, she'd been told, grew deep in the oldest growth forest and was very special to the Elves. Sweeka, close by, conversed intently with the most elegant of the Elves Yanda had seen, his golden skin accented by dark sweeping brows and a delicious, curving mouth. The Elf stood and bowed, his satiny clothes, subtle shades of burgundy, cut to perfection, as Yanda bent to scoop the sleeping Zami from his nest.

"Thank you," she said, adding in the Elven she was slowly picking up, "*Arshvon.*" Good night."

Sweeka stood and Yanda leaned to touch the sky-blue forehead of Sweeka, who'd taken to Zami and was quite often the one to watch him.

Yanda saw both Beri and Tenali watch her as she passed through the garden, waving good-night to the gathering at the table before she left through the archway.

Tenali looked hopeful and she knew he awaited an invitation but she wanted to be alone, to think, or not to think at all.

Approaching their tree, Zami woke and put his little hands on her shoulders, his eyes locking with his mother's. With a shared smile, they rose through the air, three levels to their sleeping quarters. Yanda braced a booted foot at the platform's edge as she grabbed a vine and pulled them on.

A few other Fugitives had already settled, writing or looking at devices. She envied them the use of tech. Gisli had offered to fix a network for her that would be impervious to Krid's spies, so she could call home. But she worried too much about the possibility of him tracking any contact she might have with her daughter. "I can wait a little longer."

"Your daughter would love to see your face, hear your voice, know you're safe," Tlalit had coaxed.

But it was more. Her adoptive mother—Omshi—had never approved of her going to the city, becoming a surgeon, leaving Seiti each week. Yanda dreaded her scoldings. There had been something more to it, but Omshi would never explain.

She let Zami down to crawl on the soft mats and carpets to the area they shared with Vatu.

"I left early," Vatu said. "They don't really need my input."

Yanda scooted to the head of the bed—pillows nestled against the enormously wide tree trunk—and nursed Zami.

"How was the rest of the meeting?" Vatu asked.

Yanda shrugged. "Long. And rather useless."

"I thought about coming back but we had a very full day."

"Did you? What did you do?" She found herself longing to hear about something other than solving the planet's problems.

Vatu described supporting the dozen who kept the sphere strong. "They had to repel several attacks by Krid's soldiers."

"While we were meeting?" Yanda asked in shock.

Vatu nodded.

"Do you think someone knew there were powerful Elves missing from the Circle and decided to take that time to test the dome?" Yanda asked with dread. It was rhetorical. How could Vatu know. Her heart filled with darkness for the Elves' beautiful world, so vulnerable.

Vatu asked, "What was it like? Being in the Circle?"

"Amazing. Hard." Yanda changed Zami to the other breast as she tried to describe the sharing of minds, building strength within that sometimes felt like it might hit breaking point.

"I wonder if they'd ever let me try." Vatu went on one elbow, chin on her fist. With swimming and healthy air, she'd become a different creature, vibrant colors streaming along her skin with her emotions, nubs sometimes lying soft into her hair so that they could barely be seen.

"They should. I'm sure you'd be a powerful addition. And it's a truly unique experience."

"Is it like the Withum celebration? When we felt all one-mind, with the Neyla and all?" Vatu's expression looked dreamy.

"That was a fine feeling. But definitely different. Just to be enjoyed, or to grow closer to the others, while the Circle is demanding. It takes concentration and feels like a huge responsibility."

"So there wasn't much of a solution at the meeting?" Vatu asked.

"Not really." Yanda scooted the now sleeping Zami under the covers and lay by him. "We have bits of a plan but some big disagreements. No matter what, there's a fight. Krid will use toxifying weapons. We're left still keeping the Neyna under a dome. Even Shalt's wholeness holds possible threats." Yanda felt exhausted, and out of her depth.

"Maybe if the Stone is whole, It can fix it all."

"Shalt was whole when the invaders blew out part before." Yanda hated to be a downer, but she felt down, without much hope.

"True. You look very tired."

"I am. I think I'll sleep." Yanda said, yawning. "Who knows when I can again?"

"Why?" Vatu gazed at her suspiciously. "You mean to help in the Circle?"

Yanda shook her head. "I feel Shalt calling. I think I'll have to go there, meld minds with the Stone."

Chapter 29

Tenali watched Yanda in the underground courtyard alcove, kissing Sweeka and gathering her son. He watched her pass by the long table saying good-night, with an extra look toward him, and blown kiss, watched her leave the garden area through the archway, entering the lower level of the underground bunker and disappearing out of sight.

His mother started to speak to him but he stood and made his excuses. He felt he knew anything his mother would say. "Forgive your grandfather. You have to understand." Blah, blah, blah.

Others were leaving. The meeting was officially coming to a close. He saw Gisli jam plaz sheets into a bag, a dissatisfied look on his face. Moments later, Tenali stood outside the shelter building, sensing Yanda reach her tree with Zami in her arms. He thought about going to her.

What they had shared was beginning to wrap itself around his heart. Merne had been a loving but distracted mother, often off to Dondar, setting up a system to monitor and eventually fight off the colonizers. She'd left the raising of him to the Elven community, which was traditional, yet fell short of Neyna family connection. Zamani had always been there, but was also distant, with his responsibilities as leader, one of the Elders, imparting the old ways to newer generations.

Yanda seemed to fill a hole. She'd suffered some of the same sense of alienation. First, they'd shared their early memories of abandonment. Now, just yesterday, she'd traveled with him through his adult life in a way he'd never shared with anyone. Constantly on the move, he'd taken lovers here and there across the universe, but rarely grew close to any. A few of his crewmembers became like family, but there was a limit to what they discussed on their long voyages from one planet or moon or solar system to another.

He started down the path toward the Fugitives' tree, meanwhile sending a tendril of thought to the Circle, to check the situation with the dome.

"It's not good," Wondu told him as she sat in the Circle, channeling the strength of their combined minds. "Fighting off the attacks is wearing, even if we keep changing shifts for fresh minds."

Tenali broke the connection, feeling resolve building, and turned direction. Calling a *karsh* to him, he also sent a mental cry across the Ballan Sea to Mnenu, his best friend among the Neyla.

"Meet me with a boat. I don't want to swim that far."

"You couldn't swim that far if you tried," Mnenu laughed.

Tenali heard him excuse himself from a wild and raucous game of *ralashal*, played with small painted shells. They usually bartered for objects with no intrinsic value, just a fleeting desire. Or to be the next one to organize a game. Money was not a thing among the Elves, who had stayed far from the influences of city and trade systems throughout known space. They did collect some tech.

Tenali watched in Mnenu's mind as he walked the short distance to his rig and pushed it out onto the open sea. There was a strong wind. He put up the sails and shot out over the waters.

Tenali sensed his friend was happy to have the sea to himself, under the three moons, all still high in the sky: blue Eshet, green Talal, and smallest, pale yellow-orange Salit.

Soon Tenali spotted the little boat in actuality, not through Mnenu's eyes, from the *karsh* winging swiftly above, and told it to descend.

This *karsh*, which some of the Neyna called *Fetu*, circled down and settled on the deck of Mnenu's catamaran-type boat with its carvings and brightly painted fantastical sea creatures. A string of globe lights swung in the sea breeze, casting flashes of light onto carved masts, and the tall, cocky sea Elf who stood waiting for him, hand on the tiller.

They embraced in the fashion of Terlondian Elves, touching temples, then foreheads.

Mnenu steered toward Tenali's starship, hidden under the sea near their underwater city, assuming he wanted to leave the planet.

Chapter 30

As night fell, Yanda rubbed prickly eyes, sleep-deprived, and dragged herself from her bed.

"I'm coming, too." Vatu jumped up.

"It won't be comfy. Not like up here."

Vatu laughed. "I've told you about my home. We live in caves. I'm part amphibian, really. I put these covers over me as... I don't know. Window dressing."

Yanda smiled. "Seriously?" But she felt warmed not to go alone.

She did not know what would happen next. Maybe Zami would be safer not coming with her, but she wasn't leaving him. She worked a warm one-piece onto her boy, who rubbed groggy eyes as she tucked him into his carrier.

When they reached Shalt's caves, an encampment was already set up. To one side, globe lamps glowed warm colors. Tlalit bent over, laying covers on a camp bed near a cavern wall.

Dividers hung, suspended in air, creating rows of enclosures. Yanda could see into all of them but chose not to if it looked private.

Merne met Yanda and Vatu at the center of the cave and showed them an area not yet occupied, accoutered with a small crib-bed, two adult ones, and warm globe lights floating overhead. Yanda was about to settle the still sleeping Zami when Sweeka and three other Elves approached.

"We have the children in the underground nursery. Can we take Zami there?" Sweeka asked.

Yanda hesitated. Couldn't she keep him here, close to her? She looked around at the dark, cold cavern. Where would he play? In the bunker, they had the fun gym with plubber balls, soft mats, and climbing structures all the way to the ceiling. She nodded and transferred him, sling and all, to the tall, tatted, nose-studded Elf. She kissed his plump cheek, a tear forming.

The four youngish Elves whisked him away up the track, out of the caves. Her eyes followed. What am I doing here? she asked herself. I should have Zami and Seiti living a sweet life in the country, with my surgeon's salary and status, somehow all combined.

She thought of Tenali. She hadn't seen him yet. As Vatu lined a bedside table with her usual sentimental objects from home, Yanda wandered past the other sleeping booths, at least half a dozen. Chin and the Jejods had a large one, closest to the exit ramp. Tik crouched now, high on a ledge, eye level with the outside entrance.

But no Tenali. She sent out mental feelers, through the Elf trees, into Vashal, further out, to the coastline. Nothing.

Zamani came lightly into her mind, questioning. "Are you searching for my grandson?"

"How could you tell?" she asked, mildly irritated.

He hesitated. "I can sense when someone I... care about is sending out."

She almost asked, "How can I learn to hide that?" but he probably heard the question anyway. Maybe as long as she shared a planet with him, this would be the case.

"He's not close. He's gone to his ship," he said, sending regret, or apology that he had known first.

He's not leaving. Not without me, she told herself. He just wants to get ready, in case. She masked these thoughts from Zamani, hoping what Shouma had taught her gave her at least that much strength of mind. "Where are you?" she asked him. She hadn't seen him in the caverns.

"I have a small den, toward the back of the caves. We've had it for hundreds of years, my father before me. Would you like to see?"

It seemed an odd time for sightseeing. "I think Shalt is feeling urgent," she said, but he brought her to him anyway.

Small den hardly covered it. Zamani stood facing her in a corridor, intriguing relief paintings between woven hangings. She felt soft carpet under her boots. Fresh air funneled in while float globes warmed her. There was an ancient feel to this place: carved columns, recessed fixtures of unguessable use or meaning. They walked along the hallway until Zamani opened a deeply carved door and they entered a sitting room with desk and bed.

"Do you hide here?" she asked.

"At times," he answered, smile tugging at his mouth. He indicated a large, foamy chair for her to sit in.

She took it, gazing around at the many shelves, full of antiquities, and off-planet treasures. These made her think of his unkind remark to Tenali, asking if he was bribing the Neyla to befriend him. "Why don't you join the rest of us?"

"I brought you here because there's a preparation for working with Shalt that our ancestors knew. It might help strengthen you for what is to come."

"What do you think is to come?" she asked, though bringing Shalt's fragments back and fighting off Krid were obvious answers.

"I don't know the extent, exactly. Maybe, beyond helping Shalt to be whole again, you can play some role in holding, sustaining against incursion. Shalt will have more, when you can fully take in the Stone's communication."

"I see." She waited for him to initiate this training.

He held out a hand to her. "It's further in."

She stood. "You just wanted to show off your collection first?"

He smiled, a small enigmatic press of the corners of his mouth.

On the far side of the room, a hidden panel opened at his touch. A hallway took them to another small chamber, fully paneled in rich wood inlay. There sat a very old Elf. And that was saying a lot since most of the Elves were old, in the way Yanda had always understood the word. He sat in a chair carved like a tree, beckoning them forward. Zamani drew stools close for her and himself.

"I am Decru," the silver-haired Elder Elf said to Yanda. "Take my hand, child."

The long bony hand of the wizened Elf sent waves of energy into Yanda like she'd never felt, even from the most powerful of sentients.

If she'd thought the circle of stone seats at the peak of Vashal had shown her new parts of herself, the synergy created by holding Decru and Zamani's hands was like a bolt of lightning. It hurt for just a moment and her heart surged to panic point just before a larger feeling filled her.

Shalt spoke into that place, filling all her senses. She was one with Shalt and all the Elves and allied beings, with the grove and land around them.

Then her vision moved outward, beyond the dome, to where Krid was encamped, surrounded by tanks and aircraft. They had cut trees for fire. Shalt sizzled, heart broken for the trees that had drunk from the waters fed by minerals of sister and brother stones.

Surprise could not have described her emotion as she watched Krid lifted into the air, along with a locked box that rested on a table near him in his tent.

Shalt, with Decru's help, brought him through the dome's outer membrane, carried him through the cavernous space, and down the hole to the Stone's surface.

Yanda, Decru, and Zamani now stood on the Stone as well—vast, curving away into darkness like a small moon, smooth but for huge chunks exploded out of the otherwise unmarred expanses.

Krid stared around him. His eyes stopped on Yanda, lip curled, though he seemed otherwise frozen, sitting on his camp stool. "Where's our son?"

"Not our son," Yanda said, glad that she was not alone. She felt Zamani, close behind her, to one side, while Decru stood, straight and tall, at her other shoulder.

"You became pregnant while in my care. Who else got to you? Beri?" His face flamed. "I already had a grudge against the thief. Now..."

"Quiet, man. Beri had nothing to do with *our* son," Zamani said.

Krid turned his ravening, red-rimmed eyes toward the tall handsome Elf, leader of the Neyna. He tried to send a blast of pain into their minds but it backfired from the shielding surrounding Yanda and the two Elves.

Yanda had a feeling that never before had he felt the force of his own mind-weapons. For once, he could not prevent others' punishments, by running, hiding on uninhabited moons, building his collection of tools, some of which clanked in the folds of his many-pocketed trench coat. He flinched in horror at the agony.

Chapter 31

"The Stone says stop the attacks on the barrier to this realm," Yanda translated, feeling Shalt's shout through every cell of her body.

Krid, still reeling from his own assault, brought pained eyes to Yanda, uncomprehending. Finally he sneered. "The stone says. Right."

"Very clearly," Yanda said.

Zamani and Decru nodded.

"Or what?" Krid pinched out the words, his head held at a cautious, pained angle. "The stone is damaged. Can it still be powerful?"

Zamani spoke. "It can harm. That's what's left. What it is hampered from, since the blasts"—he gestured toward the rough holes exploded out of the Stone's beautiful, opalescent-green surface—are the emanations of loving energy that help all the creatures and life on this planet."

"Ah." Krid tsk'ed, starting to shake his head and stopping abruptly with a wince. "But that's not even what I want the stone whole for."

"What a surprise." Decru spoke for the first time. He leaned against a tall, wood staff with an owl carved out of the top, looking pensive and disgusted.

"So, let's just get this show on the road," Krid snarled. "Call back all the pieces. Or I level this forest of yours. I assume there's a forest here as I heard there was one of old. Quite enchanting, with treehouses and the like. Would you like to save that?"

The three glared at him, not deigning to answer.

"Come. Let's be honest. I have enough troops out there to wear you down, and allies in the city, ready to order more. Does this rock have the power to fight all that? Every kind of weaponry."

Yanda felt Tenali's voice in her mind. "Put Krid in a dampening cell."

Yanda thought back, "Don't we need him to tell his forces to stop first?"

"That's taken care of."

What did he mean, taken care of? But Tenali's connection with her was broken.

Chapter 32

Within Vashal, the minds In the Circle felt a sudden surge of energy. For the first time in any Elf's memory, from deep within sea caverns, a similar circle of seats, occupied by Neyla, brought its hive-mind to combine with the Neyna.

"Let us make a dome around Krid's forces," the leader of the Neyla, Som, requested.

Neyna minds imparted the knowledge of how to form a protective barrier and together the two groups, powered by the two Power Stones, formed an invisible membrane that stopped all weaponry from penetrating. Beams of firepower dropped at the edges, forming pools of toxic air and water that began to move toward the perpetrators. They ran toward the far edges, trying to leave, but were held in with their weapons and toxic air.

Tlalit, in the Circle, set about syphoning the toxins into a large bubble with its own membrane. "I hate to introduce this to the universe but there's a planet where they've been perfecting the reversal of such materials. We'll send it there if they allow."

Zamani's mind, from Shalt's cavern, was tethered to the Circle. He said to Krid, "We're doing for your soldiers what you would not offer to anyone. Removing from their midst the dangers they brought."

Krid's face remained unmoved.

Shouma, Dele and Bonden lifted Krid up from Shalt's surface. He was still held in the cocoon Shalt had wrapped him in, no movement but the flicker of his eyes, the grimace of his lips. They moved his inert figure along to cells in the far back wall of the cave, below the Elders' rooms.

"Let's get Shalt's pieces here without delay," Decru said.

Shouma, Bonden and Dele glided down to Shalt's surface. The three lay, face down, fanned out on the green Stone, Yanda making the fourth spoke on their wheel. Zamani and Decru held vigil.

Monitored by the dozen powerful minds in the peak of Vashal, along with those in the Neyla Circle, undersea, a hole opened in the dome and Yanda helped Shalt begin calling the Stone's shards back.

Shalt's surface began to purr, pulsing a light the lemon yellow of delight. Yanda held hands with the three other Fugitives. Her senses, linked fully with Shalt's core essence, uncovered fragments across the universe. As soon as they were detected and started to be drawn toward Terlond, Bonden wrapped each in a protective cocoon, like fiberglass so that they might make their swift journey across space. When the cocoon was safely on, Shouma began hopping them, making them disappear and appear again closer. Gisli tracked these, having set the resonance of the stones into

Merne's AI system. They glowed as tiny dots on a grid, just as the sentient minds had shown up on her screen in Sheffed. As well as the interstellar travel, the cocoon would get the fragment through the planet's outer atmosphere without harm, while also preventing attack or capture. Any slightest touch would send the Stone fragment to a place set up in a far star system by Shouma.

The four found they could take sleep breaks, lying on the warmed Stone. Shalt or one of the others would alert them if there was a problem.

The first of these had come when a stone fragment, moving too fast through space, began to overheat and threatened to burn up. Hence, the cocoon.

Dele discovered she could help Shouma move pieces of Shalt closer by hopping them *between*.

And so it came to be that Yanda and Shalt began to pull dozens of Stone shards across the universe. Toward dawn, the first came into range on the grid, approaching Terlond. Slicing through the atmosphere, it traveled inexorably toward the hole in the dome, then down into the caves. This first was a fist-sized chunk that hurtled in through the thirty-foot hole.

Yanda felt Shalt's elation as its second piece—the first being the sliver from Tenali's brain—soared toward the Stone's gaping wounds and took its place, hovering just outside of where it had sat for millennia, not yet touching since it needed pieces to surround it.

More arrived, at intervals, all sizes from boulder to tiny flake.

· ——— ··· ——— ·

Meanwhile, Gisli and Tlalit kept watch over Dondar and Sheffed, with their surveillance system and the help of the mages and other sentients on their side, to make sure no other forces arrived, as Krid had threatened. The Elves had allies in government offices. Krid, in a cell dampened by psi-blockers, had no effect on anyone's mind, as far as they knew.

• ——— • • • ——— •

Late the next evening—though Yanda could not tell day from night, deep in the cave—almost all the fragments had arrived and gone to where they belonged, fitting perfectly, even pebbles, dust and grains fine as sand, returning to their ancient placements.

Shalt was nearly whole—but for the large fragment kept by Krid in a box that rested on Shalt's surface. No doubt he had brought it with him to be part of his moment of glory, with his forces standing by to watch, as he controlled the power Shalt would represent, once complete.

But no one could open the box. It could not be broken or sawn, chiseled, or lasered.

Krid was brought from his cell.

"Open the box," Zamani demanded.

"Couldn't figure it out, could you?" Krid looked haggard but smug.

"Get Beri," Yanda suggested.

Shouma glanced at her. "Why Beri?"

"He knows objects."

Within an hour, Beri entered the caves and was floated down to Shalt's surface.

"Can you tell what Krid might have used for this box?" Yanda asked.

Krid glowered at Beri but was unable to move or send mind-messages. A startling-looking male Elf stood just behind Krid, hand on his shoulder. Features hawklike, skin color cobalt and darker, he wore a striking cape, its shoulders arcing with metal spikes, and mean hob-nail boots. When his eyes met Yanda's, she felt a chill and was sure he kept Krid in check. *Scaton.* She felt his name pushed into her mind. By whom? Him, she thought.

She pulled her eyes away from his drilling gaze with difficulty. Her head needed a rest. As Beri dropped to cross-legged by the chest, Yanda, Shouma, Bonden and Dele rested. They had pulled some comforts to Shalt's broad expanse and now lay on cushions, trays of food between them, watching as Beri put his hands on the box's sides, fiddled with seams for hidden latches, ran his fingers along edges, pressed, and finally scratched the surface with his nails, listening. He pulled out a device, tapped in information and ran it along the surfaces.

Krid watched all this, lips curled in a satisfied smile.

At last, Beri said, "It's made of Mingalian stone. Krid probably has the clasp, of the same stone, calibrated to a frequency only he knows."

"Vatu." Yanda sent her Mingal friend a mind-call. "Do you think you could work with this stone. It's from your planet?"

The blue-green Mingal descended from the cave above to join them. She sat by the strange box, across from Beri and rubbed her hands on it. Pressing fingers inside her wrist, she activated sensors that called home on a device in her lap. Yanda heard a fluting sound as Vatu held the box and sent frequencies into it, holding a sound device to it for the *seron*—scientific priests of her home planet—to run through all the possible vibrations and resonances found in nature there. They fed her more to try and she ran them over the box, sometimes whistling them with her lips close to the wood-stone.

Krid's smile dropped away, replaced by alarm. This was his bargaining chip, his favored object!

Suddenly, the clasp released and the lid popped open.

Krid tried to lunge forward as a small slab of rock floated up and out of the box, moving toward its place with great speed.

Yanda could see, through Shalt's senses, that it settled next to the sliver that had been inserted into Tenali's brain, and both slid into place among their fellow stones, shifting slightly to make room, then settling with perfection.

Yanda and the others—in the Elven forest of Rotoul and the undersea city of Zotoul, Elves, Fugitives, Allies—all felt a small movement ripple across Shalt's vastness as its entirety shook into place, once and for all.

Above, in the cave and beyond, in the Elven woods, a cry was heard as Yanda and the others stood up, shouting.

Yanda dropped to her knees and kissed Shalt. Brilliant colors raced across the Stone like lightning streaks. Hoots and bird calls could be heard in the distance as the land felt Shalt's full presence return.

Epilogue

It was hard to contemplate the job being over. Nevertheless, now that it was, Yanda felt a barely tolerable anxiousness to be in flight to Alland, to her daughter. She stared across the land at the spaceport from the tree house, wondering what transport might arrive that could take her to Alland. Merne and Zamani had promised.

Zami played near her feet in the viewing perch, in a woven playpen, with many toys the Elves provided.

Tenali approached quietly, and only when he sat beside her on the bench in the view area facing north did she notice him. She started.

"Ready to go home?" he asked.

That was never easy to answer. Yes, she wanted to see her daughter. But leave this place? Her friends? When would they see each other again? Take up her old life? She knew things now, about herself. There was much more she didn't know, that she hadn't even known she didn't know. What was this Xentu business? "I'm ready to get my daughter." That statement held a lot of meaning. It meant she would get her and bring her to live with her, for always. She would never again put career first. "I'm ready for Zami to meet his sister."

The baby looked up at the sound of his name and grinned, crawled to her, knew and climbed up. She lifted him to her chest and he lay his head against her, studying Tenali.

The Elf-man touched his soft cheek. "And then what?" he asked her pointedly.

"I guess I'll figure that out when I get there."

"Zamani's not going to want his son leaving for long."

"I know that," she snapped a little harsher than intended. She softened her voice. "I need to not have that kind of pressure on me right now. I have big decisions to make." She turned so her knee came up between her and Tenali. Zami climbed down again. "I helped restore Shalt to wholeness. I gave up a year of my life, a year of my daughter's life, and a surgery career. I think I've done my part. Yes, I gave birth to a half-Elven son." She sighed. "And I may not want for him to grow up on Alland. It's not a place for the unique, with abilities. Though I don't think that's entirely fair. There are many talents on Alland, being suppressed. I should be willing to fight for change there."

He took her hand and held it between his. They were sturdy hands, not as long and tapering as the true Elven ones. "I get it, my love."

He'd never called her "my love." She almost yanked her hand away with her usual suspicion. Would he try to capture her, too? But she didn't.

He must have felt tension for one of his brows went up, but he kept her hand firmly. "I don't intend to put pressure on you. I love you, yes. I won't deny that. I haven't had a bond like this, ever."

Her hand started to pull ever so slightly.

He gripped it, grinning, and scooted closer, laying a kiss at the edge of her mouth. "I'm going to take you home. And then we'll talk."

"But—"

He moved in for a fuller kiss.

She relented, melting into it for a while. At last, she pushed him back gently. "But I'll be racing off the ship to get my daughter. Whatever we talk about over the weeks of travel there, I won't know what I want to do. I won't commit to anything."

He held up his hands in surrender. "Got it. I'll wait for you or I'll go. We can be in touch. You just tell me and that's the way we'll do it."

"I'll want you to go. Give me some time."

His throat moved up and down with a swallow.

"I'm not saying it to be mean. I just... really want to feel clear to make decisions about my life. And I don't want you making decisions around me."

"It's clear. I accept it." He stood, expression a study of "I'm not mad."

"Where's your ship?" she asked. "I don't think it's at the spaceport."

"I never land there." He squatted to ruffle Zami's curly brown hair. It hadn't taken on any of the interesting tones most of the Elves had in their hair. Yet neither had Tenali's.

"When can we leave?" she asked.

"Will a day give you enough time to say good bye to everyone?" he asked.

"Yes." Her heart swelled and began beating fast, adrenaline racing through her. She nodded.

He left her.

· ——···—— ·

That evening, a banquet was set out in the largest tree, where the seating was formed into scallop shapes descending toward the stage. Globe lights floated everywhere.

The Fugitives had their own table. The Ten and Zami circling a long flat surface, carved naturally with Elven hands. It was filled with delicacies special to the occasion.

"Are there ships for the rest of you?" asked Yanda.

"Some of us," Beri answered. "Tlalit says she's buying one. She may need to hire a captain for the first flight but then wants to learn to do it all herself. It's being delivered any day now."

"And she'll ferry you all home? I could wait and do that?" Yanda looked around at their dear faces, loathe to leave them any sooner than need be.

Beri put a hand on her shoulder. "I think we're going the other direction first. Shouma has a granddaughter she's very worried about. A dire health condition. Chela's going along to help. Bonden may go, too."

"To maybe come up with an apparatus to save her?" Yanda asked, feeling sad she knew nothing of any of this, that she was not involved in the next phase with her Fems.

"Yeah. Also one or two of the Elven healers. I'm going to catch a ride from there. The Jejods can, as well. It's not that far to their moon." Seeing the look on Yanda's face, he added, "You could come later, Mirror. Visit me on Romden." He shrugged. "It's not that great, though."

"Are you kidding? I wouldn't miss it." She squeezed his

hand. "Keep in touch, Beri. Okay?"

He gave her a crooked smile, his neck reddening.

She turned to Vatu. "And Mingal?"

"That's farther," Vatu said. "It's okay. I can wait a bit longer."

Yanda studied her. "You could come with me to Alland, but you'd have to hide yourself the entire time. It's not that xenotypes never come there. But... I don't trust my world."

Vatu nodded. "I understand. Anyway, I think this is a trip you need to do on your own."

"Another time, if you're determined, I'll show you where I grew up." She hugged Vatu, chest nearly bursting with emotion to be parting from her friend.

The Elves stood and began to sing. Their ethereal harmonies rose, making chills run up Yanda's spine. Zami stood on her lap and entered in, sweet notes pouring from him in the Elven language. Yanda stared at her son.

Face glowing, Zamani stepped toward their son and held out his arms. Yanda lifted him up. Zamani set him on his tall shoulders so that he was standing. All eyes turned toward the tiny half-Elf boy singing his heart out, enthralled.

"What were you singing about?" she asked her little boy when he was back in her lap.

He beamed at her. "Song of the Salamander!"

• —— • • • —— •

Next day, Tenali brought his ship from where it had been, on the far side of the undersea city of the Neyla. He landed in a wide field near the beach where they'd celebrated Withum.

Yanda held onto each of her fellow Fugitives, hugging, crying, promising to stay in touch.

At last, she and Vatu hugged in a long embrace. She turned and climbed the ramp into Tenali's ship, the Lark. This time, she was the only passenger and was there by choice. Even so, it brought a strangling sob to Yanda's throat to see the cabins, one of which had held her with the power-dampening metal collar at her throat.

Tenali had a bare bones crew for this journey of just a few weeks and no other business but carrying Yanda home. He'd put flowers in light sconces along the walls of the eating area.

For the weeks of the trip, when Tenali was not at the controls, they played cards and board games. Tenali could increase gravity in one room at a time, making everything easier, or most things.

The other crew members kept to themselves.

When the ship slowed, approaching Alland, she saw, for the first time, that, from space, her planet had a brownish color with a slight touch of green, as though partly covered in lichen.

"Not the most beautiful planet." Yanda wrinkled her nose. "Terlond is such a bright blue, being mostly ocean. Except the patch of brown that's Dondar and Sheffed."

"Alland is impressive for its tech and sciences," Tenali said from his seat at the control panels.

"Yeah, and look at what that's led to. Prejudice. Suppression of anything not about science and technology."

Tenali laughed. "You don't sound very fond of it."

"I never belonged there."

"It's where you learned to be a surgeon. That'll be useful, whatever else you want to do."

"I want to be able to use those skills only when other forms of healing aren't enough." Yanda's eyes shone bright with passion.

They watched out the windows as the ball that was her planet took on more form and texture—low foliage cut into patterns by narrow channels of water.

"Kind of like an eyeball. You know, the veins," Tenali said in all seriousness.

Yanda laughed so hard, she had to wipe tears. "Yeah. My planet, the eyeball. I can hear the poetry now."

The ship settled slowly onto a platform. "I'd land elsewhere but it's not allowed." Tenali threw up his hands.

"They know you well here, don't they?" Yanda asked, and her stomach churned a little with the memories of this ship, at this port, stealing her away.

"Quite well, yes." He shrugged, not looking at her.

⋅ ———⋅⋅⋅—— ⋅

By evening, they were on a train crossing the countryside to Yanda's childhood home. Tenali stared out, fascination clear on his face.

Pulling into the station at Balyou, Tenali gazed around. He had no trouble fitting in with the all-human—or at least all-human appearing—population. He'd done that for decades as interstellar ship captain.

To Yanda, it was a non-descript town, mostly single-story dwellings and shops. She couldn't understand why Tenali studied it so closely.

Yanda had almost nothing to carry. The Fugitives had gifted her with a few small items that fit easily in an Elven bag given to her by Merne and Tlalit. This she clutched close to her side.

"I'll just get you to your house and then go back to the city," Tenali said as they walked along the main street. He held Zami.

Yanda nodded, too anxious to speak. "Okay." She was

anticipating seeing her daughter. Would Seiti be mad at first? Of course she would. Yanda would sweep her into a hug anyway, even if she had to chase her.

Several blocks from the station, Yanda turned up a flagstone walk. The door opened and a craggy-faced man stepped out. A sturdy woman with serious demeanor followed.

Yanda rushed to hug them, then introduced them to Tenali and Zami.

"We didn't make up bedding." Omshi gripped her hands in front of her, anxiety playing at lines by her eyes. No smile touched her aging lips.

"I'm catching the train back." Tenali spoke the universal language with ease.

Yanda peeked past them. "Where's Seiti?" She climbed the steps, calling, "Seiti!"

Omshi took her arm, holding her back as she started through the doorway. "She's not here." Her lips pressed into a frown.

"Not here. What do you mean?" Yanda felt panic rising.

Her adoptive mother kept her voice neutral, almost a monotone. "We think she went to look for you."

Yanda read blame in her mother's eyes. She remembered the reprimands about living in the city, only coming home for weekends and holidays. "Just 'til I get going. I'll work long hours and get ready for her to go to a private school here in the city," Yanda'd said. But she'd felt torn. There was greater surveillance in the city, and from a very young age, Seiti's powers had been greater than hers. Or at least more obvious. "How long? Where would she have gone?"

"Maybe a month. We heard a rumor that she paid a medium. I have no idea where she got the money." Omshi glanced sideways at Nedri. "Must have been the *nefters* in those camps outside o' town."

Nedri remained silent but his eyes looked broken hearted.

Yanda had considered letting Tenali take Zami back to the ship with him. She wasn't sure how well he could hide his Elf-ness. But he was doing well. Now she made up her mind. She loped down the steps and scooped Zami from Tenali. "This is my son," she announced. "I'll be staying to find Seiti," she announced. She turned to Tenali. "I'll be in touch as soon as I find her. Can you wait a little while?"

"You're going to leave again?" Oshmi snapped.

"I don't know." With a sinking feeling, Yanda watched Tenali walk away down the block, back to his ship.

Glossary

*note: ah is used for ah sound vs a in apple;
emphasized syllable is in caps*

A

Abat (a-BAhT'): beer of Terlond.

Aktat (ahk-TAHT'): bird-like Jejod, middle sister.

Alland (all-LAHND'): Yanda's planet: no trees, no oceans, high tech

Allee (ah-LEE'): language of Alland.

Allies: those helping the Elves in Dondar and Sheffed, to help the escape of the captives, The Ten.

anti-grav and stasis: state to maintain balanced life on spaceship.

Apat (ah-PAHT): "come" in Neyna

Arda (AHR-dah): leaf similar to grape, rolled around grains

Arjan (ahr-JAHN) (soft "g" like in Asian): fellow surgeon on Alland

Arkus (AR-kuhs): Rogue mage, ally to the fugitives.

Arkut (ar-COOT): Elf child of the Neyna.

Arsat (ar-SAHT): young Elf; teen-like; helps with childcare.

Arshvon (ARSH-von): good night or sleep well (v close to b) in the Neyna language.

Ash-don (ASH-dawn): Power stone of the Neyla, Shalt's

equivalent.

Aspar (A-spar): bright colored fruit on Terlond

Assal (ah-SAHL): thin, pinched Terlondian servant.

Arsat (ar-SAHT): young elf with tats and piercings who watches the kids.

Asborn (AZ-born): female Neyla

Awanenu (ah-wah-NAY-noo): the Stone's sister.

B

Ballan (ball-LAHN) Sea: Terlond's sea between sea elves underwater city and the only continent.

Balyou (BAL-you): Yanda's home town on Alland

Beatty (BAY-tea): surgeon on Alland.

Bend: young elf with tats and piercings who watches the kids.

Beri ("berry"): journalist, fellow captive on Farn and Terlond, from Romden.

Blaz (blahz): corrupt planet with trafficking, slaving, forced labor.

Bonden (BON-den): magical crafter, inventor; can move people through objects; from Qontaq.

C

Café (ka-FAY) Selene (seh-LEHN): where Beri and Gisli met, in Dondar.

Caffa (KA-fuh): form of coffee on Alland

Calden (KAHL-den): Terlondian groundsman

Celly (SEL-ee): plastic surgeon on Alland, friend of Yanda; indiscernible age and springy orange hair.

Chala (CHAH-lah): Elven coffee

Chechons (cheh-CHONES): large humanoid species on Mingal. Can chew stone to build.

Chela (CHEH-lah): healer, fellow captive.

Chinkendit: "Chin", fem soldier; captive.

Circle: 12 stone seats at the pinnacle of the Pyramid

Citadel: Krid's building in Dondar.

Clarin (KLEHR-in): Alland seasoning.

coos (KOOS – rhymes with goose): purplish-red fruit.

Decru (DEH-kroo): silver-haired Neyna Elder; mainly occupies the underground labyrinth extending back from Shalt's caves.

Dele (DAY-lay): one of the Ten captive fems; Fugitive; musician; can move objects with her mind; from Qontaq.

Dew (doo): plump Terlondian servant

Dondar (don-DAHR): only city on Terlond

drufus (DROO-fuhs)– tall tree like a redwood, in the language of the Neyna.

E

Elf: tall, humanoid, with magical abilities, strong connection with nature. Tapering leaf-like ears, many colors of skin and hair; swirling irises.

Elf-fires: burn without consuming fuel by drawing small amounts of energy from nature.

Elznap (EHLZ-nap): little-known star-system, difficult to get to. Asteroid belts, electric storms throw instruments off; where the Sonda are from.

Erlon (ehr-LON, air-lawn): another missing people, like the Xentu.

Erzon (air-ZAHN): moon of Prokit; Tlalit loves it for its broad thinking, artists, musicians.

Escapees: Krid's captives; ten fems who escaped.

Eshet (eh-SHEHT): blue moon, one of three of Terlond.

F

fajan (fah-JAHN – soft g like in "Asian"): Neyna word for

"lover."

Fardling (FARD-ling): a form of knitting on Terlond.

Farn (fahrn – rhymes with barn): moon where Krid keeps captives, he owns a small dome city.

Fataq (fah-TAHK): soldiers of Terlond.

Fedu (FEH-doo): sea creatures of Terlond

fems: word for humanoid females.

Fetu (FEH-too): a karsh that seems to have become sentient.

Fugitives: the ten fems escaped from Krid.

G

Gerhog (GEHR-ogg): Beri's "boss" in Dondar, leatherwork.

Gisli (GIZZ-lee): wiry young man, skin a purplish brown; of Tellot.

Goncha (GAHN-chah): tiny planet; small spiritual population, mostly untouched by other civilizations.

grilaff hekom (GRI-loff HEH-kum): spider's venom in the language of the Neyna.

H

Hazmat (HAZ-mat): protection against hazardous materials.

Hintas (HIN-tahz): single-person electric cars.

J

Jat (JAHT): bird-like Jejod, oldest sister.

Jejod (juh-JOD): bird-like humanoids; warriors.

Joe Hoskins: surgery patient; bellhop at a local Allandian hotel.

Joli (jo-LEE – soft g as in Asian): 7-foot primanoid; dark red fur, black at the tips.

Jallis (JA-lis): moss used by the Neyna for bedding, stays soft.

K

Kaffe (KAF): coffee-like Terlondian drink.

Kapok (KAY-pahk): tree with wide root base.

Karsh (carsh): flying birds apparatuses, part magic part mechanical, built by the Neyna.

Kodok (KOH-doke): Alland seasonings

Konkle (CONG-kuhl): Yanda's boss in surgery.

Kran (cran as in cranberry): local grain drink on Terlond

Kridenit Sonn (kri-DEHN-it): "Krid"; dark mage; collects beings and objects with powers.

L

Lambra (LAM-brah): musical instrument of the Elves

Lark: spaceship that took Yanda from Alland.

M

Magali (mah-GAH-lee): surgeon on Alland.

mage (mayje): sorcerer from birth; powers in the genes.

manifest: starship's travel schedule.

Mans (mans): Rogue mage, ally to the fugitives

mantazos (mahn-TAH-zoes): banana-like fruit Elves fix in myriad ways.

Merne (muhrn): shopkeeper, Techie elf, Zamani's only daughter.

Mingal (meeng-GAHL): Vatu's isolated planet near the edge of the known universe.

Mingalian. (meeng-GAHL-ee-uhn): of Mingal.

Mnenu (mm-NAY-noo): Neyla (sea elf)

N

Nedri (NEH-dree): Yanda's adoptive father

Nefter (NEHF-tuhr): nomads

Neyla (NAY-luh): sea elves of Terlond

Neyna (NAY-nuh): forest elves of Terlond

Neyleyna (nay-LAY-nuh): both neyla and neyna

O

Omshi (OHM-shee): Yanda's adoptive mother

Once Bright: Merne's booth in the market.

P

Pata (PAH-tah): eggplant dish.

Plaz (plaz – rhymes with jazz): synthesized material from natural sources; anything from sheets of paper to furniture or accessories.

plubber balls (PLUB-bur): large exercise balls of the Neyna made of natural materials, can hold a form.

Primanoid (PRIME-muh-noid): sentient, part primate, part human

Prokit (PRAH-kit): planet, its moon is Tlalit's favorite place.

Psi-blockers (SIGH-blockers): suppress mind powers.

Q

Qontaq (KAHN-tahk): planet with where great mind powers are respected.

Qontaqian (kahn-TAHK-ian): of Qontaq.

R

Ralashal (rah-lah-SHAHL): a Neyla game played with small painted shells.

Romden (RAHM-den): Beri's planet. Known for universities, scholars and libraries.

Rotoul (roh-TOOL): Neyna Elves' forest home.

S

Sadthis (SAD-this as in thistle) Terlondian primate species, in the language of the Neyna. Long haired, long tailed.

Salit (sahl-LEET): pale yellow-orange moon; Smallest of the 3 moons of Terlond sana (SAH-nah): ecstasy in the Neyna language.

Sandu (sahn-DOO): planet with large freighter business.

Santu (SAHN-too): a Terlond fruit, color bright pinkish red

sarfan (SAHR-fahn): Terlondian word for millennium

sarsefi (sahr-SEH-fee): lovemaking in the language of the Neyna.

Sarwil (sahr-WIL)—biggest tree at the heart of Neyna community, their *World Tree;* has a stadium.

Satiyati (sah-tee-YAH-tee): sweet Allandian spice.

Scaton (SKAY-tahn): startling male Elf, features hawklike, his color cobalt blue and darker, striking hob-nails boots. Can damper Krid's mind powers.

Seiti (SAY-tee): Yanda's daughter, 6 at the start

Selky (SELL-key): Yanda's nickname on Alland based on her last name Selkedon.

senon emu tinon (seh-NON eh-MOO tee-NONE): Elven phrase meaning "I want you"

Seron (SEH-rone): scientists, philosophers, spiritual leaders on Mingal.

Shalt (SHAHLT – rhymes with salt): the Neyna Stone.

Sheffed (SHEF-ed): slum of Dondar

shifi (SHIF-fee): soft wind from the southwest

Shouma (SHOO-mah): elder captive, strongest mind powers; can move from place to place instantly, make herself and others invisible.

Shrapels (SHRAP-uhlz) Hospital: where Yanda works as surgeon on Alland

Skarth (SKARTH): main city on Alland where Yanda was a surgeon.

snook (snook – rhymes with look): game with spongy ball.

Som (sohm – rhymes with Rome): leader of the Neyla.

Sonda (SAHN-duh): Shouma's powerful race, from Elznap.

Sonder (SOHN-duhr): coin in Dondar

Sophis Tetra (SOH-fis TEH-truh): powerful stone of the planet Goncha

Squerbs (squerbs – rhymes with herbs): duck-like bird on Terlond.

sunine kutitu (soo-NEE-nay koo-TEE-too)– kitten with sharp claws, in the language of the Neyna

Sweeka (SWEE-kah): young Neyna Elf who helps with young elves.

tafag (tah-FOG) rolls: like a corndog; Terlondian bean curd dish.

T

Talal (tah-LAHL): green moon, one of three of Terlond.

Tellot (tehl-LOT): planet of fragile, semi-tropical climate and nonviolent culture.

Tenali (tuh-NAH-lee): Merne's only son; half-Elf; known as Tennan when Captain of the Lark.

Terlond (tehr-LOND): planet of the Neyna Elves; only has one small continent, the rest is ocean.

Terlondian (tehr-LOND-ian): of Terlond.

Tesu (TEH-soo): sea creatures of Terlond

Telori (tell-LO-ree) Sector: farthest of the Known Universe.

Tik (teek): bird-like Jejod, youngest sister.

Tlalit (t-LAH-lit): Merne's partner; techie; sits in the Neyna Circle; tangerine hair cocatieled into a crest.

Toray (toh-RAY): A tiny gnomish being, thin arms, a pale mushroom color, lives in the mountain caves.

Tuk-tuk (TOOK-took): tiny primate native to Terlond.

V

Vashal (vah-SHAHL): mountain with the crystal pyramid, site of the Power Circle.

Vatu (VAH-too): from Mingal, shapeshifter. Semi-amphibian.

W

Withum (WITH-um): sweet-smelling white flower, name of festival, promotes mind-share.

Wondu (wohn-DOO): elder Elf female who sits in the Circle.

X

Xentu (ZEHN-too): Yanda's heritage; mysterious powerful race; have not been seen for millennia.

Y

Yanda (YAHN-duh) Selkedon (SEHL-kuh-duhn): Main character, surgeon, raised on Alland; called Yandawi by the Elves.

Z

Zamani (zah-MAH-nee): leader of the Neyna Elves; Zami's father.

Zami (ZAH-mee): Yanda's half-Elf son; hair burnished magenta at the tips at 6 months

zarsh (zahrsh): a filmy natural fabric of the Elves.

zhoun-zhoun (ZOON-zoon): Dele's flute-like instrument, of the planet Qontaq.

Zotoul (zoh-TOOL): Neyla sea elves underwater city.

MARIE JUDSON

A Far Cry

Lost Xentu, #2
A Fantasy Sci-Fi Series

Watch for *A Far Cry*, Book 2 in the Lost Xentu series

Coming out in December 2023

… Yanda bobbed on sea waves, terrified. Though she'd learned to float and swim a little in the pools of Rotoul, her home planet had no oceans. Who knew how deep the water beneath her was? Now she sculled water the best she could, trying to keep salty brine from going up her nose or down her throat as wavelets hit her from one side, then another.

All was black around her, with the sound of endless, moving water.

Why had she chosen this particular approach? she asked herself with rising panic as she pumped her legs against bottomless waters without rest.

Something bumped against her arm and she curled away, gasping with terror, heart pounding painfully.

Gentle mind-waves immediately filled her head. "Not danger," the *tesu* transmitted to her. She remembered the mind-feel of the sentient sea creature from her boat-ride and uninvited swim in this same sea more than a year ago.

More *tesu* gathered around her.

"You're tired," one said.

"A bit," she admitted, spitting out ocean water that was becoming harsh in her throat.

"I am Te-weet," the creature told her. With her sight, that could penetrate darkness as well as solid surfaces, she saw Te-weet was a luminous shade of aquamarine. The *tesu* slid under her arm, bumping its way against her until she pulled on, gripping the dorsal fin.

A blow hole in front of her spouted splats of water that

sprayed her face gently. She laughed as they shot across the water. "I have to bring Zami to do this," she thought, feeling less alone, more in equilibrium with the vast sea that spread in all directions.

"I take you to boats," Te-weet said.

Boats? This wasn't exactly what she'd imagined. But what *had* she pictured? The city of the Neyla was underwater. Tenali had told her the buildings were held in place by huge kelp roots. She recalled his mouth on hers, giving her oxygen, as they descended together. How had he done that without a tank? Did he have hidden gills? Or had it been spirit travel? Then why did he need his mouth on hers? Regardless, her heart raced at the memory.

But he'd left her. Dropped her off on Alland and deserted her, without a word. Why? She'd thought he cared about her and Zami. Her son, his... uncle! Technically. But Elves live hundreds of years so strange relationships like that weren't unlikely.

The pod of *tesu* approached an atoll where several boats bobbed, tied, cresting waves. They had the marvelous carven boughs of the one she'd ridden in last year.

"Can you climb up?" the dolphin creature asked, hovering in place with its powerful tail.

There was no ladder in sight. Why hadn't she gotten lessons in transporting herself, from Bonden, or Dele, while in the Elven forest?

Holding Te-weet tight around the neck, she used her sight to peer through the side of the boat. A strong rope ladder lay coiled on the deck.

Think! she berated herself. I can move obstructions in a person's body during surgery. But that's tiny bits of congestion, blood clots. Not a heavy bundle of rope. Gripping her hands together, she willed the rope to rise. It budged incrementally.

"I see in your head you move ladder. You fine witch human," Te-weet extolled her efforts. "Get it little higher. Kala jump, grab."

Yanda stretched her head one way and the other to loosen her tight muscles. Then, holding tight to the *tesu*, she set her sight again on the woven hemp and put her will into it rising. A tip showed above the ledge as the boat's hull dipped toward them. Quick as lightning, a *tesu* the hue of a pale moon, opalescent, shot into the air and nipped the coil, tugged hard. The ladder fell over the side just before the hull facing them lurched upward. Te-weet swam closer and Yanda grabbed the rough sides of the ladder that strained against her, rising higher.

Pulling her wet weight onto the lower rungs, she climbed. "Note to self. More climbing exercises in our routines when I get back to the rebel camp." Incrementally, Yanda made her way to the top, straining. Reaching the boat ledge at last, she found hand-grips and, with monumental effort, managed to pull a leg over. "Not impressive agility," she thought, as six *tesu* watched, heads bobbing in the water below.

Now what? she wondered. Shiver on this boat 'til someone decides to go on an excursion to sea? It seemed to be closing in on night, though maybe it was close to dawn. She didn't know the moons on Terlond well enough to tell time. After all, she'd been inside most of the time for a year and a half on this planet, then deep in the Elven forest, where she'd been mostly pre-occupied with stopping Armageddon. What did it mean when pale blue Eshet hovered on the horizon? Which horizon was it on? How could she tell direction from out here?

"We tell Neyla," Te-weet called to her, answering her quandary.

"Thank you!" she called to them. What if they hadn't come along? She couldn't start to imagine.

What was she doing there? The only Neyla she'd gotten to know at all had infuriated her; frankly she hoped never to see Mnenu again after he'd knocked her off the boat, dragged her under water with him, thinking it a fun joke. That was her first time ever in deep water. He'd been so arrogant. No apology. Maybe he'd moved away, left the planet. She hoped so.

Her teeth chattered. She wished she at least had Mnenu's way of drying instantly by a mere touch of his hands.

She wrapped her arms around herself and waited. For what? This was absurd. They didn't know her. They might take her as an enemy. The Neyna had been alienated from the Neyla for decades, with nothing but hostility between them. They'd know she was tied to the Neyna, from when she held the Power Circles with them to pull the Great Stone's pieces together, while keeping Kridenit's attacks at bay.

Suddenly a head popped up over the boat ledge. Startled, Yanda gasped and backed away.

A tall Sea-Elf stepped onboard with ease. She was lovely, etched in moonlight. Tiny seashells outlined her face, embedded in her lavendar flesh. "I'm Malu." The Sea-Elf embraced Yanda. "I remember you from the Withum Festival, on the beach last year. You're cold. Here." Her hands, pressed to Yanda's shoulders, instantly dried her, even her hair.

"Thank you. You know my name then, I guess." Yanda glanced back out at the choppy sea waves. "It feels nice to be dry but I guess we'll just get wet again." She spluttered a laugh, then wiped snot and seawater from her nose. *Jeez. Why can't I be cool like this fount of Elven grace?*

"It will be better if you learn to transform to *lanten*." Malu disappeared into a small cabin on the deck.

"*Lanten?*" Yanda asked, following.

Malu came out holding a skull-shapped hood attached to tube and large gourd shape. "We'll train you to transform —we call it *lanten*—if you stay with us long enough." Malu held out the hood. It reminded Yanda of the breathing apparatus Bonden had invented for Vatu, to keep out the toxic air of Dondar.

Yanda slipped it over her head, panicking briefly as it

sealed to her skin around the neck, like seaweed drying. The bulb part strapped over her shoulders, connected by the tube. She breathed in, pulling fresh air.

"Here we go." Malu picked her up and jumped over the side.

Yanda had to suppress angst and think quick as they sank, Malu pulling her downward. Panic ensued, despite Yanda's efforts to stay calm. She tried to adjust to the breathing apparatus, making herself breathe slowly as they plunged deeper into black waters.

Te-weet and the other *tasu* hovered over them, now barely discernable. Yanda sent another mental thanks to them as she slowly gained a sense of confidence that she would not drown.

Malu swam on, pulling. Yanda did her best not to hamper their progress, kicking her feeble, human feet, filling her lungs from the tube.

After a while, she made out lights in the watery depths.

As they drew closer, she spotted balls glowing in windows. There were arches. A sort of castle took form ahead of them, descending endlessly into the depths. How else to describe it, with its towers and turrets? Like in storybooks she'd read to Seiti.

"We have a special chamber in the caves for those without gills," Malu explained in mind-speak as they skirted the underwater city.

Yanda's muscles were aching by the time they arrived at dark spots in a submerged mountain. A large black hole loomed ahead. They entered it and Malu formed a glow-globe that floated in front of them.

They navigated tunnels until coming to rubber-like coverings through which they pushed, coming into a series of chambers, the last and highest glowing with heat bulbs. There was no water here. Yanda heard the surf shushing close by in rushes, pounding, then whispering, but the room was dry, sealed off. It had a bed, a desk, even carpets and woven wall hangings.

"I can take this off?" She dug her fingers under the seaweed seal at her neck.

"Here." Malu tucked her fingertips beneath the edge and it loosened.

Yanda gasped with relief as the hood was dragged from her head.

"Tenali stayed here when he first came to us," Malu said.

Hearing the name, Yanda tensed, the familiar ache rushing into her belly, then her heart: he deserted me.

How did the Neyla know of her connection with Tenali? But of course they would. He'd called for the boat that brought her to the Withum Festival. He seemed friendly with Mnenu. "Did he?" she remembered to respond. "And when he comes now? He no longer needs it?" She found herself wondering if he'd learned to transform like the Neyla into sea creatures. Mer-Elves?

"He hasn't been, for a long time," Malu replied.

Did she sound wistful? In fuller light, Yanda saw that Malu's teeth also had tiny, sparkling insets of mother-of-pearl, or something iridescent that caught the light at angles, shining with colors. She was a sight to behold, moving with supple grace, through air as though still in water. Her feet, though humanoid, had appeared as a single tail in the water at times, connected, then parting. Now they moved on stone surfaces with ease, fitting to rough or smooth rock, delicate yet strong, almost tensile.

Yanda remembered Mnenu's feet, in front of the fire at the Withum Festival, semi-transparent, without discernable bones.

"I hope you'll be comfortable here," Malu said. "I'll bring you sustenance, and tomorrow, you'll meet more of the Neyla. There's a larger chamber like this. It's a bit of a hike and swim from here."

"How far is the Stone? Ash-don?" Yanda found herself asking.

Malu's brows creased briefly in a fierce frown, then

cleared to a neutral expression. "Further still," she said smiling, and hugged Yanda. "You'll find bed clothes and other comforts in the cupboards. Bath chamber is just there."

She indicated a door made of some material Yanda couldn't identify—was it cut from a huge shell?—stood closed, near the bed.

"I'll say good-night. Give me a mind-call if you need anything. I'll be back with food. My sleeping place is not that far away. I can be with you in no time at all."

After Malu left, Yanda had to wonder if, in fact, she was a sort of prisoner. After all, where did they think she had come from? They may have seen Tlalit's ship drop her.

Why did they think she was there? Did they perceive her as a threat to their Power Stone, Ash-Don?

She'd have no idea how to get out. Really couldn't leave, could she? She checked for the breathing apparatus. Malu had left it. But surely she'd get lost in those caves. She could always mind-call for help. But what if she couldn't?

Yanda found the catch to open the small bathroom chamber, and used it. It held an intriguing set of shapes, all sea-shell-like, that served the various needs of the human, or human-esque body. She managed to figure out how to spray warm clear water. There were towels of a fabric that drew off moisture nicely, made from sea sponge, perhaps.

When she came out, she found a tray of food, left by Malu, she assumed.

She donned the sleep gown, a soft clingy textile akin to satin but stretchy, and climbed into the bed. It was surprisingly dry and comforting.

But soon she became acutely aware that water surrounded her, and rock.

Breathe, she told herself. Where did the air come from? With her sight, she searched through the walls of her little dry cave and found vents that traveled all the way up to where a volcanic island protruded from the sea. Did it always protrude, even at high tide? Would it always keep water out? She hadn't seen any mountain protruding—any sort of island—when she'd been out at sea with the *tesu*. But then how far can you see when you're among the waves? Or was it kept glamoured, shielded from intruders' eyes?

Feeling alone, she started to push her mind, automatically, out across space to seek her son. Then stopped. "He'll be fine," she assured herself.

Instead, she sent out feelers for any sentient life within a close range. And found a familiar mental register that took her utterly by surprise…

About the Author

Marie Judson, a Northern California native, is an avid fantasy and sci fi reader herself. She's been a coffee roaster, a high school teacher and a college professor. Find her blog and more of her books at:

www.mariejudson.com